Praise for Beth Kendrick's Novels

New Uses for Old Boyfriends

"[Kendrick's] newest [is a] perfectly tailored tale of love, family, friendship. . . . Kendrick's gift for creating endearingly flawed characters combined with her impeccable sense of comic timing ensure that her books will always be in fashion with discerning readers." —*Booklist* (starred review)

"Another enchanting, heartwarming Black Dog Bay–set story of reinvention and romance. . . . The lightly magical town feels like a welcome vacation to a favorite resort. Kendrick has a light, breezy writing style that manages to take readers on unexpectedly poignant journeys with some startling twists and turns on the road. An astute and charming look at friendship, love, and self-discovery." —*Kirkus Reviews*

Cure for the Common Breakup

"Beth Kendrick has reminded me once again exactly why I love her books so much. *Cure for the Common Breakup* is packed with humor, wit, and a lot of heart. A charming and exceptionally entertaining story! I can't recommend this book highly enough." —Jane Porter, national bestselling author of *The Good Wife*

"Beth Kendrick has written a sharp, sassy, surprisingly emotional story that will make readers laugh out loud from page one and sigh from the heart at the end. Light and lovely perfection!"
—Roxanne St. Claire, *New York Times* bestselling author of the Barefoot Bay series

"Utterly delightful! Summer Benson will charm and disarm her way into the hearts of readers as easily as she does the residents of Black Dog Bay."
—Meg Donohue, *USA Today* bestselling author of *Dog Crazy*

"Kendrick's impeccable sense of comic timing and flair for creating unforgettable characters make this effervescent novel a smart bet for romance readers everywhere, while the novel's deft integration of the topics of family, friendship, and community ensure it can easily attract a broader readership as well."
—*Booklist* (starred review)

"In *Cure for the Common Breakup*, you won't be short on laughter, romance, or drama . . . a fun, lighthearted, romantic, and hilarious novel that is perfect for your summer beach read. The protagonist is sassy, spunky, and snarky. I loved each of the characters." —*The Gazette* (Cedar Rapids, IA)

continued . . .

"Kendrick's writing is witty and captivating, and her characters are an endearing swirl of complexity.... The plot whistles along, taking a few unexpected turns that make the inevitable happy ending more textured and satisfying. With snappy dialogue and a breezy tone that still manages to support emotional depth, the author keeps us turning pages and rooting for Black Dog Bay and everyone in it." —*Kirkus Reviews*

The Week Before the Wedding

"Kendrick proves she is the leader of the pack when it comes to fashioning cheekily clever love stories, and her latest will delight readers with its delectably acerbic wit and charmingly complex characters." —*Booklist* (starred review)

"In an engaging story about matters of the heart, Kendrick perfectly captures the struggle between who we really are and who we want to be. With its endearing characters and page-turning plot, this novel balances humor and emotion in a way that begs it to be read in one sitting." —*RT Book Reviews* (4½ stars)

"A delightful romp with depth." —Heroes and Heartbreakers

The Lucky Dog Matchmaking Service

"Graced with a stellar cast of captivating characters (including an adorable pack of scene-stealing canines) and written with both sharp wit and genuine wisdom, Kendrick's latest effervescent novel is a hopelessly, hopefully romantic treat." —*Booklist* (starred review)

"If the title does not grab your attention, Kendrick's writing will.... An engaging, thoroughly enjoyable tale of finding soul mates of the four-legged and two-legged varieties.... When you put this book down, you will have a smile on your face and warmth in your heart." —*RT Book Reviews* (4½ stars)

"Kendrick not only shines in portraying the subtleties of female friendships, but also at rendering the unbreakable bond between man (or woman) and dog." —*Publishers Weekly*

"If you like dog stories, romance, a little kick to the characters, and a story with a happy ending, try this book ... a funny, pleasant story.... [It] makes one want to go and seek out other Beth Kendrick books." —*Deseret News* (Salt Lake City, UT)

The Bake-Off

"With her usual literary flair, Kendrick delivers a scrumptious literary confection expertly spiced with humor and seasoned with just the right dash of romance." —*Chicago Tribune*

"A warm, winning story about the complications of sisterhood—and the unexpected rewards."   —Sarah Pekkanen, author of *Catching Air*

"A sweet, fun, and entertaining look at family, love, and the perfect pastry. . . . Fans of women's fiction, foodie fiction, and novels about sisters will delight in Kendrick's descriptions, vivid characters, and fast-paced, hilarious dialogue. A book that often had me laughing aloud—and wiping away a tear at points."
                                                                    —Write Meg!

"This story is sweet like a great dessert—just the right amount of sugar and spice. It's a story that celebrates both sisters and the therapeutic benefits of baking."   —*News and Sentinel* (Parkersburg, WV)

"Wonderful! Kendrick manages to cook up a tender, touching, and very funny story about the complicated relationship of two sisters torn apart by their own stubbornness and brought back together by love and pastry. With a fresh plot and richly layered characters, *The Bake-Off* is a winner."
                              —Ellen Meister, author of *Farewell, Dorothy Parker*

Second Time Around

"Kendrick deftly blends exceptionally clever writing, subtly nuanced characters, and a generous dash of romance into a flawlessly written story about the importance of female friendships and second chances."   —*Chicago Tribune*

"A funny, charming story about the power of female friendship."
                    —Kim Gruenenfelder, author of *Keep Calm and Carry a Big Drink*

The Pre-nup

"Witty, juicy, and lots of fun! Say 'I do' to *The Pre-nup*."
            —Susan Mallery, *New York Times* bestselling author of *Yours for Christmas*

"A smart, funny spin on happily ever after!"
                                      —Beth Harbison, *New York Times* bestselling
                                              author of *Driving with the Top Down*

"In the exceptionally entertaining and wonderfully original *The Pre-nup*, Kendrick writes with a wicked sense of humor and great wisdom about the power of friendship, the importance of true love, and the very real satisfaction of romantic revenge done right."   —*Chicago Tribune*

Also by Beth Kendrick

put a
ring on it

BETH KENDRICK

NEW AMERICAN LIBRARY

NEW AMERICAN LIBRARY
Published by New American Library,
an imprint of Penguin Random House LLC
375 Hudson Street, New York, New York 10014

This book is an original publication of New American Library.

First Printing, November 2015

For more information about Penguin Random House, visit penguin.com.

LIBRARY OF CONGRESS CATALOGING-IN-PUBLICATION DATA:

Kendrick, Beth.
Put a ring on it / Beth Kendrick.
pages cm.—(Black Dog Bay novel; 3)
ISBN 978-0-451-47418-6 (softcover)
1. Single women—Fiction.   2. Man-woman relationships—Fiction.
3. Marriage—Fiction.   I. Title.
PS3611.E535P88 2015
813'.6—dc23   2015018142

Printed in the United States of America
10 9 8 7 6 5 4 3 2 1

Penguin
Random
House

For Kresley Cole,

with love and proof of life

acknowledgments

Special thanks to Jill Edwards of the Estate Watch and Jewelry Company in Scottsdale, Arizona, for sharing her knowledge of fine jewelry with humor, charm, and style.

Hugs, kisses, and cases of the finest champagne to . . .

Danielle Perez, Amy Moore-Benson, Marty Etchart, Anna O'Brien, Jenn McKinlay, Chandra Years, Amy Serin, Tai Burkholder, and Joe and Bridget Lavin. You make my life sparkle.

put a *ring* on it

chapter 1

"*G*ive me the ring back."

Brighton Smith choked on a sip of lukewarm coffee as she stepped out of her fiancé's blue sedan. She looked over her shoulder with a stunned smile. "What?"

"You heard me." Colin clenched the steering wheel so tightly his knuckles went white. "I want the ring back."

Brighton felt her smile fade as traffic whizzed by beneath the overcast morning sky. "You don't mean that."

"Yeah, I do."

"Colin, you . . ." Brighton trailed off as she considered how long it would take her to say everything she needed to say. How long it would take to listen to everything Colin needed to say. "Listen. Let's table this discussion for right now. I'm late for work, you're leaving for the entire weekend, and neither of us has eaten breakfast. We'll sit down and work this out after we've had some protein and some time to calm down, okay?"

"I'm tired of waiting." His voice was tight with tension. "This is it, Brighton: now or never."

She took a slow, deep breath as her mind raced. "This isn't fair and you know it."

Colin held out his palm. "Give me the ring back."

"No!" She covered her bejeweled ring finger with her other hand.

"Yes. I'll find someone else—someone who will appreciate it. Someone who will appreciate me." He waved his palm at her. "Give it back. Now."

So she did. She had to work to get the slim platinum band past her knuckle, but when she finally managed, she dropped it into his outstretched hand with regal, icy dignity. "Call me when you're ready to talk about this in a rational manner."

"I'm done talking," he said. "And I'm done waiting. I'm sick of all your rules and restrictions and terms and conditions."

She snatched up her briefcase from the passenger seat and strode toward the office building, pausing to glance behind her. Colin's car was still idling by the curb. He was still watching her and clutching the diamond ring.

She should turn around and rush back to him, she knew. They shouldn't part like this when he was about to leave town. She always tried to fight fairly, to avoid drama, and to seek productive solutions. But Colin had just lashed out with no warning right in the middle of their morning commute. She felt bewildered and hurt . . . but also furious.

She had a meeting in ten minutes, and she knew that it took an average of seven and a half minutes to make it through the lobby, wait for the elevators, and arrive at her office on the fifth floor.

She straightened her shoulders and kept walking.

When she walked into the insurance firm's corporate headquarters six minutes later (the elevator doors had opened just as she arrived in the lobby), her assistant glanced up from her computer with evident concern.

"Good morning." Sherri put down her coffee mug and pushed back her chair. "Are you okay?"

"Absolutely." Brighton shifted her briefcase from her right hand to her left, then reached up to touch her necklace, earrings, and shirt collar to ensure everything was in place. "Why?"

"Nothing." Sherri kept staring. "You look pale."

"Everything's fine," Brighton said firmly.

"Uh-huh." Sherri's gaze slid down to Brighton's suit jacket. "You've got a little stain there. Looks like coffee."

Brighton frowned down at her black wool lapel. "Yeah, the ride to work was kind of, um, bumpy."

Sherri got to her feet. "Let me get you a paper towel."

"No need." Brighton motioned for her to sit back down. "I keep a stain stick in my desk drawer."

"I should have known." Sherri smiled as she handed Brighton a pile of papers. "Here's the report you wanted me to print out."

"Thanks." Brighton prepared to head into the firm's weekly Friday morning meeting.

"You're welcome." Sherri cleared her throat as she turned her attention back to her computer monitor. "And seriously, if you need to talk or anything . . ."

"Don't be silly." Brighton squared her shoulders. "I don't need to talk; I just need to work. Everything's under control."

chapter 2

"Where's your ring?" Claudia Reilly nudged Brighton as they sat down next to each other at the huge oval conference table.

"Um . . ." For a brief moment, Brighton yearned to confide in Claudia, who was her closest friend at work. They'd started in the actuarial department on the same day three years ago, and they'd bonded over late-night analyses, networking happy hours, and night-before-deadline computer crashes. "It's at the jewelers. One of the prongs was loose, so they're fixing it and cleaning the stone."

"Oh." Claudia tapped her pen against her yellow legal pad. "I'm surprised you didn't just fix it yourself." She turned to Francine, the claims processor on her left. "Brighton's a woman of many talents, you know. She makes jewelry when she's not working miracles with Excel worksheets."

"Really?" Francine helped herself to a croissant from the platter of pastries in the middle of the table. "I had no idea."

"Oh, I'm not really . . ." Brighton stared down at her paperwork as heat flooded her face. "It's a hobby. I dabble."

"Stop being so modest. Check it out—she designed my wedding rings." Claudia stretched out her arm so Francine could admire the diamond- and emerald-studded bands. "They get more gorgeous and sparkly every day."

Francine leaned her chair back to address Brighton. "You made those?"

Brighton nodded, still studying the typeface on her financial report.

"*You* made those?"

Claudia laughed. "Try not to sound so shocked."

"No, it's just . . ." Francine paused for another bite of croissant. "No offense, Brighton, but you never really struck me as the creative type."

"I'm not," Brighton said. "Claudia's husband told me exactly what he wanted. I just tried to capture his vision."

"Did you design your own ring when you got engaged?" Francine pressed.

"No." Brighton bowed her head so that her long dark hair hid her face.

"Why not?"

"My fiancé knows I have simple tastes. He picked out a lovely solitaire. It's classic. It's just what I wanted." Brighton winced at the sharp edge in her voice.

Their boss entered the room, dimmed the lights, and launched into a PowerPoint presentation packed with graphs and statistics. Ordinarily, Brighton would have been scribbling notes, asking questions, trying to look at the data from as many perspectives as possible. But today she couldn't concentrate.

She couldn't even sit still. As the presentation dragged on and on, she shifted in her seat, laced her fingers together, and tried to convince herself that everything was going to be fine. Lots of couples had tiffs before the wedding. Colin hadn't meant all those things he'd said about her. And even if he had, she didn't deserve it . . . did she?

The back of her neck felt like it was breaking out in hives.

As the speaker pulled up another red and blue bar graph, Brighton's cell phone vibrated in her blazer pocket. She shoved back her chair, raced out to the hallway, and prepared to make amends with her fiancé.

But Colin wasn't calling. She didn't recognize the number with the 302 area code.

"Hello?" she whispered as she turned toward a window overlooking the brick building next door.

"Brighton! Hey! I'm so glad you picked up!"

Brighton frowned, trying to place the soft, feminine voice on the other end of the line.

"It's Kira. Long time no talk, huh?"

"Kira!" Brighton's tension ebbed away as she thought of her old roommate. "It's great to hear from you. How's it going? I bet you're the best therapist in all of Florida."

"Well, that's why I'm calling, actually. I'm not in Florida anymore. I'm back in your neck of the woods . . . kind of. I just moved to the Delaware beach. Tiny little town called Black Dog Bay."

"What are you doing at the Delaware beach?"

"Long story, but I was unpacking this morning and I found all these old pictures of us on spring break junior year. That road trip to New Orleans."

Brighton smiled at the memories. "Ah, our misspent youth." The two of them had been inseparable in college, but after graduation, she'd accepted a job in New Jersey while Kira had gone off to graduate school in Florida. She tried to remember the last time they'd talked face-to-face. "I'm glad to hear from you. Every time I get one of those alumni magazines, I want to call you, but . . ."

"We're all so busy these days. Believe me, I get it. But now that we're so close geographically, we have no excuse. I'd love to catch up with you sometime."

"Definitely. But listen, can I call you back in a bit? I'm technically in the middle of a meeting right now—"

"Of course! Sorry to interrupt."

"No, no, I'm really glad to hear from you. I miss you."

"Come visit," Kira offered. "I mean it. My spare bedroom is all yours, anytime."

"That's very generous of you." Brighton glanced at the conference room door. "I'll definitely take you up on that one of these days."

"Great. So when are you coming?"

Brighton blinked. "You mean, like, what day?"

"Yeah. Check your calendar and tell me when you have a free weekend."

"Absolutely. Will do. I'll be in touch." Brighton clicked off the call and stared down at the phone screen, willing a text from Colin to appear.

Nothing. The feeling of hives on her neck spread down her shoulders and back. She couldn't bear another moment in this dry, muted, fluorescent-lit office. And the meeting wouldn't be over for hours. She took two steps toward the conference room but couldn't force herself to reach for the doorknob. The very thought of bar graphs and small talk made her physically ill. The sensation of hives gave way to cold sweat and nausea. There was only one thing to do, and she'd never done it before. Not at work, not in college, not even in high school. But the time had finally arrived.

Brighton forced out a raspy cough as she prepared to play hooky for the first time in her life. When the meeting adjourned for a five-minute break, she rejoined Claudia at the conference table.

"Where did you go?" Claudia demanded. "You missed a whole fifteen minutes on equity-based guaranteed policies. It was riveting, I tell you. You pay for the whole seat but you'll only need the edge."

"I'm not feeling well." Brighton covered her mouth with her elbow and faked a sniffle.

"Here." Francine pulled a travel-size packet of tissues out of her red leather messenger bag. "You okay?"

"Yeah." Brighton schooled her expression into what she hoped was a believable grimace of pain. "Just a sore throat. And I'm feeling a bit feverish." She thought wan, pallid thoughts and hoped her complexion would follow suit. "I think I better go home. I don't want to get anyone else sick."

Francine looked worried. "Maybe you should go see a doctor. There's an urgent care two blocks away."

A pang of guilt shot through Brighton as she collected her pen and paperwork. "I'll be fine. I just need to lie down for a little while."

Claudia pressed the back of her hand to Brighton's forehead.

Brighton flinched.

"You do feel pretty warm," Claudia said.

"I'm not surprised." Francine clicked her tongue. "With the hours you've been working, plus all the wedding planning, you need to slow down. Stress affects your immune system, you know."

At the mention of wedding planning, Brighton started coughing again.

"Go home." Francine backed away from the germ zone. "Take it easy and get better."

"I have an amazing recipe for chicken soup," Claudia said. "I'll e-mail it to you and Colin can make it for you tonight."

"He can't. He's"—*not speaking to me at the moment*—"studying all weekend. Prepping for the bar exam."

Claudia's eyebrows lifted almost imperceptibly. "Again?"

This time, Brighton didn't have to fake her distress. "Third time's a charm, right?" She desperately wanted to tell Claudia the truth, to ask for advice and reassurance, but telling the truth would make everything real. She'd have to admit her doubts and fears. She'd have to admit that her life plans were on the verge of falling apart.

So she stopped talking and made her exit in a dramatic display of hacking and wheezing that sent her colleagues scurrying for hand sanitizer. As she waited for the elevator, she glanced at her reflection in the polished brass doors: low-heeled patent pumps, subdued black blazer and skirt, modest cream silk blouse, and an akoya pearl necklace with matching earrings. She looked like the sensible businesswoman she was. Bland and boring and always predictable.

The elevator doors opened and she joined a trio of somber-faced executives hunched over their cell phones, tapping away at urgent e-mails.

And then she realized she couldn't drive herself home. Colin had taken her to work this morning. Right before he picked a fight and demanded the engagement ring back.

Outside, the heavy gray clouds threatened rain at any moment. Brighton stepped to the curb, lifted her ringless hand to hail a cab, and tried to decide what to do. She would go home, of course, but then what? Wait by the phone for Colin to come to his senses? Call him and beg forgiveness for whatever he thought she'd done wrong? Go to the appointments she'd made with caterers to taste cakes for the wedding Colin had just called off? She had the entire weekend stretching out ahead of her.

What the hell did normal people do with free time?

While she waited for a taxi, she pulled out her cell phone and called the only person she wanted to talk to right then.

"Hey, Kira, it's me. I just looked at my calendar, and let me ask you . . . How sincere were you when you said I could come down there anytime?"

chapter 3

No wonder high schoolers all over the nation cut class every day.

The sun came out from behind the clouds as Brighton crossed the state line and left New Jersey for Delaware. She slid on her sunglasses and rolled down her window, glorying in the damp breeze. She had a hastily packed overnight bag in the backseat, a box of protein bars in the glove compartment, and plans to meet one of her oldest friends at some bar called the Whinery. So simple, but so gratifying.

Soon, she could smell the salty tang of the Atlantic in the air. While she navigated the stop-and-go traffic in her white Subaru (white cars were ten percent less likely to get into accidents than cars of other colors), she kept her phone in the cup holder beneath the radio.

The silence of that phone not ringing was deafening.

Brighton forced herself to stop obsessing about that morning's fight and start focusing on her upcoming reunion with Kira. Her friend sounded exactly the same as she had back in college—still sweet, still smart, and still unable to turn away from anyone in need. The warm, bubbly blonde had gone from being everyone's friend and confidante to beloved dormitory resident assistant to clinical psychologist. Brighton couldn't wait to hear all the news and reminisce about the old days. A break in routine would be good for her. This little weekend jaunt was indisputable proof that she was capable of spontaneity and surprises.

In your face, Colin.

As soon as she saw the white clapboard sign painted with the black silhouette of a Labrador retriever and the words WELCOME TO BLACK DOG BAY, Brighton's whole body relaxed. Traffic cleared up, sunlight sparkled on the ocean, and she located the wine bar with no problem.

Since she still had an hour before she was supposed to meet Kira, Brighton decided to explore the charming little town square. A weathered bronze statue of a shaggy dog stood next to a white gazebo, beyond which the boardwalk stretched out to the sea. As she started toward the sand, she noticed that the local restaurants and shops seemed to adhere to a common theme: the Eat Your Heart Out bakery, the Retail Therapy boutique, the Rebound Salon, the Jilted Café.

All the passersby were dressed for the beach in denim and flip-flops. Brighton knew she looked completely out of place in her buttoned-up cubicle couture, but she didn't care—she'd spotted a store window featuring a display of glittering gems. The little wooden sign above the door read: THE NAKED FINGER.

She opened the door and stepped into a small, quiet showroom featuring ice blue walls, discreet but strategically angled lighting that brought out the sparkle in each gemstone, and a young proprietor with warm brown eyes, glossy dark hair, and a vintage-looking silk floral shirtdress.

"Hi, I'm Lila." The brunette greeted Brighton with a smile. "Did Marla send you?"

"No." Brighton shook her head. "I'm not sure who that is."

"Oh, sorry. You just had that look."

Brighton blinked. "What look?"

Now Lila started to look flustered. "Nothing. Sorry."

"No, tell me. Who's Marla? What look?" It was so unusual for anyone to describe Brighton as anything other than "professional," "practical," or "smart" that she was dying to know what this total stranger saw in her.

"Marla owns the Better Off Bed-and-Breakfast," Lila explained. "She refers her guests to me all the time."

Brighton had to laugh. "The Better Off Bed-and-Breakfast? The Rebound Salon and the Jilted Café? What's going on with this town?"

"Last year, there was a national news story that said Black Dog Bay is the best place in America to get over your breakup. So we get a lot of recently single visitors. We call them heartbreak tourists."

Brighton started to put the pieces of the puzzle together. "Hence, the Naked Finger."

"Right. I deal with all the wedding rings and other jewelry that women don't want or have to sell after a breakup. I just started the business a few months ago."

Brighton peered at the pieces beneath the glass countertops. Bracelets and pendants and watches and oh so many diamond rings. "How's it going?"

"Great." Lila beamed. "Better than I expected, actually. I've been in sales for a long time, but it never ceases to amaze me how much money people are willing to spend on clothes and accessories."

"But jewelry's more than an accessory." Brighton studied a pair of art deco emerald earrings. "It's very emotional."

Lila nodded. "That's true. Every piece in here has a history. Some clients want to tell me the stories, some don't want to talk about it at all." She pointed out the box of tissues by the cash register. "Either way, I try to be supportive."

"So you buy the pieces and resell them?" Brighton asked.

"Well, I try to convince clients to reuse the stones in a new setting, but sometimes they don't want to. Sometimes, a client just wants to be rid of them, which I get. Been there myself."

"You have?" Brighton regarded the proprietor with renewed interest. Lila looked so polished and perfect, it was easy to assume she'd never had to endure heartbreak or disappointment.

"I sold my own wedding rings, once upon a time." Lila glanced down at her left hand. "That's when I found out that jewelry doesn't hold its retail value. It's kind of like a new car; once you drive it off the lot—"

"Wait. Is this what I think it is?" Brighton spied a heavy silver ring on the counter, and she couldn't stop herself from interrupting.

Lila picked up the ring and handed it over. "You tell me. I've never seen anything like this before. A heartbreak tourist dropped this off this morning and I've been trying to figure out what it should appraise for."

Brighton held the massive ring aloft so she could examine it from all sides. Although the silver shank was sized for petite hands, the prongs were wide and sturdy. They had to be to support the red stone skull and the green, blue, and purple cabochons. This was a badass rock star of a ring, a ring that demanded brazen confidence from its wearer.

She admired the craftsmanship but didn't try it on.

"The owner is staying at Marla's," Lila went on. "She said her ex-boyfriend gave it to her and she needs to get rid of it before she uses it for evil."

Brighton started to smile as she examined the sides of the setting. "That's what she said?"

"Those were her exact words. She insisted I keep it overnight in the safe. I've been trying to figure out how old it is and what I should offer for it."

Brighton felt a small surge of triumph as she located a pair of narrow silver hinges. She ran her fingernail along the side of the sneering red skull until she felt a tiny clasp give way. "This is a poison ring. I haven't seen one of these in years."

Lila looked alarmed. "A poison ring?"

"Check it out." Brighton lifted one edge of the red skull, revealing a shallow silver compartment beneath. "These were all the rage back in the sixteenth century. You could put poison in here and use it to kill your enemy or yourself."

Lila looked horrified. "Really?"

"Really." Brighton marveled at the craftsmanship of the piece. "That's what the owner meant when she said she didn't want to use it for evil."

Lila gazed at her with renewed interest. "How do you know all that? Are you a jeweler?"

"No, I'm in insurance."

"You deal with poison rings in insurance?" Those big brown eyes had gone from sweet to speculative.

"My grandfather was a bench jeweler. He did it all: stone setting, engraving, wax carving, forging, polishing. I used to help him when I was a teenager." Brighton closed her eyes for a moment, flooded with feelings she couldn't quite label. And didn't want to. "Once upon a time, I wanted to be a jewelry designer." She opened her eyes. "Back before I understood that being a responsible adult requires health benefits and retirement plans and mortgage payments."

Lila stepped back, sizing her up. "But you're not a heartbreak tourist?"

"No, I have a fiancé." Brighton tucked her hand into her pocket. "I'm just visiting a friend from college."

Lila continued to look her over with that appraising, acquisitive gleam. "Do you have any interest in staying for the summer season? I've been looking for a designer to coordinate with my bench jeweler."

"I'm only here for the weekend, and then it's back to reality. Sorry." Brighton turned toward the door. "I should get going so I'm not late to meet my friend."

"Where are you meeting her?"

"The Whinery."

"What a coincidence—I'm headed that way, too. I'll walk with you." Lila grabbed a fifties-style black leather handbag from beneath the counter. "What's your name?"

"Brighton." In an effort to head off the inevitable questions, she explained, "As in Brighton Beach. The one in Brooklyn, not Britain. My mom had a thing for New York in the eighties."

Lila laughed. "So did mine. Welcome to Black Dog Bay, Brighton. Here's hoping you'll decide to stay for a bit."

"It seems like a lovely town, but I really can't. I have to be back to my office on Monday—places to go, people to see, reports to write, accounting rules to research." She paused. "I swear it's not as dull as it sounds." *It's duller.* "But in any event, I have to get back."

Lila gave her a knowing smile as she flipped the sign on the glass door from OPEN to CLOSED. "That's what they all say in the beginning."

"Look at him. Who is *that*?"

As Brighton followed Lila into the crowded bar, she heard a trio of women laughing and murmuring.

During their phone conversation, Kira had described the Whinery as "a cute little spot to people watch." She had neglected to mention the profusion of pink, toile, and crystal chandeliers. There were silver bowls of chocolate candy dotting the glossy black bar top and a curly-haired female bartender pouring fruity cocktails. Everything in there appeared sugarcoated and sweet . . . except the clientele, who were less interested in the wine list and more interested in verbally undressing one of the male patrons.

"That's the man I've been looking for all my life," one woman declared. "Or at least for this weekend."

The guy on the other side of the bar was impossible to miss. Tall and broad shouldered, he radiated masculinity amid all the pastel frippery. He was so handsome he looked like he should be shirtless on the cover of a romance novel, all strong jawline and smoldering dark eyes and tousled dark hair. But good looks alone couldn't account for all the attention he was receiving. He exuded a confidence and charm that could not be denied, that *forced* you to notice him.

And then he turned to face them and the trio of women in front of Brighton practically swooned. They snatched up their wineglasses and started toward him, fluffing their hair and swaying their hips. It was like the guy had switched on a tractor beam. The Death Star in jeans and a worn leather jacket.

As soon as the first trio left, another trio materialized to continue the fangirling:

"Look at his face."

"Look at his eyes."

"Look at his hair."

"Look at his *watch*." Brighton squinted, trying to discern the details in the dim lighting. "Is that . . . ?"

"*That* is Jake Sorensen." Lila waved to the bartender, who slammed down her stainless steel cocktail shaker and motioned them closer. "Designated rebound guy for all the newly single women."

Brighton couldn't take her eyes off the designated rebound guy's wrist. "Incredible."

"Pretty much," Lila agreed. "He's filthy rich, he's charming as all get out, and he looks . . . well, he looks like that. Although he's usually smiling, which makes him look even better, if you can believe it." She shot a sidelong glance at Brighton. "You're not hyperventilating and dissolving into a puddle of lust? Way to buck the trend."

"What?" Brighton was still staring at his wrist. "Oh. Yeah, I don't really go for tall, dark, and handsome. I prefer well-read, low-key, and loyal. I'm boring like that. And also engaged." *I think. I hope.*

"Me, too." Lila clapped her hand over her mouth. "Well, not yet. Not officially. But soon."

"Good for you. You shouldn't rush these things," Brighton murmured. Why didn't more people understand that? "Patience is a virtue."

"It's not really so much about patience; it's more about our insane work schedules. I've been busy getting the Naked Finger up and running and my boyfriend, Malcolm, works with Jake. Speaking of which, brace yourself." Lila rolled her eyes like an exasperated but indulgent older sister as Jake Sorensen strode toward them. "He's headed this way."

Some of the women who had been eyeing Jake started glaring at Brighton and Lila. Lila seemed oblivious, but Brighton wasn't used to being the object of anyone's envy or hostility. Blending into the background was more her deal. She studied the drink specials on the chalkboard above the bar until Lila made the official introductions:

"Jake Sorensen, this is Brighton Smith. She just arrived for a weekend visit."

Base, carnal desire surged through Brighton, shocking in its immediacy and intensity. One second she was reading about champagne cocktails; the next second she was struggling to keep her hands to herself. She hadn't even made eye contact yet and she wanted to peel his shirt off.

Then for God's sake, don't make eye contact.

"Hi." She jerked her chin in a kind of a side-nod and kept her gaze focused on his wrist. "Is that a 1950s Patek Philippe?"

"It's 1953." He lifted his wrist so she could inspect the watch. What had once been a flawless Swiss timepiece had become nearly unrecognizable with age and neglect. The brown leather band was cracked and scarred. The stainless steel lug and case had blackened. The crystal covering the dial was cloudy and scratched so badly, she couldn't read the manufacturer's name. But she appreciated quality when she saw it. "How'd you know?"

"The lugs." She pointed with her index finger but didn't trust herself to touch. "They're extended and curved downward. That's really rare. They only made that design in the late forties and early fifties."

"I would have figured you for a Rolex guy," Lila chimed in, cheery and chipper and apparently oblivious to the pheromones. "That watch is . . . underwhelming."

"Just had a meeting with my financial advisers." Jake was speaking to Lila but focused on Brighton, who didn't dare look up. "They're all about understatement. Except when they're swilling my forty-year-old scotch."

"Sounds like a fun day." Lila's tone softened. "Is that why you look stressed?"

Brighton was still hunched over his hand, but she could *feel* his gaze on her head. She noticed the tan of his skin and the smell of his leather jacket, and the Death Star tractor beam almost kicked in.

Almost.

She straightened up, took a step back, and stared over his shoulder at the glittering crystal chandelier.

He stepped forward, closing the distance she'd just created. "What can I get you to drink?"

"Oh, nothing, thanks. I don't really drink." She forced herself to pretend that his face was a solar eclipse. *One glance and you'll burn your retinas.*

"That's too bad," Lila said. "They have some really great cocktails here. There's one with champagne and fresh orange juice and vermouth—"

"You're an antique watch expert who doesn't drink." Jake shifted his body so his arm was less than an inch from hers. If she relaxed for even a second, they'd be touching.

Brighton tensed up. "That's right. I like Swiss precision and I don't like to lose my self-control." Halfway through the sentence, her vigilance lapsed. She looked at his face.

"Good to know." He finally smiled, slow and wicked, and she tingled in places she didn't know she could tingle. She suddenly felt alluring and aglow, and she wanted more of that feeling. More of him.

"Hey." Lila wedged herself in between them and leveled her index finger at Jake. "Don't start with her."

He seemed to take this admonishment as a personal challenge. "Why not?"

Lila looked at Brighton, who couldn't dredge up any kind of verbal response. Her brain had shut down. Her good sense had deserted her. Her hormones, however, were very much present and accounted for.

"Because she's too good for you, that's why," Lila informed him.

His dark eyes flickered. For a fraction of a second, something surfaced behind all that seduction and calculated charisma. It happened so quickly that Brighton almost missed it, but she *felt* a pulse of emotion pass through her like a heartbeat.

She looked down at her naked fingers. When she glanced back up, he had sidled into the perimeter of her personal space again. He didn't make any move to touch her; he didn't try to engage her in conversation. But he was looking at her as if he could see right through the pearl necklace and silk blouse and wool suiting.

"I'm serious." Lila swatted him on the shoulder. "Go pick up one of those women over there. They're dying to be picked up, and I know you know it."

He gave Lila the same eye-rolling routine she'd given him earlier. "Don't tell me what to do, Alders. I'm buying. What're you drinking?"

"Oh, nothing, I'm fine. I'm about to drive home." Lila couldn't suppress a girlish little smile. "Takeout and a movie with Malcolm."

Jake signaled to the bartender. "Throw a bottle of Sea Smoke in a bag, Jenna. The pinot noir. Thanks."

The bartender batted her eyelashes and hastened to do his bidding.

Lila shook her head. "Jake, you don't have to do that."

"Here." The designated rebound guy of Black Dog Bay handed the bartender a credit card and passed the bottle to Lila. "Enjoy your date night."

"That's really fancy wine." Lila's expression was part amused, part dismayed. "You can't just—"

"It's not for you; it's for Malcolm. I made him work twelve-hour days all week."

At this, Lila turned a bit salty. "Yes, I noticed."

"Then you know he earned it." He took Lila's elbow and steered her toward the door. "You have a hot date to get to."

"But—"

"Bye." He escorted her out to the sidewalk, then returned to Brighton by the bar. "You sure you don't want a drink?"

Suddenly, she did. She wanted a drink and so much more. But she couldn't have it. She was a smart, levelheaded, and *engaged* woman.

To remind herself of this fact, she reached up and touched her tasteful pearl earrings. "No, thank you."

He looked at her for a long minute. Then he glanced down at the watch that was practically rotting away on his wrist. "Anything you want. Pick your poison."

"No." Her voice came out very prim and proper.

He accepted her curt refusal with a nod, then turned away from her. The music changed from Ben Folds Five's "Song for the Dumped" to Sara Bareilles's "Gonna Get Over You," and the front door swung open.

"Brighton!" A woman waved and started across the room.

Kira. Thank God. Brighton rushed to greet her friend.

"Ooh, look at you in your fancy suit, Miss Corner Office. You're positively glowing!" Kira held Brighton at arm's length before engulfing her in a hug. "You must be in love."

Brighton hugged back. "Right in the middle of planning a wedding, actually."

"I knew it!" Kira squeezed Brighton again. "I need to hear everything. Who he is, how you met, when you knew he was the one."

And just like that, they were back in sync. It felt as if no time had passed, no distance had separated them. They picked up right where'd they left off years before. A little spark of hope kindled in Brighton's heart, and this time, when she told herself that everything would work out, she actually believed it.

Relationships are resilient. Love can endure.

Kira seemed to sense the sudden shift in her mood. "You all right?"

"Mm-hmm." Brighton tucked her hair behind her ear. "Let's get a table."

That's when Kira noticed Jake Sorensen. "Ooh, look at *that* guy. Let's sit by him."

"Let's not." Brighton spotted an empty table on the opposite side of the bar. "Follow me."

chapter 4

"Sorry I kept you waiting." Kira sat down at a tiny café table in the corner. "I don't usually work this late on Fridays, but I just opened the practice and I hate to turn away new clients."

"Don't apologize," Brighton said. "It's nice to have a bit of free time. I got to walk around and see the town. This place is adorable."

"Isn't it?" Kira grabbed the wine list and studied the selections. "The perfect place for a fresh start."

"And the perfect place for a psychologist." Brighton grinned. "The woman who owns the Naked Finger told me Black Dog Bay was named the best place in America to bounce back from your breakup. Opening a practice here was genius."

Kira put down her menu and focused on her friend. "So you were at the Naked Finger?"

"Yes, and you'll never guess what they had." Brighton launched into a detailed explanation of the poison ring. "It was so cool."

Kira smiled. "I'm so glad you're still designing jewelry."

"Uh . . ."

"Remember that silver bracelet you made me sophomore year? With the sea glass we found on the beach? I still have that in my closet somewhere."

"I don't work with jewelry much anymore. I sold my soul to the corporate world."

Kira looked disappointed and a bit reproachful. "But what about your grandparents? I thought you were going to take over their business one day."

"My grandparents died a few years after we graduated." Brighton sighed. "They left their jewelry business in its entirety to my mother."

Kira's eyes softened. She knew enough about Brighton's mother to know what was coming. "And then what happened?"

"She ran it into the ground. My grandfather spent forty years building that business and my mom bankrupted it in eighteen months." Brighton shook her head. "I begged her to keep the overhead expenses down, but she couldn't do the hands-on work and she hated the book-keeping side of things. So now she's back to teaching part-time and I'm an actuary."

Kira waited a beat, then changed the subject. "And how's your sister?"

"Back in school. She's in an accelerated accounting program. My mom's bitterly disappointed in us because we refused to follow the artist's path. What can I say? We like to eat."

Kira tapped her finger on the top of the laminated wine list. "So you're an actuary."

"Yes." Brighton smiled wryly. "Don't be jealous."

"What does an actuary do, exactly?"

"I minimize risk for the insurance company. I figure out how much we should charge different entities for different policies, based on all kinds of statistical models and behavioral patterns."

"Sounds . . . juicy." Kira didn't try to hide her skepticism.

"It's very interesting," Brighton insisted. "Plus, I get to travel."

"Ooh, like to check out overseas markets? Africa? Asia?"

"Um, more like Cleveland and Chicago."

"But what happened with the jewelry?" Kira asked. "I know you loved it, and you were so good at it."

"I was never all that serious about it." A hint of defensiveness crept into Brighton's voice. "It was fun, but it was never going to go anywhere."

Kira waited, her head tilted. "Uh-huh."

"Let's be real, Kira. Who actually grows up to be a jewelry designer?" Brighton pointed out her own accessories. "I don't even have cool jewelry anymore. It's all tasteful gold pendants and dainty little earrings."

Kira rested her chin in her hands, never glancing away from Brighton's face. "You've changed."

"I haven't." Brighton spread out her hands. "I'm exactly the same. The eternal designated driver. Except now I have an office, a lovely condo, and an awesome dental plan."

"And a fiancé," Kira reminded her. "What's his name?"

"Colin."

"I want to hear all about him." Kira rotated her hand to indicate that Brighton should start talking. "Go."

Brighton swallowed and tried to figure out where to start. "Well. We met at a networking breakfast two years ago. He got me the packet of sugar for my coffee."

"Romantic."

"It kind of was—he had to fight a line-cutting mortgage broker for it."

"Your knight in shining armor." Then Kira asked the question Brighton had been dreading: "What does he do?"

"He's a . . . Well, he's going to be a lawyer once he passes the bar.

He's cramming all weekend, holed up with his study group." Brighton clasped her hands next to her cheek in a mock display of sentimentality. "The actuary and the attorney, riding off into the sunset together. We'll live happily ever after with our spreadsheets and our 401(k)s." She felt a bit chagrined, and her friend seemed to pick up on this.

"Hey, if you're happy, I'm happy," Kira assured her. "*Are* you happy?"

Brighton finally cracked. "Listen, if I tell you something, can you keep it a secret? Put it in the vault of psychologist confidentiality or the former roommate bunker of trust or whatever?"

"Of course."

Brighton glanced around and lowered her voice. "Do you ever do couples' counseling?"

Kira remained totally blasé. She must have heard this lead-in hundreds of times. "With some of my clients, yes."

"Well, how do you know who's going to make it long term and who's not?" Brighton gripped the wrought iron tabletop with both ringless hands. "There have got to be signs, right? Red flags that you can see even if the couple can't?"

Kira settled back in her chair, her blue eyes kind and patient. "Why do you ask?"

"Because Colin . . ." Brighton ducked her head as her eyes flooded with tears. She knew she shouldn't be talking about this, especially to someone she hadn't seen in years, but she was desperate for an outlet for all her anxiety and confusion. "We had a huge fight this morning—a really ridiculous, petty fight—and he asked for the ring back."

Kira reached across the table and rested her hand atop Brighton's. "Tell me everything."

"The whole thing was so stupid." Brighton dabbed at her eyes with a pink paper napkin. "*So* stupid."

. . .

In retrospect, Brighton could pinpoint the source of the fight as nutritional in nature. Neither she nor Colin had eaten a proper breakfast. Although she was typically fastidious about starting her day with an egg white frittata or a Greek yogurt smoothie, Colin had offered to drop her off at her office on his way out of town and she'd barely managed to brew coffee before he'd arrived because her mother had called the second she stepped out of the shower.

"Hey, Mom. How's the new job going?" Brighton had held her breath, half-afraid to hear the answer. Her mother had just moved from a low-paying adjunct teaching job in Indiana to an even lower-paying adjunct teaching job in Iowa.

"Okay." Despite the early hour, her mother had sounded alert and upbeat. Perpetual optimism, no matter how dire the circumstances, was her mother's best and worst trait. "Settling into the new apartment." Halfway through a description of the new teaching position, Brighton asked the question she always asked:

"Any chance this one'll turn into a full-time position?"

"I brought it up to the department chair, and she started in about budget cuts and belt-tightening. You know how it goes, honey."

"I do know how it goes." Brighton stifled a sigh. Her mother had been painting and teaching art history part-time for the past thirty years. She had never had dental insurance or paid vacation time, but she had always done what she loved. She'd encouraged both her daughters to do the same—to live fully, to create and appreciate art.

And when she needed a root canal or a car repair, Brighton sent a check.

"The good news is, I get to teach Tuscan altarpieces this semester. Giotto and Cimabue and Duccio."

"Tell them I said hi. Listen, Mom, I have to go. Colin will be here any second—"

"Sorry, hon, I know you're busy. I just wanted to ask . . ."

Brighton waited for the rest of the sentence. "Yes?"

"Nothing. It's just that Cat's tuition is due, and . . ."

"I paid it online last night." Brighton poured coffee into a travel mug, wincing as a drop of hot liquid spilled on her thumb. "Did you really think I'd forget?"

"No. I never worry about you. You're so responsible."

Brighton screwed on the travel mug's lid and ran her hand under cold water. "Even though I live inauthentically?"

"We can't all paint masterpieces," her mother replied. "Every artist needs a patron."

Brighton's door buzzer sounded. "I've got to run. Love you, Mom."

"We need to talk," Colin announced as the car merged onto the highway.

Commuter traffic was heavier than usual due to construction in the left lanes, and Brighton braced one hand against the dashboard as Colin slammed on the brakes to avoid rear-ending the car in front of them. "Please be careful," she said. "What do we need to talk about?"

"The wedding." He cursed under his breath at the hulking SUV that was tailgating the car. "You're stalling."

"I . . . what? How can you say that? I'm setting up cake-tasting appointments for tomorrow."

He shot her a sullen sidelong glance. "You keep moving the date back."

"Colin." She took a moment to suppress all the hurt and surprise. "The hotel called and said they wouldn't be done with renovations on the original schedule. If you want to change reception venues—"

"Do you?"

"Not really. We made a plan and I think we should stick to it."

"*You* made a plan." He laughed, the sound dry and bitter. "You always have a plan and a backup plan—just in case things don't work out."

Brighton stared out the window and reminded herself that he was under a lot of pressure right now. "What's that supposed to mean?"

"It means that you're hedging your bets by dragging out the engagement."

"Hedging my bets?" she repeated. "What does *that* mean?"

"Nothing."

"No, tell me."

"Nothing." He switched from surly to sheepish. "Sorry. I'm just stressed about the bar exam."

Brighton reached over and rested her fingertips on his forearm. "Honey. Don't get upset, but I have to ask you something: Did you skip breakfast today?"

"Yes," he admitted. "But that has nothing to do with this."

"With what? I don't even know what's going on." She turned off the radio. The insistent ding of the turn signal ticked off the seconds while she waited for him to respond.

He shook her hand off and resumed muttering under his breath.

"Look." She put her hands on one knee. "I know prepping for the bar sucks. But it'll be over soon, and you'll never have to take it again. Want me to quiz you?"

"No."

"Oh, come on. As long as we're stuck going five miles per hour, we might as well go over real estate holding law again." She lowered her voice to a breathy whisper. "For every question you get right between here and the office, I'll make the dinner of your choice. Even that strawberry rhubarb pie I swore I'd never make again."

"Then we're both going to starve, because I can't understand the real estate statutes to save my life."

"Don't be like that," she implored. "You can do this. I know you can! You—" She sucked in her breath as the minivan next to Colin's car edged closer. "Sweetie, you're supposed to let him in." She pointed out the van's blinking yellow turn signal.

"No way. I had to wait in line; so should he."

Brighton abandoned all attempts at pie bribery and shifted into actuary mode. "But if everyone in our lane lets one car from that lane in, it's faster and more efficient."

Colin hunched his shoulders and set his jaw.

"It's called a zipper merge." Brighton kept her tone light. "They've done studies."

"I don't care. I'm not letting him in."

"Can I just tell you about the research I read on—"

"No." He'd gone cold and hard and almost unrecognizable. "Doesn't your brain *ever* shut off?"

She turned in her seat to face him, bewildered. "What's going on with you? Why are you being so . . . ?"

"I'm fine." He turned away from her, scowling toward the minivan. "Although I would like to know why you always get to make the rules and the schedule."

She drew back. "We're supposed to be a team; I thought we agreed. You're the one who said you wanted to pass the bar before—"

"The bar is bullshit, Brighton." He hit the steering wheel with the heel of his hand. "The zipper merge is bullshit! All of your rules and excuses and expectations are bullshit!"

She twisted the diamond solitaire on her ring finger. Colin had never raised his voice to her before. Never. Where was the man who rubbed her feet and prided himself on his Sunday morning omelet-making skills? What had become of her late-night *Jeopardy!*-viewing buddy? "Don't yell at me. Why are you yelling?"

"Because nothing's ever enough for you." His voice dropped from a yell to a barely audible whisper, which was even more unsettling. "I know what you think. You think I can't pass the bar."

Brighton felt something inside her snap. "That's not true. I *know* you can pass the bar."

"Then why are you making our whole future dependent on my passing some stupid, bullshit test?"

"I'm not!"

"Fine. Then let's scrap the whole wedding and go to the courthouse on Monday."

She blinked. "I have to work on Monday."

"See? Right there." He sounded perversely satisfied. "I know why you want such a long engagement. You don't want to be married to a loser who can't pass the bar." He turned up his palm. "Give me the ring."

"What?" She clapped her hand over the diamond solitaire. "No."

He stomped on the brake and laid on the horn as the minivan merged in front of them.

"What is *wrong* with you?" Brighton cried. "You're going to get shot in a road-rage confrontation. Don't you listen to the news?"

"This is why I'm yelling!" Colin's face reddened as a vein pulsed in his forehead. "You always have to be right. You always have to know the statistics. You always have to follow the rules."

Brighton cringed as the minivan's bumper came within millimeters of the hood. *"It's a zipper merge!"*

"Fuck the zipper merge."

And Brighton completely lost it. "People like you are the reason that traffic is at a standstill. You think you should be the exception. You think you're above rules and statistics, but you're not." She had a sudden, adolescent urge to unbuckle her seat belt, slam out of the car, and walk the rest of the way to the city. Except there was no sidewalk here and she was wearing heels. "If you want to talk about the wedding like a rational human being, I am happy to do that. But don't blame me because you can't pass the bar exam."

"Then don't blame me when I give your ring to someone who wants to marry me without my precious bar results."

"If you . . ." She took a moment to collect herself, smoothing her hair and crossing her ankles. "You know what? This conversation isn't going anywhere productive."

"You need to call it, Brighton." He opened and closed his hands on the steering wheel. "Now or never."

"*Not* now or never," she said. "We made a plan and I would ask that you respect that for the next seventy-two hours. If you still feel this way on Monday morning, we can reevaluate at that time. Now, eat a protein bar before we both say things we're going to regret."

"And then he started yelling that I had to give the ring back. He was furious, and I still don't know what I did."

"It doesn't sound like you did anything," Kira said.

"I haven't heard from him since," Brighton confessed, checking her phone for text messages yet again. "It's been hours. I tried to call him, but it went straight to voice mail. So I ditched work for the first time in . . . ever and drove down to see you." She tucked her phone back into her handbag. "So what do you think? Should I call him again? Try to smooth things over? Or tell him I'd never want to marry someone who throws a temper tantrum over a zipper merge?"

"Well, I have no idea what your relationship's like," Kira pointed out. "I don't know him. I don't even know you anymore, apparently."

Brighton sniffled. "You have a PhD, yes? You have to know *something*."

"Do you guys fight a lot? Is this part of a pattern?"

"Not at all. We're both very calm and rational. We don't yell, we don't call each other names—there's no drama." Brighton settled back in her chair. "That's what I like about our relationship. He's very direct, no surprises. But this bar exam stress has been killing us."

She paused. Kira let the silence settle in around them.

"The problem's not Colin," Brighton finally admitted, to herself as much as to her friend. "It's me. I'm completely burned out. He's burned out on the bar, but I'm burned out on *everything*—my work, my schedule, my whole life. I just don't have anything to give right now. I feel . . . I don't know. But I can't keep going like this." She blew out a breath. "Anyway, enough about me. I want to catch up with you. Tell me what you've been doing since graduation."

"Going to school and working, mostly." Kira shrugged, but something in her tone didn't match her placid expression. "Just opened my practice, and that's pretty much consuming every waking moment right now."

"But it's going well?" Brighton pressed.

"Professionally, it's going great."

"Good for you." Brighton felt a small stab of envy that her friend had dared to do what Brighton had not—take a leap of faith and pursue her passion, health benefits and pensions be damned. "How did you first find this town? It's pretty out of the way."

Kira suddenly seemed fascinated by the frosted glass sconces on the wall. "I first came out here for vacation last summer and realized that there weren't a lot of counseling options in town, which seemed like a big oversight, considering the population. I spent a week at the Better Off Bed-and-Breakfast and they had a few informal support groups for the heartbreak tourists, but no licensed professionals. So I wrote up a business plan and stepped in to fill the void."

Even though she was pretty sure she was venturing into none-of-your-business territory, Brighton asked, "You came here as a heartbreak tourist yourself?"

"Yes." Kira kept gazing up, her eyes clear and calm. "I was married. And then I wasn't married."

"What happened?" Brighton crossed her arms, preemptively outraged with the man who had done her friend wrong. "Did he cheat on you? Yell at you for no reason? Pick petty fights about traffic maneuvers?"

Kira's gaze never wavered. "He died."

Brighton covered her mouth with her hand. "Oh, Kira. I'm *so* sorry. I had no idea."

"Don't feel badly—it's not like I made an announcement in the alumni class notes." Kira traced the edge of the table with her finger. "I should have told you when it happened. I wanted to reach out, but I didn't want to keep going over and over the details. I kind of shut down for a while. But I'm trying to start fresh, and this seemed like a good place."

"I can't believe I didn't know any of this," Brighton said. "You were like a sister to me. How did we get to the point where you get married and widowed and I'm completely oblivious?"

"We got out in the real world and we got busy." Kira's phone buzzed and they both startled. "Speaking of which . . ." She frowned at the screen. "It's my office. Which means it's a client emergency. Brighton, I am so sorry—"

"Take it." Brighton waved away her friend's apologies. "I'll order us some wine."

"Be right back," Kira promised, and darted for the door.

Brighton took a deep breath and tried to absorb the enormity of everything she'd just confessed. She had made her life choices so carefully, accepting the reality that success in one area required sacrifice in another. She had thought everything through and selected the career and the relationship that were most likely to last.

And now she felt nothing.

Then, from within her purse, she heard her cell phone chime with the ringtone she'd programmed for Colin's number. She remained numb as she pressed the phone to her ear and said the words a sensible, even-tempered girlfriend should say in this situation: "I'm so glad you called. I feel awful about leaving things the way we did this morning."

She paused to let him talk, then frowned and pressed the phone to her ear. "Hang on, I can't hear you . . . You're where? You're *what?*" She got to her feet and covered her other ear with her free hand. "Hold on, let me go outside. It's crazy in here and I can't hear a thing—it sounded like you said you got *married*, ha-ha!"

chapter 5

"I'm sorry." Colin's voice cracked. "I don't know what to say, Brighton. It just happened."

Brighton froze midstride on the sidewalk, the pale glow from the streetlamp behind her and the vast darkness of the boardwalk and ocean stretching out in front of her. "You're yanking my chain. You are not serious."

Colin was talking so fast, she could understand only half of what he said. "We were taking a break from studying . . . decided to go grab dinner . . . drove to this steakhouse by the shore . . ."

Kira gestured from a few yards away that she had to go to her car. Brighton waved her friend away and tried to make sense of what Colin was saying.

"Why were you at the Jersey shore?" Brighton grimaced at her own tone. She sounded like his mother. "You're supposed to be studying federal practice and procedure."

"We were watching the game." Colin sounded so far away through the staticky connection. "I wasn't doing anything wrong, I swear to God . . . And then I saw her."

Something in his tone made Brighton draw in a sharp, deep breath. She'd never heard so much emotion in his voice. Certainly never when speaking to or about her.

She knew that she didn't want to hear the answer to this question, but she also knew that she had to ask it. Brutal honesty was always preferable to living in denial. "Who, Colin? Who did you meet?"

"Her name's Genevieve." He was gasping and choking. "I can't explain it. I looked at her and I just knew."

Brighton glanced up at the cloud-covered moon, feeling unnaturally calm. "Are you *crying?*"

"It was this instant connection." He was definitely crying. "We started talking and one thing led to another and . . ."

"Wait." Brighton raised her palm as if calling a meeting to order. "How long have you been at the shore?"

Sniffle, sob. "Four—no, five hours."

"And you already . . ." She pulled her shoulders back. "What did you do, Colin? Sleep with some woman you just met?"

"We . . ." *Sob, sputter, hiccup.* "We got married."

Brighton was officially out of things to say.

"Brighton?" Colin sounded a bit more coherent. "Are you still there?"

She had no contingency plan for this.

So maybe it didn't happen. Denial kicked in, easily overpowering all the brutal honesty. "Colin." She said his name crisply. "Is this a joke? Put down the tort law and tequila and tell me you're kidding."

He started sobbing again.

"I'll take that as a no." She knew she should probably start crying, too, but a cold, eerie calm had settled in. "You're serious? You *married* somebody else?" Her eyes widened as another thought hit. "Is she wearing my ring?"

"I'm sorry." He sounded shattered, absolutely broken by his own decisions. "It was love at first sight."

"Love at first sight? *Love at first sight?*" Brighton pulled her hair back with her free hand and looked around for a gutter to retch into. "What is *wrong* with you?"

"I knew you wouldn't understand." He stopped sniveling, and a note of defiance crept into his voice. "I followed my heart."

"Love at first sight and following your heart." She had to laugh. "This gets better and better. Let me tell you something, Colin. The human heart? Is a moron. That's why it has to stay down in your chest pumping blood while your brain is up in the executive suite making decisions."

"You're mad," he stated.

"You think?! You lose your mind over a damn zipper merge, you demand the ring back, you ignore me all day, and then, when you finally do call, you tell me that you married some woman you just met at a steakhouse? I mean, *what?*" She shivered as a cool, damp breeze blew in from the water. "How does that even work, logistically?"

"The courthouse is open 'til five." His voice was now tinged with both pride and hostility. "It was my idea, so don't blame her."

"Oh, I don't."

"I know this is . . . awkward, but I wanted you to hear it from me. No lying, no sneaking around."

"This is real?" She had to keep asking. "You're serious with all this?"

"It's real. I'm married."

There ensued a long pause while she tried and failed to process his confession. "You married someone else because of a zipper merge."

"I'm sorry, Brighton."

"Don't be." She stopped shivering as adrenaline rushed through her. "I don't want your pity. I hope you and what's-her-name—"

"Genevieve."

"—are deliriously happy together. But odds are, you won't be."

"You're bitter." He sighed, paternal and concerned. "You have a right to be."

"I'm not bitter; I've just read the research on divorce rates. One to three years of dating is the sweet spot for marital longevity. Not one to three hours."

"I don't care what the research says. When you know, you know," he informed her. "And maybe one day, you'll find someone who's a better match for you." He sighed again, then got down to the business side of the breakup. "Text me when you've had a chance to calm down. I still have a few things at your apartment. There's no hurry, but—"

She hung up on him and drew back her arm to fling her phone into the sand. She stopped herself in time, forcing her body to relax. Destroying her phone wouldn't solve her problem. It wouldn't teach Colin a lesson or make him realize that he'd just made a massive mistake.

But she'd find something that would.

She tucked her phone into her purse, located a tube of lip gloss, and strode purposefully back toward the bar.

From the moment Brighton stormed into the Whinery, she could feel the pull of the tractor beam from across the room.

Her heart was pounding, and she made every effort to silence her brain up there in the executive suite of her skull. *The CEO is fired for the night.* Adjusting the lapels of her black blazer, she threaded her way through the crowd of starry-eyed women. "Hey," she said to the back of Jake Sorensen's leather jacket. "Is that drink offer still good?"

He made her wait for a beat, then turned around to face her. With one look, her anger subsided, washed away in a surge of hormones and unspeakable impulses.

"I'm not supposed to talk to you," he drawled, his dark eyes glinting with amusement.

Brighton crossed her arms over her chest. "Says who?"

"Lila Alders." He smiled at her and her whole body felt fizzy. "She said you were too good for me."

Brighton scoffed. "That's just one person's opinion. Lila doesn't even know me." She lifted her chin in defiance. "Buy me a drink."

He stood up, offering her his barstool. "You said you don't drink."

She slid onto the stool. "I usually don't. But people change their minds—just ask my fiancé." She stopped and corrected herself. "*Ex*-fiancé."

"She'll have a glass of champagne," Jake informed the bartender.

"Champagne is for celebrating," Brighton pointed out as the bartender handed her a delicate glass flute.

"You are celebrating." He raised his glass, which appeared to her untrained eye to contain scotch. "Here's to changing your mind."

Brighton took a sip of the light, bubbly booze, then put down her glass with a sharp clink. "We dated for two years and he just broke up with me over the phone. Because he met someone else. Like five minutes ago." She finished the rest of the champagne in two big gulps.

Jake slid his scotch over her way.

"Thank you, but I really, truly don't drink hard liquor. I'm only making an exception for the champagne due to extraordinary circumstances." She leaned toward Jake, her eyes narrowing. "Get this: He *married* the woman he just met five minutes ago."

He loomed over her, so tall and so good-looking and so very obviously bad for her. "Damn."

"I know." She threw up her hands, brushing her fingers against the sleeve of his jacket. "Some random woman named *Genevieve*."

Jake went completely motionless. The smoldering, speculative spark in his eyes flickered out.

"Yeah, that was pretty much my reaction, too." Brighton dug

into one of the little silver candy dishes and helped herself to a handful of miniature Krackels. "Two years versus two seconds. He said he took one look at her and he 'just knew.' What the hell does that even mean?"

Jake devoted all his attention to her, shutting out the music and laughter and carousing with his intensity. The way he looked at her made her feel like the only person in the world. She realized that this was a practiced technique of a lifelong lothario, but she didn't care.

So what if he was a player? Right now, she wanted to be played with.

"How could he do this?" She pounded the bar top, nearly upending her empty champagne flute as the bartender handed her a full one. "We have one stupid fight about a zipper merge, and then, bam! He calls me crying, he's made a binding legal commitment to someone else, the end." She shoved another piece of chocolate into her mouth.

Jake looked incredulous. "He was crying?"

"Yes! And I love him. I tried to be a good girlfriend, I really did. I spent so much time helping him study that *I* could probably pass the bar exam at this point!" She could feel the champagne starting to take effect, and she helped herself to another sip. "But none of that matters, apparently, because she's 'the one.' I can't compete with 'the one.'"

Jake dismissed this with a quirk of his brows. "I give it three months, tops. He'll come crawling back."

"I don't want him to come crawling back!" Brighton declared, although she wasn't sure this was true. "I never want to see him again." She startled a little as her text alert chimed. Kira was checking in:

This is going to take a while. Sorry X1000. Be back asap.

When she glanced back up, Jake was still watching her intently. "That's a pretty serious suit you've got on."

"Yeah, 'cause I'm seriously successful." She narrowed her eyes. "That's what pisses me off about this. He kept harping about how I wanted to marry a lawyer, but I never cared about that. *He* was the one who couldn't stand the fact that he failed the bar."

Jake seemed skeptical. "A lot of women would care about that."

"Yeah, well, I'm not one of them. I want a partner, not a sugar daddy." She made a face. "Gross. I'd never want to be dependent on a man like that."

"Maybe that bothered him," Jake suggested. "Maybe he wanted you to need him."

"Then why'd he propose?" Brighton challenged.

"Why'd you say yes?" Jake shot back.

"Because." Brighton nibbled her lower lip, considering. "He was the guy I always saw myself marrying. Stable. Sensible. Like me."

Jake smiled down at her again. "He's not that stable if he married a stranger with no warning."

"Touché."

"Maybe that's why you liked him." His tone turned conspiratorial. "You want a little chaos on some level."

She shifted in her seat, acutely aware of the whisper of her silk blouse against her skin. "I don't. Trust me."

He nodded. "Okay."

"I *don't*. I like ten-year plans, balanced portfolios, and predictable outcomes."

"Okay." He kept watching her as though she were the most captivating woman on earth.

"So what am I supposed to do now?" she said. "What would you do if this happened to you?"

"*I* would spend a solid decade drinking and buying expensive shit and socializing with strangers." He started to say more, then thought better of it. "Hypothetically."

Brighton snapped out of her emotional death spiral and regarded him with renewed interest. "Hypothetically, hmm?"

That smoldering, speculative spark had returned in full force. "You know what you should do?"

"What?"

"You should marry a stranger, too. That'd show him."

Brighton burst out laughing. "Yeah, right."

"I'm serious. He'd never get over it."

"Please." She took another fortifying sip of champagne. "Do I look like the kind of woman who marries a stranger?"

"You could do it."

"No, I couldn't. I won't even wear a thong."

His gaze intensified.

"Sorry. Overshare. See, this is why I don't drink." She tipped back her head and pressed her fingertips against her temples. "Ugh. What am I going to do?"

"That's the great thing about being single—you can do whatever you want."

"What do I want?" She mulled this over for a moment. And then the answer presented itself. "A shot of whisky."

He frowned. "But you just said . . ."

"Forget what I said. I changed my mind again. Come on, do one shot with me."

He rested his hand on the bar behind her. "This is a bad idea."

"Good." She angled her shoulder until she pressed into his arm. "It will change the whole trajectory of today. Instead of remembering this as the night Colin married someone else, I'll remember it as the night that I did shots of whisky and threw up all over the hot guy with the great watch. Bartender, two shots of . . ." She turned to Jake. "What kind of whisky is good?"

"You're going to hate it all," he predicted.

"Okay, well, what kind will I hate the least?"

"Try this." He handed her his glass. "It's Macallan."

She peered down at the amber liquid. "I thought that was scotch."

"It's scotch whisky." He smiled at her evident confusion. "What we call scotch is really whisky from Scotland."

"What?"

"As opposed to whisky from Kentucky, which is bourbon, or whiskey from Ireland, which is whiskey with an *e*."

"Whisky, Scotch, and bourbon are all the same thing?" Brighton stared at him. "My mind is blown. I learned something new today."

"Great. Now taste something new." He tapped the glass in her hand.

She took a tiny sip of the Macallan and gagged. "Maybe I'll stick with champagne."

"That should cut down on the throwing-up factor." He caught the bartender's eye and signaled for a refill of Brighton's glass.

"You are a refreshing change of pace from the men I normally meet." She rested her cheek against his arm for a moment, then picked up his wrist and tried to discern the time through the watch's cloudy, scratched glass faceplate. "You could fix that, you know," she murmured up at him. "*I* could fix that."

For the first time, he moved away from her, freeing his wrist from her grasp. "I don't want to."

"Why not?" she demanded. "It has so much potential. It could be amazing."

"Potential is a myth," he said. "I'd rather deal with the here and now."

"Me, too." Her whole body felt flushed, and for a moment, she imagined she was a different kind of woman. The kind of woman who could work a skirt suit and closed-toed pumps like a backless dress and stilettos. The kind of woman who let good-looking bad boys buy her drinks on a school night. "The here and now is really working for me."

Two and a half glasses of champagne later ...

Brighton shrugged out of her suit jacket and rested her bare elbows on the glossy black bar top. "This is the best night ever!" She beamed at Jake, who now sat on the stool next to hers. Their shoulders, arms, and thighs pressed together as they surveyed a growing collection of empty glasses. "Are you having fun?"

He paused long enough to drain the rest of his Macallan. "Yeah."

"Good—you definitely did not look like you were having fun when we first got here."

"I'm making up for it now."

"Oops." She frowned as she felt one shoe slip off her foot and tumbled to the floor. "So? What next?"

He inclined his head. "You tell me."

"No, no, no. I've made enough bad decisions already today." She yawned. "*You* tell *me*."

"If you're done here, I can call a car to take you back to wherever you're staying."

"That's it?" She couldn't keep the disappointment out of her voice. "You chat me up, buy me drinks, and now you're just sending me back to breakup purgatory?" She shook her head in despair. "It's this outfit, isn't it? And the pearl earrings? And the fact that my name isn't Genevieve and I don't wear thongs?"

He opened his mouth to respond, but she cut him off by pressing her index finger to his lips. "It's because I'm a normal person with a normal job and a normal life and you're, like, some indolent rich guy who looks like he should have a British accent and a vast estate in Provence."

His lips twitched. "I'll take that as a compliment."

"You're also clearly bored out of your mind."

"I assure you, I'm not bored right now."

"No, I mean in general. *Ennui*: You have it." She gave up searching for her shoe as she sank back in her seat and crossed her legs. "So don't waste the whole night buying me drinks and being agreeable. *Do* something with me." Her voice held a note of rebellion she hardly recognized. "I dare you. Do something with me that you've never done with anyone else."

He gave her a look she couldn't quite decipher. "I've done a lot of things with a lot of women."

"I'm sure you have. Hence the ennui." She circled the crystal of his disintegrating watch with her index finger. This time, he didn't pull away. "Get creative. As long as we don't end up in a cop car or the emergency room, I'm game."

An obviously drunk guy wearing a white baseball cap and the desperate miasma of an over-the-hill frat boy descended upon them.

"Jaaake," he slurred. "Jake, my man, Jake Sorensen."

Jake acknowledged him with a nod and a tight half smile. "How are you, Buddy?"

Buddy turned to Brighton with a leer. "Who's your lady of the evening?"

Her champagne buzz evaporated as she assembled all her social defenses. "Brighton Smith." She tried to appear sober as she offered a handshake.

Buddy blinked at her with bleary eyes. "That's a weird name."

She and Jake exchanged a look. "So I've been told."

"You look like you're all business, honey." Buddy's breath smelled like the floor of a tavern. "Are you hooking up with this guy or taking a deposition?"

"Good seeing you, Buddy." Jake got to his feet and offered his hand to Brighton. "We're on our way out."

"I bet you are." Buddy practically fell over in his attempt to convey *wink-wink-nudge-nudge* solidarity. He recovered his balance, then warned Brighton, "Don't get attached."

Brighton gave him a flat, cold stare.

"This guy isn't relationship material." Buddy slung one arm around Jake's shoulder. "You and me, man. We're alike."

Jake had to use both hands to extricate himself from the man-hug. "See you later."

"We're both *wounded*." Buddy grabbed Jake's shirtfront. "No one understands us."

Brighton stifled a laugh. Jake looked appalled.

As Buddy rambled on, Brighton collected her bag and lost shoe. Jake finally escaped the existential frat boy's clutches and hustled her out of the bar. "Sorry about that."

"No need to apologize." Brighton couldn't help laughing at his obvious horror. "I understand. You secretly wounded man-whores have to stick together."

He scrubbed his face with the palm of his hand. "Buddy and I are not the same."

"Well, obviously not. You're way better looking."

"That's true."

The note of challenge crept back into her voice. "Back to what I was saying. Defend your title as 'designated rebound guy.' What are you going to do for a type A corporate drone whose trusty, dependable fiancé just married some stranger with no warning?"

Jake looked at Brighton. Brighton looked at Jake.

"Let's get married," he suggested in the same tone he might use to ask if she wanted to grab a soda.

She held his gaze for a long moment. "You're insane. And drunk."

"So are you," he pointed out. "You said you wanted to do something I've never done with any other woman."

She maintained eye contact, trying to assess how serious he was.

He looked pretty serious.

"You're bluffing," she said.

He didn't blink. "Try me."

"You don't even know my middle name." She furrowed her brow as she considered the logistics. "And it's Friday night. Even if we did agree to get married, there's no possible way. All the courthouses are closed."

He pulled out his smartphone with an air of determination. "Prepare to watch an indolent rich guy get to work."

chapter 6

"Are you *sure* this is safe?" Brighton asked for the third time as she checked her seat belt and crossed her ankles.

"Yes." Jake settled into his expansive leather seat. "Calm down. You said you were game, remember?"

"But small aircraft have a terrible safety record." Brighton had to speak up to be heard over the hum of the engine.

"Yeah, Gulfstream is famous for cutting corners." Jake shook his head. "It's a miracle I'm still alive."

"You mock me, but I speak the truth." Brighton ticked off the facts on her fingers. "Statistically, private planes are at much higher risk for loss of control, mechanical failure, collision with terrain . . ." She clutched the sumptuous padded armrest. "Aren't you looking forward to being married to a woman who memorizes aircraft safety statistics?"

"We're not married yet," he reminded her. "If you want to talk stats, I'd say there's a ninety-five percent chance you'll lose your nerve before this deal is actually done."

"No way," she swore.

"We'll see."

"I've never been on a private jet before." Brighton surveyed the gray leather upholstery, the polished walnut wall panels, the luxurious cashmere throws, the flat-screen TV. "This is crazy. Who the hell are you that you have your own jet?"

"It's not mine," Jake said. "Technically, it belongs to my company."

"Indolent Rich Guy, Inc.? Seriously, how did you get all this?"

He merely smiled in response and nodded at the bottle of red wine on the table. "You should try that. It's great."

"I can't. Not if we're actually going to go through with this." She tightened her seat belt one more time for good measure. "You have to be sober to get married in Vegas. All those Hollywood movies about drunken weddings are factually inaccurate." She tapped her phone screen. "So says Google."

"What?" He sat up straighter. "What the hell is the point of going to Vegas to get married in the middle of the night *sober*?"

"I'm just guessing, but maybe they don't want people making terrible choices with random strangers because of too much champagne."

He considered this, then shrugged. "It'll be fine. Keep drinking if you want."

She shook her head. "But—"

"Even if there's a sobriety checkpoint at the altar, I know a guy."

"You know a guy?"

He pulled out his wallet. "Benjamin Franklin."

"Seriously?" She rolled her eyes. "You think you can buy your way around the rules?"

Again with that heart-melting smile. "You say that like it's a bad thing."

"Well . . ." Brighton held out her glass for some wine. "I guess if I'm going to be irresponsible, I might as well do it right."

"That's the spirit." He took a sip from her glass, then passed it back to her.

"So . . . one of the drive-through chapels?" she suggested.

"I like it."

"And then we can go get fries."

"Done." Jake pulled out his phone. "I'll have a plan in place by the time we land."

"You can plan an impromptu wedding after drinking this much?" She stumbled over the pronunciation of "impromptu."

"I haven't had that much."

"Yeah, I guess I'm drinking enough for the both of us." She blinked. "Are we really doing this?"

He didn't glance up from his phone. "It's your call."

"Because I'm only doing this for spite, you know."

He nodded. "I know."

"You don't have a problem with that?"

"Nope."

"But . . . I'll be your *wife*." The word sounded so strange in her mouth.

"That's usually how it goes after a wedding."

She tilted her head, assessing him through the shadows. "Why are *you* doing this?"

He held up his index finger and started talking on the phone. For the next few minutes, Brighton gazed out the window at the blinking lights on the wing while Jake talked marriage license logistics.

"So what are we going to do for the next few hours?" Brighton asked when Jake hung up. "Besides go through all the wine they have on board? It's a long flight, right?"

"A few hours." He reached into a drawer and produced a deck of cards. "Want to play blackjack?"

"Sure. Give me a quick rundown on the rules."

He gave her an incredulous look. "You don't know how to play blackjack? A midnight Vegas trip is wasted on you."

"Tell me the rules. I love rules. And I'm really good with numbers and statistics."

He seemed skeptical.

"Come on, tell me the rules and deal the cards. You might want to go grab some Kleenex, because I'm going to beat you so bad, you'll be crying just like my bar-exam-failing fiancé." She hiccupped. "*Ex*-fiancé."

After losing her twentieth game of blackjack, Brighton's memory of the night's events got a bit blurry. Which was too bad, because she was sure that arriving at a private airfield and being whisked away in a limo were very exciting and glamorous.

The good news was, she was no longer thinking about Colin— or anything else related to her real life. In a matter of hours, she'd gone from total burnout to jet-setting party girl.

"My shirt has red wine on it," she lamented as the limo cruised down the neon-lit Vegas strip.

"I'd say that's the least of your problems right now." Sprawled out on the seat next to her, Jake was trying—and failing—to conceal the fact that he was completely wasted.

"You may have a point." She kept dabbing at her cream-colored blouse with one of the wet wipes she always carried in her bag. Looking at her naked fingers under the traffic lights reminded her: "What are we going to do for rings?"

"Whatever you want. After we hit the drive-through, we can go pick something out. I'll buy you the biggest, blingiest diamond in Nevada."

"Eh, I'd rather get fries." As if on cue, her stomach growled. "I'm starving. Besides, I doubt we'll be married long enough to actually wear the rings. It'd be a waste."

His expression was almost pitying. "It's not a waste if it's fun."

"Yeah, but . . ." She threw up her hands. "How long do you think we'll last, anyway?"

Jake shrugged. "Haven't really thought about it."

"We have to last longer than Colin and his new bride," Brighton decided. "You can date other people if you want to, but there's no way I'm filing for divorce until he does."

"It's good to have a goal."

"This is a huge mistake," she said cheerfully. "But you know, it's kind of exciting. Getting drunk. Marrying a stranger. I have a feeling . . ."

"Yes?"

She flung out her arms. "This is the beginning of what shall be known as my screw-up summer. I'll act out and make mistakes and not care what anyone thinks." The whole world was spinning. All she could see were streaks of dark and light and bright colors. "I'm really looking forward to it."

"You'll have stories to tell your grandkids one day."

"Oh, I'll never be able to tell my grandkids anything about it. That's the point." She stifled a huge yawn. "Thanks for being the catalyst for chaos and self-indulgence."

He patted her knee. "Happy to help."

Brighton bounced in her seat as the limo arrived at a white sign emblazoned with two interlocking yellow rings. "We made it." She reached across the seat, took Jake's hand in hers, and stared deep into his eyes. "Last chance to bail."

"I'm not bailing," he vowed. "I'm in if you're in."

"Then get your bribery cash out and let's do this."

But there was a line at the drive-through—a rusty pickup truck and a red convertible idled in front of the limo.

"Damn," Brighton muttered. "There should be a VIP lane at the drive-through chapel. Can't your people get us an E-ZPass?"

"We're looking at a ten-minute wait, tops."

"I know, but we need to get this over with before I lose my nerve." The pickup truck's brake lights flickered, and Brighton bounced in her seat. "Okay, here we go. Five minutes and counting." She fumbled for her bag. "I swear I had a stain stick in here somewhere."

"Let it go." Jake pulled her other hand into his.

She leaned in toward him, basking in the hormones and the buzz. "We're about to get married and we haven't even kissed yet."

"I can cross that off your list right now." He tilted his head.

But she forced herself to pull back. "Not yet. We waited this long. Might as well wait five more minutes 'til we make it legal."

He laughed. "An old-fashioned girl."

"Practically Victorian." Brighton dug her cell phone out of her bag and turned on the camera feature. "As long as we're stuck in traffic, I have a few texts to send a certain ex."

chapter 7

"Urgh." Brighton woke up a few hours later, completely disoriented. Her mouth—her entire head, really—tasted like vinegar. She heard the rustle of a fast-food wrapper when she shifted her feet. Her wool blazer smelled faintly of cigarettes and her skirt was bunched up around her thighs.

But she was covered in a soft, featherweight cashmere blanket. Her head rested on a fluffy pillow. She was stretched out in all her hungover glory on the leather seats of Jake Sorensen's private jet.

She was . . . married?

She lifted her head and propped herself up on her elbows, blinking as the plane's interior came into focus through the dim lighting. Jake was slouched on the other side of the cabin, gazing down at the screen of a laptop computer.

She licked her lips and cleared her throat, but her voice still sounded like she'd been singing karaoke at the top of her lungs all night. "Hey."

"You're awake." He pointed out a bottle of water on the table next to her. "Hydrate."

"I feel like . . ." She rubbed her forehead with the heel of her hand. "I'd say I haven't felt this hungover since college, but I've never felt this hungover, ever." She paused to gulp some of the cool, fresh water. "Did we . . . did we go through with it?"

"We did." He closed the laptop and gave her his full attention, but the sensual smolder had been replaced with an almost detached friendliness. Something had happened between pulling up to the drive-through chapel and now; they were no longer boozy partners in crime. Now they were two adults who had just met.

Who happened to be married.

"Did we kiss?" she asked.

He furrowed his brow. "I think so. Right after I introduced the officiant to Benjamin Franklin and right before you passed out."

She covered her lips with her hand. "How was it?"

"Brief. Official. Wine-flavored."

She tugged her blanket tighter around her shoulders. "How are you still awake?"

He shrugged. "I'm supposed to be looking over some work documents."

"You're working." The reality of everything they'd done slammed into her. "It's our wedding night and you're working? That's not very indolent of you."

"I'm *supposed* to be looking over some documents," he clarified. "I'm actually watching a documentary on giant radioactive wolves."

Brighton scrambled into a sitting position. "Like, science fiction?"

"No, they're real. It's about what happened to the wildlife at the abandoned Chernobyl site."

"Is that . . . related to your job?"

"Not even remotely."

"Okay." She blinked a few times. "You like nature documentaries?"

"I do when they're about radioactive wolves." He lifted the shade so she could see the golden morning sunlight. "We won't be landing for another hour. You can go back to sleep, if you want."

"What kind of work do you do that you can afford all this?" she rasped. "Private jets and teams of people to do your bidding wherever you go?"

He didn't reply. She could hear the steady drone of the engines and the hiss of air from the overhead vents.

Just when she started to wonder if she'd inadvertently offended him, he asked, "Do you like to talk about your job when you're hanging out at bars or flying to Vegas?"

"No," Brighton admitted. "But that's because my work is really boring."

He nodded. "My work is really boring, too."

"Boring and completely legal . . . right?" She laced her hands together and squeezed.

"Completely," he assured her.

"It better be. Because, so help me, if I find out later that you're some sort of drug dealer or Mafia kingpin, I'm going to be pissed."

"If I were into drugs or organized crime, I wouldn't be spending my summers in Black Dog Bay." The warmth had returned to his voice and his eyes. "Everybody knows everything about everybody else, and they all talk."

"Good. I just want to make sure you don't have a criminal past. Or a criminal present, for that matter."

He mirrored her solemn expression. "If it makes you feel better, a wife cannot be forced to testify against her husband. So if I *were* a criminal, marrying me is actually reducing your odds of getting caught up in all the legal proceedings."

Her eyes widened and her palms started to sweat. "The fact that you know that does not make me feel better."

"Relax. I'm just torturing you."

"Well, knock it off and reassure me that cocaine and arms trafficking didn't pay for this plane."

He finally relented. "Sand paid for this plane."

"What?"

"Sand, concrete, and gravel."

"Elaborate, please."

"I started out supplying concrete for construction contracts." He looked and sounded completely bored with this topic of conversation. "That's how I made my first million."

"First million's the hardest, right?" Brighton paused. "Or so I've heard."

"Then I branched into gravel, and now I supply sand for corporate and military contracting jobs in the Middle East. The end."

"You send sand to the Middle East. Like, the desert?"

Jake nodded. "The sand over there is too fine for sandblasting concrete. We use a proprietary processing method and ship it over."

"You built this"—she gestured to the cashmere and the polished walnut panels and the leather upholstery—"out of sand and gravel. That's kind of . . ."

"Redneck. I know."

Where had that come from? "'Redneck' is not the word I would use to describe you."

He watched her expression. "Disappointed I'm not part of a seedy underworld syndicate?"

"No," she said, a bit too quickly.

"What about you?" he countered. "How do I know *you* don't have a criminal past?"

"Seriously?" She glanced down at her outfit. "Look at me."

"I'm looking. The suit and the pearls could be a façade."

"They're not."

"For all I know, you could be an undercover cop or a Russian spy."

"No." She sighed. "I am exactly as buttoned-up and responsible as I look."

"You just flew off to Vegas to marry a stranger."

"A stranger who *doesn't* have a criminal past or a loan shark after him." She snuggled back into her cashmere cocoon. "Ooh, so rebellious."

He laughed and closed the window shade. "Baby steps."

Just as she was drifting back to sleep, Brighton sat up straight, gasping. "Kira."

"Who?" Jake asked.

"My friend Kira. I was at the bar with her last night. She has no idea what happened to me." Brighton scrambled to straighten her skirt and grab her purse. "I need to call her right now. Can I use my cell in flight?"

"Sure."

Brighton entered her password to unlock her phone, then gasped as she looked at the image on the screen. "Oh no. Oh no no no."

"What?" Jake moved to sit next to her. He still smelled freshly laundered, with just a hint of woodsy cologne. It was like the laws of physics and hangovers didn't apply to him.

"I texted Colin last night." She felt light-headed. "After the drive-through. I don't remember any of this, but the time stamp says one a.m. Why didn't someone take away my phone?"

"Because you're a professional woman who's clearly capable of making her own decisions."

"What have I done? *What have I done?*" Brighton scrolled through the texts she had sent to her ex.

All twenty-eight of them.

Photos of the limo.

Photos of the private jet.

Photos of Brighton and Jake holding up the freshly signed marriage certificate and a bottle of champagne.

"Oh my God," Brighton whispered. "I sent these to my fiancé. I mean, my *ex*-fiancé."

Jake started laughing. "When did we get another bottle of champagne?"

And then, as if the pictures weren't bad enough, Brighton noticed the typo- and autocorrect-riddled captions she'd included with each photo:

Floying commercial is so pleb

Look at the smolder on this guy

Not to mention the hair

It's like he's the lost Hemsworth brother

Marrying a Stranger: I WIN!!!!!!

"I'm dying." She pulled the blanket over her head. "I'm dead. How will I ever go back to New Jersey?"

"You know what the great thing is about marrying me?" Jake said. "You don't have to."

Brighton yanked the blanket down. "Of course I do. What about my job?"

"Quit," he suggested. "It's your screw-up summer, remember?"

"Screwing up my summer is one thing, but I don't want to screw up my whole life."

He gave her an appraising look. "I'm willing to bet you have some vacation days stored up."

"Um. Maybe." Three years' worth. Plus sick days. Plus personal days.

"Then take some time off."

"I can't."

"Why not?"

"I don't know." But she did know. She was afraid. Afraid that if she took a break, her boss and her coworkers would realize that she wasn't indispensable. And she'd spend her vacation time doing . . . what? Admitting that she had no interests outside of work and helping her boyfriend study contract law?

"Technically, you're on your honeymoon," Jake said. And then he kissed her. Slow and soft and thorough; confident but unhurried.

When he finally tapered off, she hung on to his jacket with both hands. She wasn't thinking about work or the future or the potential fallout from her ill-advised texts. She wasn't thinking about anything. She could be content up here in the clouds, with cashmere and champagne and the lost Hemsworth brother, for eternity.

"Okay." She trailed her fingers along his cheek. "I'll take two weeks off."

Jake pulled her closer and kissed her again. "Get ready for the best two weeks of your life."

chapter 8

They landed at a tiny private airfield in the bright morning light, and when they got off the plane, Brighton noticed a black Town Car waiting next to a gray Ford pickup truck.

Brighton nodded at the livery vehicle. "Is that your car?"

Jake pulled out a set of keys. "No. The truck's mine."

"Of course; I should have known."

"Why's that?"

"Because the Ford F series pickup truck is the most popular vehicle among millionaires nationwide," Brighton said. "You fit right in with your demographic."

He smiled but seemed distracted. "I have to go take care of a work thing for a few hours. While I'm dealing with that, the driver will take you anywhere you like. If you want to go take a nap at my house, I'll give you the key." He reached into his jacket pocket.

Brighton held up her hands and took a step back. "Slow down, buddy, we just met."

"Tell it to the marriage registrar." He pressed a cold metal key into her palm. "I'll text you when I get back to Black Dog Bay, and we can figure out where we go from here."

They looked at each other for a long moment.

"I'm going to need your phone number," he said.

"Right back at you." They exchanged contact information and prepared to go their separate ways.

"Last night was fun." She pushed her windblown hair back from her face. "Thanks for helping me launch my screw-up summer."

"My pleasure." He was talking to her but looking at his phone.

"So . . . see you later?"

"High noon. And if you need anything at all . . ."

"Advil," Brighton blurted out. "Please. I'm begging you."

"Consider it done." He gave her a soft, quick kiss on the cheek that left her thoroughly frustrated. But she resisted the urge to fling her arms around him and demand more. Better to consummate the marriage after she'd showered and recovered from her hangover. All in good time.

Time, which she suddenly had in abundance. She could do whatever she wanted for the rest of the weekend. But how could she possibly top the adventure she'd just had?

She pulled out her own phone, preparing to call her sister and mother with the news. But as she scrolled through her contacts, she realized there was no way to explain what had just happened. Yes, she was technically married, but Jake wasn't really her husband. She barely knew him.

Although, as it turned out, she'd barely known Colin, either, and they'd been dating for two years. Maybe trust and love and good decision making had nothing to do with a happy marriage. Maybe it was all just a crapshoot.

If she called her family, she'd have to try to put last night's events and emotions into words. She'd have to defend her actions and reassure everyone that she was still the same responsible, thoughtful Brighton she'd always been. That she was having a romantic interlude and not a nervous breakdown.

But how could she expect them to buy that when she didn't really buy it herself?

Instead of dialing her mother, she dialed Kira, who picked up with a mixture of annoyance and relief: "Thank God you called. What happened to you last night? Are you okay?"

"I'm okay." She took a deep breath. "I'm also married."

Kira gasped.

"Meet me for breakfast and I'll explain everything," Brighton said. "Is there someplace in town that has good hash browns?"

"I can't believe this." Kira regarded Brighton with huge eyes across the laminate table at the Jilted Café. "I take one emergency client call and you end up married to the hot guy you wouldn't let me sit near?"

Brighton nodded. "It just sort of happened."

"Wow." Kira stirred a packet of sugar into her coffee and turned her attention to the rumpled, wine-stained business wear. "Tell me you didn't wear that to your wedding."

"Um . . ." Brighton pushed her napkin and silverware to one side as their server approached with hash browns and omelets.

"Oh, Brighton. You couldn't build a few minutes into your elopement schedule to buy a white dress?"

"No schedule. Like I said, it just sort of happened." Brighton held up her phone. "Check it out. Here we are waiting in line at the drive-through."

"A drive-through chapel?" Kira's hand flew to her mouth. "Oh, honey, no."

"It was amazing. Tacky in the very best possible way." Brighton grinned as she picked up her huge, warm coffee mug and sipped.

"And this is for real?" Kira pressed. "You signed an actual marriage license? You're that guy's legally wedded wife?"

Brighton nodded.

"But . . . but why? I thought you were engaged."

"I was." Brighton summarized the debacle with Colin and the magical, marriage-worthy Genevieve. "So you see, I was provoked."

"Uh-huh." Kira dug into her breakfast.

"You should see your expression right now." Brighton couldn't stop laughing. The sleep deprivation was starting to make her punchy. "If I were your client, what would you tell me?"

"You're not my client." Kira looked heavenward. "Thank God."

"Fine, but I'm your friend." Brighton winced as one of the line cooks dropped what sounded like an entire shelf's worth of glassware on the floor. "Don't hold back. Say what you're thinking."

Kira stalled by taking another huge bite. "Well."

"Come on."

Kira put down her fork and looked her friend squarely in the eye. "*Officially*, I think you've lost your mind. I think you're going to regret this later. I think you took a bad situation and made it worse."

Brighton nodded. "Keep going."

"What Colin did to you was pretty traumatic. If I were your therapist—which, let's be crystal clear, I am not—I would tell you to step back and regroup. Don't make any big decisions for at least six to twelve months."

"So . . . don't run off with the lost Hemsworth brother and a case of champagne?"

Kira picked up her fork and pointed it at Brighton. "Right. Revenge rebounds never end well."

"That's good advice," Brighton conceded. "And logically, I know I should follow it."

"Officially, I advise you to start the annulment process on Monday," Kira said. "I'm sure if you file right away—"

"What's your unofficial advice?" Brighton asked.

Kira hesitated.

"Come on. Out with it. I don't care how many years have passed—I'm still your take-it-to-the-grave friend, right?"

Kira nodded. "I did used to say that if I ever murdered someone, I'd call you to help me hide the body."

"Because I'd know it was justifiable homicide," Brighton said. "So cut the 'official' crap and let's get down to some unofficial real talk."

"Okay, let's." Kira crumpled up the empty sugar packet. "Unofficially, I have no room to talk about this kind of thing. Chris and I got married three months after we first met."

"You did?"

"Yeah. Everybody said we were nuts." Kira smiled at the memory. "My parents begged me to wait until I'd finished my internship and dissertation. His mother threatened to boycott the wedding."

"But you got married anyway?"

"At a tiny little chapel in Santa Rosa Beach." Kira shrugged. "What can I say? When you know, you know."

Brighton's stomach soured. "That's what Colin said. Verbatim."

Kira's blue eyes lit up as she reminisced about her newlywed days. "Looking back, our parents were right. We were young and impulsive. I'd never want my daughter to marry someone she'd just met."

Brighton cupped her chin in her hand. "But you regret nothing."

"We were really happy together. And we didn't know it at the ceremony, but he had a brain tumor already."

"Oh, Kira."

"The time we had together before he got sick, before all the scans and doctors' appointments and hospice . . . I wouldn't trade that for anything. I treasure every single second. I always have that, even though he's gone."

For the hundredth time since she'd reunited with Kira at the Whinery the night before, Brighton wished that she had worked harder to hold on to this friendship. If she had a do-over of the past ten years, she'd spend less time racking up connections on LinkedIn and more time maintaining relationships with the people who'd known her before she became consumed with professional achievement.

But there were no do-overs. She couldn't change her past; all she could do was try to change the future.

"My point is, real love is never a waste," Kira concluded. "The best moments of my life have been when I deviated from my ten-year plan." She shot Brighton a look.

"Don't knock the ten-year plan," Brighton said. "I snagged a big office with a window and everything thanks to my ten-year plan."

"And you snagged the lost Hemsworth brother without it."

"Well, when you put it like that . . ."

"I guess my question for you is, is this a true 'when you know, you know' situation?" Kira asked. "Did you and Jake fall in love at first sight?"

"Nope. Love has nothing to do with this."

"Then my official advice stands."

Brighton leaned in and confided, "But there's something about this guy, Kira. I don't know if it's the post-breakup rage or the sleep deprivation or what, but I just want more. I want to drape myself over him like a chinchilla coat."

Kira leaned in, too, and for a moment, it felt like they were back in their university's student union. "Go on."

"It's like . . ." Brighton closed her eyes, trying to put the sensations into words. "I had no idea that kissing could be like that. I mean, I like making out as much as the next girl, but he takes it to a whole other level. I'm still thinking about it. I don't know if I'll ever think about anything else." She had to stop and catch her breath. "I've never done

issing him is what I imagine it's like. He tastes good, he
e feels good. I'm high, Kira. High on Jake Sorensen."

Kira's smile turned soothing. "There's a clinical term for this feeling. It's called 'limerence,' and it means your brain is getting a big surge of dopamine."

"So I *am* high."

"Yeah, basically."

"I like it." Brighton tipped her head back and basked in the sunlight streaming in through the café's plate-glass window. Her hangover was gone, thanks to Advil, greasy hash browns, and all that dopamine. "I feel tingly all over. I couldn't care less about who Colin is with right now or what he's doing. Limerence is much better than love."

Kira got serious. "It's a great feeling, but it eventually fades, and then you crash."

"I'll worry about that later," Brighton said. "Like in two weeks. Right now, for once in my life, I'm going to live in the moment. I want to take some vacation time and explore this whole evil-twin lifestyle. Carpe diem. YOLO. Whatever the kids are saying these days."

"Yeah." Kira sounded dubious. "But eventually, you'll need to deal with everything that happened with Colin. Right now, you're self-medicating with a new man. You have to grieve sooner or later."

"Later," Brighton said. "I choose later."

"Then enjoy every moment of your vacation." Kira flagged down a passing server. "Hey, do you guys have any of those bear claw things with the almonds?"

"I'm so glad you called me yesterday. I've missed you." Brighton rubbed her bleary eyes and doubled down on her coffee consumption. "The second thing I'm going to do with my screw-up summer is make up for lost time with you."

"The second thing?" Kira said. "What's the first thing you're going to do?"

"Jake Sorensen."

. . .

A few hours later, ensconced in the cool, quiet interior of what Kira had dubbed "the Secret Service car," Brighton reunited with her husband.

Jake was waiting for her at the end of a long cobblestone drive-way. Even from afar, his tall, broad-shouldered silhouette radiated confidence and masculinity. When the car pulled up, he opened the passenger-side door and offered Brighton his hand. As she gazed up at the sprawling cedar-shingled estate perched on an oceanside cliff, she started to consider the real-world implications of her flight of fancy. They had signed a legally binding document without so much as a background check. This man could be a serial killer for all she knew—or worse, he could have a terrible credit score. He could be an addict, a misogynist, a cult leader . . .

He put his hand on the small of her back and led her toward the house.

"So this is where you live. It's beautiful." If he was a cult leader, at least she'd have a nice compound.

He shrugged. "It's a good investment."

The house featured dozens of windows; Brighton could see through the first floor to the ocean. The views from the second story must be incredible. "I know this is tacky, but I have to ask: How many square feet?"

For the first time, Jake seemed uncomfortable. "I don't know the exact number."

"Guesstimate," Brighton urged.

"Maybe eight thousand." He gazed up at the spacious structure with what almost looked like chagrin.

Her jaw dropped. "Damn. What do you even do with all that space?"

"Wait for it to appreciate, then sell it."

This stretch of the bay was lined with brand-new, contemporary-style houses, most of them boasting three stories with wraparound patios and balconies that faced the ocean. Though the homes were luxurious, they lacked historical charm.

"You definitely got the best lot," she said. "How long ago did you buy this place?"

"I was one of the original construction investors." He cleared his throat. Definitely uncomfortable.

Well, at least she wasn't the only one feeling nervous. "What was here before the land was developed?"

"Nothing, really. They used to call it Gull's Point. The local teenagers would come up here and have bonfires."

She glanced around at the mansions flanked by pools and guest cottages. "That seems like kind of a shame, for the town and the environment."

"If we hadn't developed it, someone else would have."

As he guided her along the stone-paved walkway, she noticed a little pond, complete with a fountain. She stopped to get a closer look and saw swirls of orange moving beneath the water's surface.

"Are those goldfish?" she asked.

He glanced back over his shoulder. "Yeah. Koi, actually. That's how this house got its name."

"Your house has a name?" She crouched down to get a better look at the fish. "I should have figured."

He pointed out the little bronze plaque next to the door: DON'T BE KOI.

"I'm going to pretend I never saw that." As she straightened up, he took her hand. "Who takes care of these little guys all year?"

"The groundskeeper." He paused. "Or the housekeeper? Probably the groundskeeper."

"Even your fish have people? I should have known."

"What kind of man would I be if I let my goldfish starve?"

She saw her opening and took it. "What kind of man, indeed. You know, I'm curious. You wouldn't mind if I ran a quick little background check on you? As a mere formality?"

"You'd be stupid not to." He turned toward her. "And you don't strike me as a stupid woman."

She could have told him about her valedictorian status, her academic scholarships, her accolades and promotions at work. She could have cited her credentials to prove her worth, but she found that she had no interest in proving her worth to Jake. Professional qualifications had no place in her screw-up summer.

"Are you going to run a background check on me?" she asked him. "For all you know, I could have a criminal record as long as your property line."

He looked intrigued by the prospect. "Do you?"

"No." But she kind of enjoyed the fact that he hadn't immediately dismissed the possibility. Which surprised her—she'd always liked being respected and held up as an example . . . hadn't she?

This was the real problem with marrying someone she didn't know. It made her question whether she really knew herself.

"You okay?" He looked concerned.

"Yeah." She forced herself to stop thinking these thoughts. "I was just—" She held up one hand as she heard a muffled sound. "What was that?"

Jake froze. "What was what?"

"I thought I heard something." She strained to pick up any sound above the gurgle of the pond's filter. "Like a dog barking."

"I don't have a dog," he said.

"That's probably a good thing, considering you don't even feed your own fish."

And then they arrived at the front door. Talk of background checks and criminal records ceased. When he paused to find his house keys, Brighton tucked her hair back behind her ear.

"So, um, so now what?"

He stilled and all she could hear was the crash of the waves and the chirp of the crickets. "You're welcome to stay in the guesthouse until you finish your background check."

She inched closer, reveling in her own recklessness. "Or . . . ?"

"Or you can come inside with me."

"Okay."

"And I'll take you upstairs to my bedroom."

Her throat went dry. "Okay."

"And I'll take off that suit and that shirt and those pearls and do hot, sweaty, dirty things to you."

She gave up trying to talk and just stared at him.

He smiled, slow and wicked, and Brighton Smith, lifelong control freak, finally lost control.

chapter 9

"I'm going to need the names and addresses of every woman you've ever slept with." Brighton lolled back against the pillows, her hair tangled, her brow sweaty, and her cheeks flushed. The bright midday sun had faded into sunset and the fading light filtered through the gauzy curtains and bathed the bed in a warm golden glow. "I'm going to send them handwritten thank-you notes."

Jake sat up next to her and regarded her with mock reproach. "You think I couldn't figure all that out on my own?"

"I think you should be giving seminars." She felt dazed with a combination of languor and lust.

"My techniques can't be taught." She could hear the smile in his voice. "I'm gifted and talented."

"Yes, you are." She shifted against the crisp white sheets, rubbing her bare ankle against his. Even if this spur-of-the-moment marriage played out exactly as the stats would predict—hell, even if she got out of bed right now, buttoned up her shirt, and resumed her regularly scheduled life without a single backward glance—she would always look back on today with a fond heart.

After twenty-four hours packed with rage and despair and spiteful selfies, she'd managed to let go and spend a few hours as the woman she wished she could always be: Free-spirited. Bold. Confident and passionate, with just a hint of a dark edge. One day with this total stranger had easily eclipsed two years with the man she'd been prepared to spend the rest of her life with.

Colin who?

That's just the limerence talking.

"You could go on late-night TV to pitch your book and DVD series." She trailed her fingers across his broad, square shoulders. "*Secrets of the Designated Rebound Man: An Instructional Lecture Series* by Jake Sorensen. We can put together a business plan tomorrow."

"If you're thinking about a business plan right now, my work here isn't done." The sheets rustled as he moved back over her.

"Mmmm." She wound her arms around his neck and lifted her face to brush her lips against his. "Can we take a quick water break? I need to hydrate."

The mattress dipped as he pulled away. "What's your pleasure? Bottled water? Red Bull? Iced coffee? Iced tea?" He ran his hand through his hair as he rattled off her options. "Lemonade? Orange juice? Wine? Diet Coke? Diet Pepsi? Craft beer? Gatorade?"

She managed to lift her head off the pillow. "Are you running a 7-Eleven out of your kitchen?"

He seemed mystified by her amusement. "I try to be a good host. What'll it be?"

"Gatorade's fine."

He nodded. "What kind of Gatorade? I have orange, lemon-lime, fruit punch . . ."

"Oh my God."

"What flavor?" he prompted.

"Orange."

He headed down to the kitchen with his sculpted cheekbones and chiseled abs and endless charm. She watched him go and wondered if perhaps she had stumbled into an alternate universe. Maybe that wine bar was a portal to another dimension? Men like Jake Sorensen didn't marry women like Brighton. Hell, men like Jake Sorensen didn't even *notice* women like Brighton.

When she rolled over onto her stomach, she noticed his banged-up watch on the night table. She picked it up and turned it over to examine the back of the casing. The metal had been engraved, although the letters were obscured by rough patches of oxidization from years of neglect. She scraped lightly with her thumbnail, trying to discern the words.

Jake appeared in the doorway, a bottle of orange Gatorade in hand. "You're obsessed with that thing."

"I'm sorry, I know it's none of my business, but it just seems wrong to let it stay in this condition." She turned the watch over and over in her hands. "You obviously have the resources to restore it."

He barely glanced at it. "I have the resources to buy a new watch."

"Yeah, but you can't buy the history and the cachet." She closed her eyes and rubbed her fingertip across the scratched crystal, trying to imagine the past owners. "You must have liked this at some point or you wouldn't have bought it."

"For someone who claims to be so practical, you're kind of a romantic," he remarked.

"Only about inanimate objects. My grandfather was a bench jeweler—I have a thing for well-designed pieces. We used to repair watches together."

He leaned against the doorframe, listening intently. He was so good at making her feel special. Even though she knew it was a practiced act, she couldn't help responding. "No wonder you can't keep your hands off it."

"We didn't do the mechanical recalibration—that's a whole other skill set." Brighton held up the watch as she talked. "But we used to replace the crystals—that's the glass part here—and polish the cases—that's the metal part here—and resize the bands. It's a lot of detail work, but it's kind of Zen. I once read that the Dalai Lama repairs watches to relax." She remembered the peace she'd felt working side by side with her grandfather in silence. She would become totally immersed in the project. As an adult, no matter how hard she worked at her corporate jobs, she'd never been able to recapture that sense of fulfillment and intensity. "Where'd you get this, anyway?"

He pushed off the doorframe and unscrewed the cap of the Gatorade. "An estate auction. I was twenty-five and drunk on good scotch."

She couldn't hide her surprise. "You had enough money to buy a Patek Philippe at twenty-five? Did you have a trust fund?"

His laugh had a dark undertone. "No. I told you, I literally made my money from dirt and rocks."

"But to have made so much, so young . . ." She waited for him to elaborate, then finally gave up. "Anyway, this watch spoke to you."

"Not really." His brown eyes betrayed no hint of emotion. "I bought it to impress people who did have trust funds. I was young enough that I still cared what they thought about me."

"Trust fund or not, you have good taste. This is an heirloom." Brighton showed him the back of the casing. "See the engraving here? Men pass these watches down to their sons and grandsons and great-grandsons. Each owner has his name engraved back here, along with the date he inherited it." She smiled up at him. "You should do that. It'd be easy to refinish."

He quirked one eyebrow. "I don't have a son."

"But you might someday." She flushed again. "Not with me, obviously, but, you know."

"I'm new money, Brighton. Heirlooms are for families that came over on the *Mayflower*." He sat down next to her on the bed and offered it to her. "That thing's going back into the drawer it came from."

She took a sip and shook her head. "This right here is why we're doomed to failure. We'd never be a match on any online dating site. eHarmony would make us go to our separate corners."

"We both like orange Gatorade." He took a sip from her bottle, then passed it back. "eHarmony can suck it."

"Okay, so we have *one* thing in common. But where do we go from here?"

"Is this a rhetorical question? We're naked, in bed, and rehydrating. To quote the little bronze plate by the front door, 'Don't Play Koi.'"

Brighton laughed and spilled a droplet of Gatorade on the pillowcase. "Oops. No, I mean, what happens in the cold light of day tomorrow? We can't keep the whole drive-through chapel and mind-blowing-sex thing going indefinitely."

"Why not? If you want to spend the rest of the summer jetting around the world and drinking champagne, we can make that happen."

She pondered the prospect for a moment. It sounded like a dream come true—for someone else. "What about you? Don't you have to work?"

"Don't worry about me. Focus on making your screw-up summer worthy of its name."

She sat up and kissed him, heedless of his stubble. Somehow, Jake Sorensen even made beard burn feel good.

And maybe that was okay. Maybe, just for a week or two (or three), she could abandon her ten-year plan and let herself follow her heart. Maybe now was the right time.

When you know, you know.

"Fourteen days and no regrets." She spilled another drop of orange liquid on the pristine white sheets. She didn't apologize or race to the bathroom for a washcloth dipped in cold water. She let the stain set and kept kissing her new husband, who tasted like intrigue and Gatorade. "But just tell me one thing: Why me? Why now?"

He gathered her up in his arms and her whole body melted against him. "Why not?"

By the time the moon crested over the dark horizon, Brighton was completely relaxed, completely blissful, and completely exhausted.

"Do you need anything?" Jake asked. "Water? Trail mix? A protein bar?"

"Sleep." She snuggled into the pile of fluffy pillows.

"I'm going to shower." He kissed the top of her head as he rolled out of bed. "Feel free to pass out."

The steady noise of waves crashing on the shore lulled her to sleep, but just as her eyes fluttered closed, her phone beeped.

She groped for her cell and peered through the darkness at the text from Kira: *Just making sure you're still alive. Sometimes the charming ones turn out to be sociopaths.*

Brighton hit "call back." As soon as Kira answered, Brighton demanded to know, "Why are you still awake?"

"Oh good, you're not dead." Kira sounded more amused than relieved. "Sometimes I have trouble sleeping. And when that happens, I like to stay up and obsess about worst-case scenarios that will probably never happen."

"Like Jake Sorensen being a duplicitous sociopath?"

"Exactly like that."

"Well, he's not. But even if he was? *Worth it*." Brighton was wide-awake again. "I need a new word, Kira. Lust, limerance, longing . . . it's all of that to the tenth power."

"Nice."

"He *is* nice," Brighton confided. "Yes, he's the physical equivalent of a Dolce and Gabbana cologne ad and he has a mansion on the beach and an apparently bottomless supply of orange Gatorade—"

"What?"

"Never mind. He has what he has and he looks how he looks, but he seems like a genuinely nice guy." Brighton paused. "Not a duplicitous sociopath. And not one of those guys who *pretends* to be nice so he can manipulate you into putting up with his bad behavior."

"An important distinction," Kira agreed.

Brighton nibbled her lower lip as she gazed up at the whitewashed ceiling beams.

"But . . . ," Kira prompted.

"But I have no idea who he actually is."

"Did you Google?"

"Of course I Googled!" Brighton was insulted. "I'm not brand-new."

"Well? What did Google say?"

"Not a whole hell of a lot. It pretty much verified everything I already know—vague references to corporate wheelings and dealings. But I couldn't find anything personal. No social media or embarrassing photos from college."

"And you still got on the plane and signed the marriage certificate." Kira clicked her tongue.

"Whatever. What's done is done, and we can always get divorced."

"That's the spirit."

Brighton noticed the flickering glow of a bonfire on the other side of the bay. "What do you think Colin is doing right now?"

"Don't go down that rabbit hole," Kira advised. "At least one of us should get some sleep tonight."

Brighton rolled over onto her side. "Do you think he's really found his soul mate? Do you think they'll be happily married for fifty years?"

"I think *your* marriage has a better chance of working out than his does. And that's saying something."

"Aw. You're sweet."

"I'm so glad you're going to stay in town for a bit," Kira said. "It's nice to have someone who knew me before."

Brighton didn't have to ask before what. She pressed the phone closer to her ear. "I'm glad, too."

"And don't worry." Kira's tone lightened. "If you end up dead in a puddle of Dolce and Gabbana cologne under mysterious circumstances, I'll know who did it."

chapter 10

$\mathcal{T}$he next morning Brighton woke up alone, surrounded by tangled white sheets and empty bottles of Gatorade. She could glimpse slices of ocean, sky, and sand through the slats in the white wooden shutters that covered the glass doors leading out to the balcony.

Before she had time to start speculating as to Jake's whereabouts, he appeared at the bedroom door. "Oh good," he said. "You're awake."

"I'm awake." She stretched both arms toward the ceiling, then let them fall back on the pillows. "I can't remember the last time I slept so well. The ocean is the best white-noise machine ever."

"I've got some conference calls later this afternoon, but I'm all yours this morning." He walked over to the nightstand and put down a mug of coffee.

She clapped her hand to her heart. "You made coffee for me?"

"I figured you might be ready for a break from Gatorade."

"Coffee is perfect. *You* are perfect." The words slipped out before her better judgment kicked in. "Which I know is impossible. Would you please just tell me what's wrong with you, already? Come on. Get it over with."

He sat at the foot of the bed, giving her his full attention without crowding her. "What do you feel like doing today? I can show you around town."

She'd come to view Jake as some sort of nocturnal, man-whoring superhero. He didn't do mundane things like show a visitor around town. He was . . . well, he was Jake Sorensen: larger than life and less than human.

Brighton tried to come up with a suggestion that didn't involve private jets or drive-through chapels. Something normal. Something she might do with Colin. "Well . . ."

"You'll need something to wear," he pointed out.

"My overnight bag is still in my car, which is still parked by the Whinery." She paused. "I hope. Maybe I can get one more day out of this suit?" She wrinkled her nose as she glanced at the floor, where her skirt, blazer, blouse, and shoes were strewn across the rug.

"You can't," he decreed.

She draped a sheet around her shoulders like an oversize poncho, clambered out of bed, and started picking up the wrinkled clothes. "I have a Tide stick in my bag. All I need is an iron."

"I don't have an iron."

"You don't *use* an iron or you don't *have* an iron?"

"I've never seen an iron in this house."

"Are you sure? Look at the shirt you're wearing right now." She pointed at his deceptively well-tailored casual blue button-down.

"Dry cleaner pressed it," he said.

"How do you know? Did you take it to the dry cleaner yourself?"

"Uh . . ."

"I didn't think so. You have a housekeeper, right?"

"Yes."

"And you have a laundry room?"

He looked almost abashed. "Somewhere around here."

"Then I guarantee you own an iron." She gathered up her clothes. "Lead the way."

"You're making this harder than it has to be," he protested. "I'm happy to buy you new clothes. You can throw out the suit and be done with it." He glanced at her strand of pearls, which was still fastened around her neck. "Keep the pearls, though."

"I'm not going to throw out a five-hundred-dollar suit just because it got a little wrinkled from sleeping on your private jet."

"But—"

"Fine, I'll find the laundry room myself." She marched down the stairs, the sheet trailing behind her like the train of a wedding gown.

As predicted, Jake Sorensen owned an iron. He also owned a top-of-the-line washer and dryer, complete with a steamy "wrinkle care" setting and magical dry-cleaning abilities. Brighton's black suit was restored to like-new condition. The cream silk blouse . . . well, luckily the blazer covered the wine stain. Sort of.

She returned to the bedroom holding her freshly steamed clothes.

"I guess I do own an iron." Jake sounded awed. "I'll be damned."

"You own an iron," she confirmed. "But as it turned out, I didn't need it. Your dryer has rendered ironing obsolete. Well played."

"We should stock the kitchen for you," he said. "Let's go to the grocery store."

Going to the grocery store was definitely a Colin activity.

Brighton sank down on the edge of the bed. "Oh. Okay."

"Don't sound so excited," he drawled as he headed back to the hallway. "See you downstairs."

As she hurried to shower and dress, she tried to identify the twisting, almost nauseated feeling in the pit of her stomach. It was the same sensation she'd had as a child after a day at the carnival, gorging herself on cotton candy and whirling around on midway rides. She was about to return to reality and she didn't want to.

But her husband (!!!) was waiting to go to the grocery store with her. So she swiped on some lipstick, combed out her damp hair, and tried to imagine what on earth a guy like Jake Sorensen might purchase in the produce section.

"Twelve-dollar strawberries?" Brighton gaped at the little chalkboard sign announcing the price of the "handpicked" berries. "No way. That's obscene."

Jake grabbed the nearest carton of berries and placed it in the shopping cart. "Do you like strawberries?"

"Yeah, but I don't like them twelve dollars' worth." Brighton reclaimed the berries and put them back with the others. She had passed several large chain grocery stores on her drive into town on Friday, but Jake had opted for a little gourmet shop by the boardwalk. Everything in there was organic and/or artisanal and/or handcrafted, with price tags to match.

Jake dismissed her protest with a roll of his eyes and placed the berries back in the cart.

Brighton called for a time-out. "Wait. Seriously. We are not buying twelve-dollar strawberries. That's highway robbery."

He grinned. "Don't think of them as twelve-dollar strawberries— think of them as hand-selected, sun-drenched, locally-sourced strawberries that *only* cost twelve dollars."

"That's a pretty good sales pitch," she admitted.

"Thank you. And I'm paying for them, so you don't get a vote anyway."

Her eyebrows shot up. "Really."

"Really." He nodded, as if this settled everything, and glanced around the aisles. "What else do you like? Sweet corn? Tomatoes?"

"Do we have to pay for the tomatoes in Krugerrands?" she asked.

"I'll take that as a yes." He tossed some vine-ripened tomatoes into the cart.

"Hold on." She trailed behind him as he worked his way through the aisles in an efficient, systematic fashion. "I'm not done with the strawberries yet."

"Yeah, you are." He all but patted her on the head.

"I am not. First of all, I can buy my own berries." She held up her hand to hold off his rebuttal. "But it's not about the money; it's about the principle."

He scoffed. "Whenever anyone says that, it's about the money. Always."

"That's not true."

He pulled her in for a quick kiss. "Stop arguing before I add a ten-dollar box of blueberries and seventy-five bucks' worth of rasp-berries."

She felt her resolve crumbling as she kissed him back. "I just feel like it's excessive and morally wrong to pay that much for what should cost three dollars. Five dollars, tops."

"I'm excessive. Deal with it." Jake moved along to the next aisle. "Let's figure out what we're having for lunch."

She glanced at a display of jam jars topped with gingham cloth and ribbons. "What do you eat, besides, like, beluga caviar and snif-ters of brandy?"

He added artisanal cheese and organic wine to the cart. "I pre-fer burgers to beluga caviar. And what the hell is a snifter?"

Brighton had to think about this. "I'm actually not sure. A bil-lionaire's shot glass?"

"Well, if it isn't Jake Sorensen!" A tiny, trim, middle-aged blonde, decked out in heels, diamonds, and a pink and green dress, rounded the corner. "I didn't realize you were still in town."

"Can't stay away." He gave the woman a smile and she simpered.

Even this blow-dried, buttoned-up, Lilly Pulitzer devotee couldn't resist Jake Sorensen's swagger. The woman was all but fanning her face.

"And will you be staying for the rest of the summer?" she asked, sidling closer as the tractor beam sucked her in.

Jake shrugged, rakish smile still in place. "Unknown."

The woman was eyeing Brighton with rapacious interest, and Brighton did her best to fade into the background and slink away to spare everyone the awkwardness of—

"This is Brighton." Jake placed his palm on Brighton's back, thwarting her escape attempt. "My wife. Brighton, this is Mimi Sinclair. The Sinclairs are building a new house a few doors down from ours."

Mimi Sinclair made a remarkably poor attempt to conceal her shock. "Your wife? Well! I hadn't heard you were engaged."

Jake leaned over and kissed the top of Brighton's head in a display of husbandly affection. "It was very recent."

Her eyebrows shot up as far as the limits of Botox would allow. *"Really."*

"Really."

"Then I suppose I shan't be hearing about your exploits at the Whinery anymore?" The woman's smile looked almost serrated. She raked her gaze up and down Brighton. "You're certainly a . . . refreshing change from his usual type, aren't you?"

Brighton started coughing.

"There must have been an official day of mourning for single women all along the Eastern Seaboard. Well, best wishes to you both." Mimi captured Brighton's hand in both of hers. Her skin felt buttery smooth, her fingernails glossy and sharp. "I'd love to send a gift. Where are you registered, darling?"

"Oh, we didn't do any of that." Brighton tried and failed to free her hand from Mimi's manicured talons. "Everything was very spur-of-the-moment." She glanced up at Jake.

"It was love at first sight," he said solemnly.

"A whirlwind romance." Brighton tried to look earnest and naïve. "What can I say? When you know, you know."

Mimi narrowed her eyes and flared her nostrils, a gossip hound picking up a fresh scent. "No ring, I see."

When Jake laughed, Brighton could feel the warm rumble against her. "We eloped to Vegas on Friday night," he said. "Just couldn't help ourselves."

"But we're going to take our time designing the rings," Brighton added. "We want them to be special and one of a kind."

"Just like our love." Jake managed to keep a straight face.

Mimi appeared both horrified and delighted. "You're quite fascinating." She continued her appraisal of Brighton. "Do you happen to have a business card or a pen? I'll be in touch directly to invite you both to dinner." She waited for Brighton to provide her contact information and then walked away, looking back over her shoulder so many times that she nearly collided with a display of gluten-free scones.

"Did you hear that?" Brighton turned to Jake. "I'm *fascinating*."

But his attention had gotten snagged earlier in the conversation. "Did she actually say 'shan't'?"

As they made their way to the bread aisle, she spotted Mimi Sinclair again. The society matron was on her cell phone, hunched over her shopping cart handle and murmuring with fevered intensity. When she noticed Brighton, she straightened up, waved, and cast a pointed look at her midsection.

"Oh my God." Brighton nudged Jake. "She thinks I'm pregnant. She thinks this was a shotgun wedding."

He shrugged. "So?"

"So doesn't that bother you?"

"Nope. Does it bother you?"

Brighton considered this for a moment. "No. Which is weird, because I'm used to doing everything in the right order. I.e., first comes love, then comes marriage, then comes the baby carriage."

"First 'shan't' and now 'i.e.'?"

She flipped her hair, which had started to frizz in the humidity. "Shut up; I'm *fascinating*."

"Yes, you are." He led the way to the baking supplies aisle. Almond flour and lavender-infused sugar galore.

"What are we going to say?" Brighton asked. "When people start asking about everything? We should set some ground rules. Get our story straight."

He turned and gazed down at her. "What are you talking about?"

"It feels disingenuous to present ourselves as a real couple."

"We're a real couple," he assured her. "Exhibit A: last night."

Brighton flushed. "Yeah, but are we really *together*? Like, exclusive?"

"We're husband and wife," he pointed out. "The vows are pretty cut-and-dried about the exclusivity thing."

She was surprised to hear this from him. "You're taking drive-through vows seriously?"

He looked equally surprised. "Aren't you?"

"Well, I mean, considering I did this for spite, drunk off my ass . . ."

"Yeah?"

"And you're known far and wide as the designated rebound guy who will never settle down . . ."

"Yeah?"

"And I still have no idea why you agreed to all this—feel free to fill me in, by the way . . ."

He watched her, waiting for her to finish.

"But okay." She shrugged. "I'm fine with it if you are."

"Then we have a deal." He moved on to the next order of business. "Let me know what you want to do about rings."

Before she could think about anything gold and shiny, she was distracted by sweet and scrumptious. "Ooh, waffles," she breathed as she grabbed a brown paper bag filled with (organic, artisanal) waffle mix.

"You like waffles?" Jake asked.

"I *love* waffles."

He tossed the mix into the cart. "Done. I'll make you waffles to go with the strawberries."

"Oh, please. You can't make waffles," she blurted before her mental censor could kick in.

He gave her an amused smile over his shoulder. "Are you calling me a liar?"

"You don't even know where your laundry room is. You have a driver and a jet and properties all over the world. You're like Bruce Wayne. Your house should be called Wayne Manor."

"And Bruce Wayne doesn't make waffles?"

"I don't think he does." She crossed her arms, trying to summon up memories of old-school *Batman* reruns.

"Just another way in which I kick Bruce Wayne's ass." He selected parchment paper with CEO-level decisiveness.

She knew she shouldn't say anything more, but she couldn't help herself. "Be honest: Are waffles the only thing you know how to make? And you make them for every woman who spends the night?"

Jake turned to face her. "You want honesty? If I made waffles for every woman I slept with, I'd cause a world waffle shortage. Panic in the streets."

"This conversation, right here? This is why I'm surprised you want to tell people we're actually married. Or why you got married at all."

"We decided it would be fun," he reminded her. "Aren't you having fun?"

"Yes," she conceded. "Because all of this is way outside my comfort zone. But you get to do whatever you want all day, every day." She glanced at the spot where Mimi Sinclair had stood. "You're famous among single women all along the Eastern Seaboard. I don't mean this in a low-self-esteem way, but you could do better than me, and we both know it."

"That sounds pretty low-self-esteemy to me."

"Start talking, Sorensen. Why'd you marry me? Why me, why now, why all of this?"

"I never took a philosophy class, but this is what I imagine it'd be like."

"Don't sidestep the question." She positioned herself in front of the shopping cart so he couldn't escape her interrogation. "I want you to tell me what's really going on."

He turned the smolder back on to distract her. She could *see* him do it. One second, she was thinking about how to make him talk, and the next second, she was thinking about stripping his shirt off and running her hands along his—

Damn pheromones.

"Brighton." Even his *voice* smoldered. "We're having a great time together. Can't we relax and enjoy?"

"If you actually knew me, you'd know how ridiculous that question is." She had to laugh. "'Relax and enjoy' is not how I operate."

"Until now. Welcome to your screw-up summer."

She edged closer to him. Closer. "Stop changing the subject."

"Let's go home and make waffles," he said. "And whatever else your heart desires."

"What about potatoes?" she asked. "Can you make potatoes?"

"Mashed, roasted, or boiled."

"What about seafood?" she challenged. "Halibut with fancy chutney? Crab cakes? Lobster mac and cheese?"

"Yes, yes, and yes."

She tried to decide if he was kidding. "How did you learn to cook like that?"

He kind of shrugged. "I was in Mexico for six months on business—this was a few years ago—and I almost got kidnapped. So after that, I had to stay in the compound all day every day, and I was bored."

Brighton was inching ever closer to him. She could smell his freshly laundered shirt. "You're making this up. This is confabulation at its finest."

He raised his hand as if taking an oath. "True story. Kidnapping corporate guys for ransom was a big thing for a while. They used to call it 'millionaire tours.'"

"Millionaire tours," she repeated.

"Yeah. It's a big thing with insurance companies—I'm surprised you haven't heard about it."

"Why were you in Mexico?" she demanded. "Specifically?"

"I was overseeing construction of a resort. I've done some projects with this Mexican billionaire who develops luxury resorts and shopping centers. Javier Mendoza. Makes me look like a pauper. My guys were supplying and pouring the concrete."

"Do I even want to know how you got connected with a Mexican billionaire when you live in Delaware?"

"I have a summer home in Delaware," he corrected her.

"Where do you live when it's not summer?" She was kind of afraid to hear the answer.

"I have apartments in New York, London, and D.C."

"The better to network with government officials who want sand shipped to Saudi Arabia," Brighton said. "And how did you and Javier join forces?"

"We met at a gallery opening–fund-raiser thing in Manhattan. I was there with a date; he was there trying to break into the East Coast old boys' club. But he never could, even though he's smarter and richer than most of them. In those circles, having money isn't enough. You have to have social currency, too. He doesn't belong to the right social clubs and he speaks with an accent, so he and I ended up talking."

"And your relationship with him outlasted your relationship with your date from that night."

"She had a good time," he assured Brighton. "But yes, Javier and I have been working together for years now."

"And almost got kidnapped."

"Good times, good times." Jake smiled at the memories. "We'd send the guards to the market for ingredients and then spend all night cooking. Javier makes the best *asado de bodas*."

"Your life is like *Proof of Life* meets *Sex and the City*," Brighton marveled. "Meets *Top Chef*."

"I'll take you to Mexico next time I go down there. You'll like Javier. When he sets a goal, he gets it done. No matter how long it takes or how many obstacles are in the way."

"Sounds like you." Brighton straightened her shoulders. "Which leads me to the next topic of discussion."

Jake finished tossing things in the cart and headed toward the cash register. She hurried to keep pace with him and gathered her hair back into a bun.

"Uh-oh," he said. "The hair is going up. Shit is about to get real."

"Yes, it is." Brighton took a deep breath. "Because if you won't talk about love, then we definitely have to talk about money."

chapter 11

"*I* feel like I should be wearing a suit for this conversation," Jake said.

"I bet you look great in a suit. I'd like to see that someday in the near future." Brighton let her mind wander for a moment. "But that's not the point. The point is money." She tried to sound brisk and businesslike.

He stopped in front of a stack of fair-trade coffee canisters and regarded her with a mix of exasperation and amusement. "What about it?"

"Well." She cleared her throat. "You obviously have some."

He nodded.

"And so do I. Not as much as you, obviously, but I've worked hard for what I have."

He nodded again.

She wanted to stop talking sense and go back to the suit fantasies, but she forced herself to keep going. "We did, technically, get married. So all boozy fun and hot sex aside—"

He grinned. "It is pretty hot."

The suit fantasies gave way to naked fantasies. "*That aside*, we need to acknowledge the reality that marriage has legal and financial ramifications."

"Tell me what's bothering you, Brighton." He rested one hand on her shoulder and maintained eye contact. "Be specific. I'll take care of it."

"This is more like a one-night stand than a marriage. Which is not a bad thing; so far it's been great." She studied the coffee labels. "But given the formalities that went down at the drive-through, we should follow up with more legal documents. We need to find an attorney who can draft a post-nup."

He blinked down at her, his expression unreadable. "You're worried I married you for your money?"

"No!" she sputtered. "Obviously not. Although, now that you mention it, in the interest of due diligence, I should ask if there's any chance you're living beyond your means and are about to go down in flames like a Wall Street investment bank circa 2007. You can tell me. I won't be mad."

He squeezed her shoulder. "No."

"You're sure?"

He kept staring at her. "Yes."

"All the more reason to make sure you're protected. You have a lot of assets to consider."

"I'll consider them. You don't have to." He gave her shoulder one last squeeze, then proceeded to the cash register, where he paid for and bagged the groceries with efficiency that rivaled even Brighton's.

"You can't be fine with all this," Brighton insisted as she trailed behind him out to the sidewalk. "You know nothing about me."

"I know we have fun." He stopped at an intersection and took her hand. "In bed and out of it."

"How can you possibly trust me?" she cried. Her agitation increased in direct proportion to his nonchalance. "Maybe I'm a consummate gold digger who's out for all I can get."

He laughed and led the way across the street.

"This isn't funny!" She extricated her hand from his. "What the hell is wrong with you? I mean, the beach house and the apartments in D.C. and New York and your corporate jet . . . are you really willing to risk all that?"

When they reached the curb on the other side of the street, he stopped, turned toward her, and did the laser-beam-focus routine. He moved closer, until she could feel his cheek brush against hers. "I'll let you in on a secret. I don't care. You want the beach house that bad? Take it. It's yours."

She pulled back, frowning. "What do you mean, you don't care? Of course you do."

His eyes darkened. "That's the secret to success. You have to not care if you lose sometimes."

She went silent in the sea-scented breeze. "Well, for someone who doesn't care about stuff, you sure have a lot of it."

His voice remained soft, but for the first time since they'd met, he seemed remote and unyielding. "I realized years ago that no matter how much I have, it'll never be enough. So now I *make* investments; I don't invest."

Brighton decided to use one of his own tactics on him—she got flippant. "Is this the part where you finally tell me about your dark and tortured past?"

She held her breath, aware that she'd just ventured into dangerous territory. She'd pushed too far and now she was going to find out what happened when the charming, casual Jake Sorensen got angry.

But he didn't do anything. He stood motionless for a moment, squinting in the sunlight reflected off a store window, and then that cold anger melted into a rakish smile.

"If I had a dark, tortured past, believe me, I'd exploit it to the fullest."

"Uh-huh."

"I work, I make money, I have fun. That's it."

Brighton crossed her arms. "I'm not buying it. You built an empire from the ground up—there has to be more to you than money and good bone structure."

"I wish there was." He looked forlorn. "If I were you, I'd get my gold digger on and snag a beach house or two while the snagging's good."

Before she could try a new interrogation technique, a voice interrupted: "Hey, Sorensen! Get over here!"

Lila had stepped out of the Naked Finger and was waving both arms to flag them down.

Brighton glanced at Jake. "You don't think she's heard about us already?"

"Everyone's heard everything. Guaranteed." He rolled his neck as if prepping for a boxing match. "Let's go."

Together as husband and wife, they did the walk of shame through the shop's glass door. The little blue showroom was lined on all sides with glittering gems and precious metals.

"Well, well, well." Lila put both hands on her hips like a parent about to ground two curfew-breaking teenagers. "So the rumors are true."

"Rumors?" Brighton feigned innocence. "What have you heard?"

"I told you," Jake said. He put down the grocery bags and gave Lila a quick hug. "I tried to tell her about the way this town works."

Lila looked both delighted and scandalized. "You two actually got married?"

They nodded.

"For real?" Lila pressed. "You signed legal documents to this effect?"

"Do you need me to send you a certified copy of the marriage certificate?" Jake asked.

"Maybe you'd better."

He nodded knowingly. "You and Malcolm had a bet going that I'd never get married, didn't you? And you just lost."

"This whole town's had a pool going for years. Why couldn't you have waited two more years? I could have made a killing!" Lila shook her fist. "Is this a sign of the impending apocalypse? Should I start stockpiling bottled water and canned goods?"

Brighton shook her head. "No need. It's temporary. We're having a fourteen-night stand."

"Thirty-night stand," Jake muttered.

Brighton ignored this. "The paperwork was just to prove a point."

"What was the point?" Lila asked. Before Brighton could respond, she glanced at their hands and practically started jumping for joy. "You don't have rings yet? You've come to the right place."

Jake's phone buzzed, and as he started reading an e-mail, he kind of lifted his chin in Brighton's direction. "She's the jewelry person. Whatever she wants is great. I'll pay."

"Ah, romance." Brighton walked over to Lila. "We don't really need rings."

"You got married, didn't you?" Lila rubbed her palms together. "This is going to be fun. You need something bold and dazzling. Something that proclaims to the world, 'I married Jake Sorensen and I'm loving every minute of it.'"

"Let's not get ahead of ourselves," Brighton cautioned. "It hasn't even been two full days."

Lila waved away her protests. "I just got in a stunning three-carat brilliant-cut solitaire. Ideal cut, VVS1 clarity, G color—"

"Three carats?" Brighton almost choked. "No, no, no. That's way too big for me. And way too expensive."

Lila glanced over at Jake. "Hi. Have you met your husband?"

"Buy it," Jake yelled from across the room.

"Read your e-mail and mind your business," Brighton yelled back. To Lila, she said, "Look at the outfit I'm wearing right now. Do I strike you as a three-carat eye-gouger kind of gal?"

"You got Jake Sorensen to marry you," Lila stated flatly. "Rules don't apply to you." She pulled out a glittering diamond ring from under the counter.

"That is gorgeous," Brighton conceded. "For someone else."

"Then how about this?" Lila handed over a small marquise-shaped diamond in a wide yellow gold band. "We can reset the stone in platinum."

"It's a little eighties."

"I know, damn it." Lila snapped her fingers, foiled again. "I have five of these now and no one wants to buy them. Marquises aren't in fashion right now."

"You have five?" Brighton studied the stone. "Could you put them together to make a new piece? Like a cross pendant? Or maybe earrings flanked with trillions?"

Lila regarded her with renewed interest. "Yes, yes I could. *If* I had a designer to do it."

"Oh, it'll be easy." Brighton waved her hand. "Bring out the pieces and I'll show you."

Lila fetched the diamonds, along with a pad and a pen. Brighton glanced at the stones and started sketching a few possible designs.

"You're going to freehand?" Lila asked, a note of awe in her voice.

"Sure. I'm not certified or anything, but I can sketch, do basic design on the computer, make wax molds, do polishing and engraving, that sort of thing."

"So you *are* a jewelry designer."

Brighton shook her head. "Not really."

Before Lila could argue, the phone next to the cash register rang. While Lila picked up and greeted her caller, Jake joined Brighton by the jewelry case. "What's going on?"

"Nothing." Brighton tilted her head and considered the placement of the hypothetical trillions. "Just fooling around."

Lila's tone sharpened. "You want me to do *what*? For *when*?" The sweet brunette's expression looked panicked. "Wait, slow down. What happened? You were where? Uh-huh, uh-huh, okay. But . . . Yes, but . . . Well, do you have a photo I could work off of, at least? I see. Listen, I'm with a customer right now. May I call you back in five minutes? Okay."

"What?" Jake asked when she hung up.

"That was some guy who lives in Bethany Beach," Lila explained. "He just lost his wedding band and he wants to know if I can make an exact replica by Wednesday at noon."

"What happens Wednesday at noon?" Brighton asked.

"He sees his wife," Jake guessed.

Lila nodded. "She's coming back from a business trip. He says he'll pay whatever I ask, but he doesn't have any pictures I can work from."

"Are you sure?" Brighton nodded at the computer in the corner. "Does he have a Facebook profile? If he does, you should look at the pictures where you can see his ring finger and zoom in."

Lila looked impressed. "Let me call him back and have him

friend me on Facebook." She hesitated as her hand hovered over the phone. "I'm going to hell, aren't I?"

Jake laughed. "Why would you be going to hell?"

"Because I shouldn't be aiding and abetting a cheater."

"Who said that you are?" Jake asked. "You don't know the facts of the case."

"Come on. This guy went carousing without his wedding ring and now he's trying to make sure his wife never finds out. I *hate* cheaters." Lila turned to Brighton. "My ex-husband was a cheater."

"You can't be sure of that," Jake pointed out. "For all you know, the ring could have fallen off and rolled away. It's unlikely, but it could have happened. Bottom line, it doesn't matter."

"How can you say that?" Brighton protested. "Don't you have any morals at all?"

Jake ignored this and focused only on the issue at hand. "If you want to run a business, you can't make value judgments on your customers."

"But . . ." Lila frowned. "But *cheating*."

Jake shrugged. "Do you want to be the cheating police or do you want to be a successful jeweler?"

Brighton recoiled a bit. "Who *are* you?"

"A guy who runs successful businesses." He glanced at his phone again. "Speaking of which, I've got to run."

"You do that." Lila all but shoved him out the door. "Run along and don't come back, because I'm keeping her."

"You can't keep her," Jake said. "She's mine."

"Then you're going to have to share," Lila informed Jake. To Brighton, she said, "You're hired whether you like it or not. Don't try to escape."

"But I'm only here for the next two weeks," Brighton said.

"Thirty days," Jake intoned as he strode out the door.

"Then you're hired for two weeks," Lila decreed. "Starting right now. Want to track down this ring on Facebook and make a wax mold?"

Brighton relented as an old, familiar surge of excitement hit. "We can probably get it done by noon on Wednesday, but we better get cracking. Does this fool happen to know his ring size?"

Lila gave her a look. "What do you think?"

Brighton nodded. "When you call him back, tell him to go to the nearest pawn shop and have them size his finger."

"God, you're good." Lila picked up the phone but didn't dial. "Is that why Jake married you?"

"I have no clue why he married me," Brighton confessed. "And I only married him to stick it to my ex. Hot rage plus hot guy equals bad decisions."

"I know all about making snap decisions because of an ex," Lila said. "But getting *married*?"

"I know." Brighton hung her head. "I'm too ashamed to tell my family."

"No, that's not what I meant." Lila kept studying her as though she were an exotic zoo exhibit. "Talk about drama! Excitement! Adventure!"

"I was reeeally mad at my ex," Brighton murmured. "And like I said, I don't know why Jake did it. There are more pieces to this puzzle, and I'm a little afraid to find out what they are."

Lila leaned back against the counter. "So what's it like, being married to Jake Sorensen?"

"It's . . ." Brighton tried to find the right words. "Easy. The opposite of real life." Being with him was so seductively simple. He didn't argue or act as the voice of reason. He didn't expect anything from her.

Because he didn't care.

But no—that wasn't fair. He'd cared enough to whisk her away to Vegas, to take her to his house and cook for her and give her the most mind-blowing orgasms of her life followed by witty conversation.

He just didn't care about her in the way that a husband traditionally cared about his wife. Which was fine, because they weren't really married in the traditional sense of the word. And they'd been together less than forty-eight hours. She didn't care about him, either.

Much.

chapter 12

Six hours later, Lila dropped Brighton off in front of Don't Be Koi.

"Sorry, that went way later than I expected," Lila said.

"Time flies when you're frantically trying to re-create a wedding ring using grainy Facebook photos." Brighton's fingers were cramping from all the drawing and detail work, but she felt elated. She'd forgotten how exhilarating it was to lose herself in a design project. The total concentration conferred a sense of peace—her busy mind quieted while her hands worked.

"We're totally going to pull this off." Lila paused. "Right?"

"Absolutely." Brighton unbuckled her seat belt. "That guy is just lucky he wants white gold—platinum takes forever to cool."

Lila checked her cell phone as a text came in. "That's Malcolm, wondering if I'm ever coming home. I better let you go inside. Tell Jake I'm sorry I deprived him of his bride all day."

"Ah yes, his legally wedded tax implication."

"I'd say you're more than a tax implication." Lila smiled knowingly. "There's something going on between you two."

Brighton waved this away. "Look at Jake Sorensen and look at me. Do you really think we're going to fall madly in love and live happily ever after?"

Lila shrugged. "Stranger things have happened."

"Name one."

"Remind me to tell you the story of how Malcolm and I got together someday."

"Is Malcolm like Jake?" Brighton asked.

"No." Lila gazed off dreamily into the distance. "He's nothing at all like Jake."

"That's why you're living happily ever after." Brighton opened the door and got out of the car. "What time do you want to get started tomorrow?"

Lila snapped out of her reverie. "Is seven too early? I'll bring coffee."

"I'll be there." Brighton waved good-bye.

"You're the best. And listen, you have to finish up the detail work, so I'll need you well rested. Try to get some sleep tonight."

Brighton closed the door and practically skipped past the koi pond, thoughts of Gatorade in her head. "I make no promises."

"Hello?" Brighton kicked off her shoes in the front hall and padded barefoot up to the master suite. The fading light cast shadows across the stair treads. "Anybody home?"

No one answered. Which, when she thought about it, was kind of eerie, because this house was clearly maintained by a substantial staff. Every baseboard, window, and countertop was immaculate. The beachfront was perfectly raked. The beds were made, the towels were folded, and the entire place smelled comforting yet expensive, with subtle notes of sandalwood. And of course, someone had to keep the massive refrigerator stocked with bottled water, iced coffee, soda, craft beer, and energy drinks.

So where was everyone?

Maybe Jake had gone back to the Whinery to find another boozy watch enthusiast. Maybe he was chatting up another freshly dumped executive worker right now. Maybe . . .

She heard the soft hiss of running water from the master suite. Someone was in the shower. Her heart rate kicked up as she opened the door.

Sure enough, the invisible housekeepers had been busy. The bed had been remade with snowy white linens and piles of fluffy pillows. A silver bowl of strawberries rested on a rough-hewn wooden bench next to a silver champagne bucket filled with ice and three bottles of orange Gatorade.

Brighton tugged her blouse out from the waistband of her skirt and knocked on the bathroom door. "Jake?"

His voice was muffled through the heavy white door: "Your timing is perfect. Come on in."

She opened the door and stepped into the palatial bathroom, which featured a huge white and silver slipper tub, a glass-walled shower almost as large as Brighton's entire bathroom, and a custom-made blue and white tile map of the Delaware coastline across one entire wall. She couldn't stop staring at Jake's bare chest. His torso was as perfectly proportioned as his face. *Somewhere, a museum is missing its Michelangelo sculpture.* His shoulder was marked with a trio of faint white scars that just added to his rugged masculinity.

She took off her earrings, placed them carefully on a stack of white washcloths next to the sink, and reached behind her to unzip her skirt. He turned off the water and stepped out of the shower. She met him on the bathmat and wrapped her arms around his neck. "Hi."

"Hi." His hands settled on her hips.

She looked at the shower. "You're done already?"

"Nope."

"But you turned the water off."

"No point in wasting water." He finished unzipping her skirt.

"I didn't figure you for an environmentalist."

"Someone's got to think of the radioactive wolves in Siberia," he murmured against her lips.

"I think it's actually the Ukraine," Brighton murmured back.

He kissed his way down her neck and starting working on her blouse buttons. "Did you try the strawberries?"

"Nope." The thin, soaked silk of her blouse clung to her skin. "But they can wait."

She could feel his smile against her cheek. "Go get one."

"I'm otherwise engaged right now."

He eased away from her, ducked out to the bedroom, and returned seconds later with a strawberry. "Taste."

She took a tiny, tentative nibble, then devoured the rest of the berry in one bite. "Oh my God."

He nodded, vindicated.

The strawberry was sweet and juicy and delicious, more so than any strawberry she'd had before. It tasted like summer. It tasted like sunshine. She had to close her eyes and support herself with one hand on the marble counter. "That is . . . I can't even . . ." When her taste buds finally settled down, she admitted, "Those were absolutely worth twelve dollars."

"I'm glad you like them." He peeled off her blouse and got to work on her bra.

"Did you *do* something to them?" Brighton ran her hands along his back muscles. "Like infuse them with dopamine?"

He quirked one eyebrow, confused. "What?"

"Never mind." She stepped out of her skirt.

He slipped off her bra, followed by her panties. Then he took her hand and tugged her toward the shower.

Her hand flew to her throat. "My necklace."

"Leave it on."

"These are hanadama pearls," she protested weakly, even as she put one foot into the shower. "I hand-strung them myself. Soap and water erodes the nacre."

He turned his smolder all the way up. "But you look so good in them."

Brighton couldn't resist him, couldn't stop touching him—but she knew an opportunity to gain leverage when she saw one. "Tell you what: I'll get in the shower and I'll do all kinds of depraved things to you and I won't say a word about nacre."

"Best marriage ever."

"*If* you let me do some work on your watch when you're finished."

He regarded her with renewed interest. "You want to fix my watch more than you want to save your pearls?"

"I want to fix that watch *bad*," she informed him with a sultry pout. "I'll do *anything*."

He turned on the shower. "You've got yourself a deal, Mrs. Sorensen."

"Pass the Gatorade, please." Brighton settled in for a long night in Jake's bed. She leaned back against the padded headboard, snuggled into his worn blue T-shirt, and stared down at the laptop propped up on a pillow.

Jake handed her a fresh, cold bottle. "Do you need a snack?"

"No thanks. Now, quit stalling and pick a color: brown or black."

Her pearls were in ruins, the bedclothes were on the floor, and the only light in the room came from the faint blue glow emanating from the laptop's screen.

His gaze flickered over the photos displayed on the Web site. "I don't care."

"Let's go with brown." Brighton tapped away at the keyboard. "It'll match your eyes."

He made some growly, unintelligible noise deep in his throat.

"I'll take that as a yes." She scrolled through the site for contact information and nudged him with her foot. "Okay, now you call and place the order."

"It's the middle of the night," he pointed out.

"Which means it's business hours in Switzerland."

"Can't we just run to Target and pick out a watchband?"

"I am going to pretend I did not hear that." She clamped her hands over her ears. "'Patek Philippe' and 'Target' do not belong in the same sentence."

"You're such a snob."

"Less talking, more dialing," she said crisply. "And by the way, I haven't changed my name. I'm still Ms. Smith."

"You don't want to be Mrs. Sorensen?"

She paused for a sip of sports drink. "It's not that I don't want to be; it's that it seems wrong to call myself that when we're not serious about this marriage."

"You seemed pretty serious about it in the shower."

She ignored this. "Besides, I built my professional reputation as Brighton Smith." She shot him a sidelong glance. "Does that bother you?"

He shook his head and surveyed the clothes littering the rug. "Did you buy anything new to wear?"

"Nope. I kind of lost track of time while I was working on the ring today. I kind of lost track of everything."

He looked at her for a long moment.

"What?" she finally said.

"You love it."

"'Love' is a strong word." She felt a bit panicky at the mere mention.

"It lets me use a different part of my brain. It reminds me of some good parts of my childhood. But it's not like I can't live without it."

"Uh-huh."

"True story." She put the laptop aside and drew her knees up to her chest. "I can stop anytime I want."

He put one hand beneath his head and used the other to trace the curve of her back through the soft, thin cotton shirt. "If you don't love this work, if you can live without it . . ."

She glanced down at him. "Yes?"

"Why do all this to my watch? Why do you care?"

"Because that watch is special," she finally answered. "It's rare and it's valuable and I want you to recognize what you have."

"I'm aware," he assured her. "That's why I bought it in the first place. Well, that, and too much scotch."

"That's not enough—I want you to *care*." She was surprised at the conviction in her voice. "I want you to invest emotionally, not just financially."

"In a watch?"

She nodded.

He patted her hip. "I hate to tell you this, but that's never going to happen."

"But I don't want a husband who can't emotionally invest. In his watch," she hastened to add. "But then, you probably don't want a wife who sent a bunch of photos of your private jet to her ex."

"Eh. I'll deal with it."

She sighed and wrapped her arms around her shins. "There've probably been a hundred women just like me in this bed already."

He smiled that heart-melting, amnesia-inducing smile. "There has never been a woman like you in this bed. Ever. I can promise you that."

"That's nice of you to say." She let the subject drop and picked up the laptop again. "Call Switzerland. Make sure you get the steel buckle."

"Got it." He groped for his phone on the nightstand.

"Tell them I'm e-mailing photos of the original watch right now. They're going to be so excited."

"They're going to emotionally invest?"

"You mock me now, but one day soon, you're going to weep tears of poignant joy over this watch," she said. "Wait and see."

He reached over to commandeer the laptop. "While we're waiting, let's order you some clothes."

"My black suit's not doing it for you anymore?"

"Oh, it's doing it for me. That reminds me, I'll order you some new pearls, too. A lot of pearls."

"You have a boardroom fetish now?"

"I guess I do." He reached for her. She reached for him.

His phone rang, startling them both.

"Who do you know with such terrible timing?" she asked.

He glanced at the screen, got up from the bed, and left the room without another word.

Probably a work call, she told herself. A sand-related crisis in Saudi Arabia.

She picked up the computer and scrolled through some online clothing stores while she waited for him to return. And waited.

And waited.

Finally, after at least ten minutes had passed, she tiptoed out to the hallway and peered over the railing. Pale moonlight flooded the vast, empty space between the first floor below her and the rafters above her.

"Jake?" she called softly. The sound bounced off the smooth white walls and varnished wood floors.

He'd left. She was all alone in this huge, empty house.

She crept back to the master suite, waited a few more minutes, and then dialed Kira's number.

"Hey," she whispered when Kira answered. "Can I come over?"

"Of course." Kira sounded drowsy. "Do you need to talk?"

"No." Brighton couldn't imagine how to explain the situation she'd found herself in. "No talking necessary. I just need to sleep."

chapter 13

"You do *not* look well rested," Lila declared the next morning when Brighton straggled in at seven thirty wearing Kira's white denim skirt and cobalt blue T-shirt. "You look completely exhausted."

"Sorry I'm late." Brighton gratefully accepted the cup of coffee Lila offered, then sat down at the design table. "Slept through my alarm."

The brunette studied Brighton with rapt interest. "So how was your night?"

"It was . . ." Brighton could feel her cheeks flushing. Even though her marriage was a total farce and less than a week old, she realized that she didn't want to admit failure.

"Words fail you?" Lila looked as though she had about a thousand follow-up questions and was barely suppressing the urge to ask them. "Good for you guys."

"Oh, we weren't . . . you know . . . all night."

Lila held up her hand. "No judgment from me. You are newly-weds, after all. And he is Jake Sorensen."

Brighton tried to smile the way she would if she had actually spent all night with him. "We stayed up past midnight ordering watchbands from Switzerland."

Lila looked a bit dismayed. "Really?"

Brighton nodded. "I'm trying to get him to invest a little bit. Emotionally."

"How's that going?"

"Well, he Googled a question about how watch hands work when he thought I wasn't paying attention. I'm optimistic."

Lila shook her head. "You should see your face when you talk about that watch."

"What do I look like?"

"Like you're falling in love."

Brighton ducked her head. "Oh, well, I . . ."

"No wonder Jake whisked you off to Vegas." Lila raised her coffee cup in tribute. "It's about time he met someone who could keep him entertained *outside* the bedroom." She clapped her hand over her mouth. "Whoops. Let me start over."

"No need to start over; let's move on." Brighton gazed down at the white leather display cases. "I'm excited to work on the ring. It's been a long time since I actually got my hands dirty."

"Speaking of your hands . . ." Lila peered across the display case. "You still don't have a ring."

"File under: 'Let's move on.'" Brighton held out the sketch she'd worked on the day before. "So what do you think? Are we ready to move on to the CAD?" The CAD, or computer-aided design, would render a virtual, three-dimensional prototype from which they could create a wax mold and eventually the ring itself.

Lila studied the sketch. "This looks great. Really great. The detail work is amazing."

"Sometimes being an obsessive control freak works in my favor."

"No kidding." Lila's gaze turned cagey. "Are you *sure* I can't persuade you to stay for the rest of the summer?"

"Tempting, but no." Brighton grimaced as she remembered she was supposed to be at her office in half an hour. "In fact, I need to call my boss right now." She took a deep breath, stepped into the back room, and mentally prepared herself to stay strong against a barrage of begging, wheedling, guilt tripping, and threats. She'd never taken two weeks off. Especially with no notice.

What if her boss yelled at her? Worse, what if he cried like Colin had?

But putting it off would just make it worse. She dialed. She tensed. She closed her eyes and rehearsed a brisk, businesslike speech in her head.

Two minutes later, she hung up the phone and sagged against the wall as a dizzy spell hit. She stumbled back into the shop with her palm pressed to her forehead and a sick feeling in her stomach.

"What's wrong?" Lila grabbed a bottle of water and offered it to her. "Are you okay?"

Brighton collapsed into the nearest chair and fought a rising wave of nausea. "I called my office. I told them I'd be taking two weeks off. I was very calm and professional about it, but very firm because I've never taken time off before."

"Wait. You worked there how long?"

"Three years."

Lila whistled. "And you never took any vacation time?"

"Not even a sick day." Brighton paused, thinking about all the awards she'd won and bonuses she'd received. "I had no idea how my boss would react when I told him."

Lila crouched down next to her. "Was he really upset?"

"You know, I thought he would be." *Inhale, exhale.* "I expected a fair amount of pushback. A huge guilt trip at the very least."

Lila's eyes were huge. "So? What happened?"

"Nothing." Brighton made a faint, hoarse sound in the back of her throat. "He was fine with it. He said business was slowing down for the summer and I could even take an extra week or two if I needed it."

"Well, that's great!" Lila exclaimed. "Isn't it?"

"Yes, but . . ." Brighton struggled to put this into words. "He let me go so easily." She stopped talking because she realized how ridiculous she sounded. Of course the huge corporation she worked for could survive without her for ten business days. She should be grateful she wouldn't be inundated with work while she was eating twelve-dollar strawberries with the hottest man on the Eastern Seaboard.

And yet.

If Colin could let her go so easily, and her boss could let her go so easily, what did that say about her?

She let her hand fall away from her face. "Now my screw-up summer is *actually* screwed up."

Lila got up and did a little jig of glee. "Screwed up? What are you talking about? This is great! Now you can work for me. This is fate, I tell you. Meant to be!"

Brighton stared numbly at the carpet.

"Can I at least persuade you to cover for me this Saturday and Sunday?" Lila asked. "My mom is going to be in New York City and I'm hoping to meet her there. We're going to hit up a bunch of vintage clothing boutiques in Manhattan and Brooklyn."

Brighton shook off her stupor and tried to rally. "That sounds fun. Where is she visiting from?"

"Depends on the week." Lila grinned. "She's a buyer for a vintage clothing dealer, so she's kind of a jet-setter. She hasn't been stateside for months, and I'd love to go spend some time with her. So, what do you say? Can you hold down the fort?"

"I'd be happy to hold down the fort if you think I can handle it."

"You can handle it," Lila assured her.

"I've never done the retail side of this job."

"Selling's the easy part. Just remember: Jewelry is emotional. People who come in here already know what they want; all you have to do is listen and give them permission to do whatever they've already decided."

Brighton looked around for a pen and paper. "Should I be writing this down?"

"No, you'll be fine. Some of them will be very upset—they need the money, but they hate to part with a diamond ring they've worn for twenty years. I always try to give them a fair price."

Brighton started taking notes on her smartphone. "Of course."

"The customers looking to buy are different. For some of them, especially the summer residents, jewelry is competitive."

Brighton glanced up. "Competitive how?"

"You'll see. Just remember: When in doubt, always suggest a larger carat weight." Lila brightened as a gray pickup truck pulled up to the curb in front of the shop. "Hey, it's your husband."

Brighton focused on her phone. "Mmmm."

Lila suddenly remembered a pressing task she had to attend to. "I'll give you two a minute alone."

As Lila ducked into the back room, Jake strode through the front door. Without preamble, he offered his hand to Brighton. "I'm sorry."

Brighton looked at his hand but made no move to take it. "What happened to you last night? Where'd you go?"

His jaw tightened. "I got a phone call."

"That much I know. Who was calling?"

"A longtime associate."

She narrowed her eyes. "Is that code for something?"

"No. I didn't want to take the call, but I had to. It was rude and

I'm sorry." When she still didn't stand up, he grabbed a chair and sat next to her. "Where'd you go?"

"My friend Kira's house." Brighton set aside her phone and gave him her full attention. "I don't like to be in your house all alone. It's so big and quiet, it's like a massive mausoleum."

"I'll be sure to put that on the listing when I sell it." He smiled wryly. "Again, I'm sorry. I will make it up to you. Let me take you out on Friday night. Black-tie thing. We'll have fun."

She softened but refused to give in so easily. "I'll consider it."

"Great." He reached over and took her hand. "So I'll see you at home tonight?"

The sensation of his skin against hers made her crave more contact. "I already made plans with Kira."

"Tomorrow night?"

"Possibly." She pulled her hand away. "Unless I have to take a phone call from a longtime associate."

He gave a brusque nod. "So you want me to win you over before Friday? Challenge accepted."

Brighton knew she was in trouble when she saw the glint of determination in his eyes. "It's not a challenge."

"Too late. Are you coming back to my house or do I have to go full Lloyd Dobler with a boom box outside your friend's house tonight?"

"Do *not* go full Lloyd Dobler." But she couldn't suppress a tiny grin.

"Then tell me when I'll see you again."

"After I finish the ring I'm working on," she relented. "Wednesday night at the Whinery. I'll bring Kira. She wants to meet you."

"Looking forward to it." He pulled her close and kissed her, soft and seductive. He kissed her like he meant it and she kissed back, too suffused with desire and longing to stay angry about how he'd treated her.

Just like every other woman he'd been with.

She stiffened and pulled away. "You should go." Before he could react, she hurried to join Lila in the back room.

"What was that about?" Lila peered out to the showroom.

"Nothing." Brighton absentmindedly rubbed her lower lip. "Hey, where can I get a gown for a black-tie ball? I need something by Friday night."

"Date night with your husband?" Lila asked. "Well, if this were *Pretty Woman*, he'd give you his credit card, you'd buy a whole new wardrobe on Rodeo Drive, and then you'd greet him wearing nothing but a tie when he came home from work."

"This isn't *Pretty Woman*. I'm not a nineteen-year-old street-walker wearing thigh-high leather boots."

Lila made a face. "That's a damn shame."

"Yes, well. Any ideas on where I should look for formal wear around here?"

"Give me five minutes on the phone and all your problems will be solved."

"Who are you calling?" Brighton asked.

"Your fashion fairy godmother."

chapter 14

On Wednesday morning, right after Lila's very grateful customer picked up his stealth replacement wedding ring ("This is great—thank you . . . and don't tell anyone, okay?"), a deliveryman arrived at the Naked Finger requesting Lila's signature in exchange for a big white carton.

"Ooh." Lila scrawled her name on the clipboard and seized the package. "Must be your dress for Friday."

Brighton looked up from the marquise-diamond cross pendant she was designing. "Already?"

"This is my mother working her magic," Lila assured her. "This is what she does. It's her love, it's her life, it's her job. That's why she wanted me to text her those photographs of you." She grabbed a pair of scissors and carefully sliced the packing tape. "I guarantee you that the gown in this box will flatter your body type and skin tone."

"She can get all that from a few cell phone snapshots?" Brighton marveled.

"Heck, yeah. Oh, and you better accessorize exactly the way she tells you, or I'll never hear the end of it." Lila dug through multiple layers of tissue paper to reveal a dainty black floor-length gown with a wide square neckline and black Chantilly lace cap sleeves. The label said *Estevez*, a designer Brighton had never heard of.

"It's from the 1950s," Lila explained. "Check out the back. Sexy." She pointed to the lace panel that would show most of Brighton's back.

The dress was beautiful but appeared so delicate, Brighton was afraid to touch it. "How am I supposed to wear a bra with this?"

Lila was still admiring the stitching. "You're not."

"Uh . . ."

"Have no fear." Lila glanced up with a reassuring smile. "My mom knows all the tricks that models use to look perky in backless dresses."

Brighton rubbed her forehead. "This is going to involve duct tape, Krazy Glue, and tears, isn't it?"

"Let's figure out what to do with your hair." Lila plucked a folded sheet of paper out of the box. "Oh, never mind. My mom included detailed instructions. With diagrams."

Brighton scanned the step-by-step "hair staging" manual with a mounting sense of panic. "This looks complicated."

"It'll be fine," Lila assured her.

"You know what's not complicated? A basic, bra-friendly little black dress from Ann Taylor. I could still go to the outlet mall—"

"No outlet malls for you." Lila cut her off with a shake of her head. "You need to step up your game."

"I have no game," Brighton pointed out. "Ask anyone."

"Sweet pea, you're Mrs. Sorensen now. You'd better start acting like it."

. . .

Wednesday night at the Whinery started out pretty much like every other night at the Whinery—lots of loud music, free-flowing cocktails, and women looking to shake things up.

"Now, remember," Brighton instructed Kira as they approached the entrance. "Your job is to talk to Jake and then give me your honest, unbiased opinion."

"Got it." Kira fluffed her bouncy blond hair and adjusted the straps of her black sundress.

"Profile him," Brighton urged.

"I think you're mistaking me for an FBI agent on a network crime drama."

"Don't play coy," Brighton said. "I know you do personality assessments."

"Yes—in my office. With standardized assessment instruments that have been statistically normed and validated. And also with informed consent."

"Can't you just ask a few leading questions?" Brighton begged. "I'm counting on you to snap me back to reality here."

"I'll do my very best."

Brighton leveled her gaze at her friend. "And if you see the merest hint of pathology or a personality disorder—"

"Hi." Jake was waiting for them at the front door of the bar, wearing a black T-shirt and jeans. He turned to Kira with a smile. "You must be Kira."

Kira shook his hand and turned to Brighton. "I approve."

"What?" Brighton hissed. "You haven't even asked one question!"

"Don't need to." Kira gave Jake a thorough once-over. "Have fun, you lucky girl."

"Hey! You're supposed to be objective! Interrogate him! Profile him!"

"You didn't tell me it was karaoke night. I'm going to ask if they have Jewel's 'Foolish Games.' That's my go-to karaoke jam." She dismissed Jake with a friendly wave. "Delightful to meet you."

"You, too," he replied.

Kira practically skipped into the bar, humming the Jewel tune as she went.

"And there goes my sensible therapist friend, Kira." Brighton moved closer to Jake and let all her hesitation and worry evaporate in a cloud of dopamine. "Why do you smell like dust?"

"I was working on-site all day." He brushed her hair back from her face. "I showered, but the grit clings to your hair."

She glanced at the jeans. "You were working on-site? Like, hard labor?"

"Yeah."

"But why?"

"It's fun. Sometimes a man needs to work with his hands."

She considered how she felt when she became absorbed in the process of creating designs and pouring wax molds for new jewelry pieces. "But aren't you the CEO or whatever?"

"That's what's great about being CEO. I get to stack cement block if I want to."

"Living the dream."

"Every day." He took in her black pencil skirt and lace-trimmed blue top. "You look great." He ushered her inside, where groups of tourists, local residents, and bar-hopping college kids were laughing and talking at deafening decibels.

"We can go somewhere quieter," Jake yelled into her ear. "Like a shuttle launch or a prison riot."

"No, let's stay." She pointed out a table in the corner. "Lila's coming later and she's going to introduce me to some of her friends."

As they approached the bar, a gorgeous, buxom blonde who

looked about twenty-five years old wrapped her hands around Jake's forearm.

"You're Jake Sorensen," she announced. Brighton could smell a hint of wine on the woman's breath. "I was wondering when you'd show up." She used her shoulders like a fulcrum to wedge Brighton out of the way.

Jake gently but firmly pried the blonde's hand off his arm and stepped back to steady Brighton.

Undaunted, the blonde resuctioned herself to him. "I've been waiting all night for you to show up."

Brighton couldn't help herself. "Do you two know each other?"

"No." It was like the blonde could hear Brighton but couldn't see her. She focused completely on Jake. "But I know who you are. *Everybody* knows who you are."

Jake turned to Brighton. "Last chance for that shuttle launch."

The blonde finally deigned to acknowledge Brighton with a nod. "Listen, I see that you've already staked your claim or whatever, but I just need to borrow him for a few hours. It's an emergency."

The woman's words were flippant, but her eyes were melancholy. Brighton felt a twinge of sympathy. People who had just had their hearts broken didn't always act reasonably—especially around Jake Sorensen. She'd learned that firsthand. "Bad breakup?" she asked.

"Gut-wrenching." The blonde gripped Brighton's arm with the same intensity she'd gripped Jake's. "I feel like my heart's been ripped out of my chest, flung on the ground, and run over by a bus. Twice."

Brighton jerked her chin toward the bartender, who was mixing up a fresh batch of pink cocktails. "You know what helps with that? A little champagne, a little vermouth, and a lot of singing Nancy Sinatra at the top of your lungs."

"Yeah, no." The blonde released Brighton and sank her manicured fingernails into Jake again. "I'm way past vermouth and Nancy Sinatra. I need this guy."

Brighton instinctively stepped away from his side. This was the natural order of the world. Who the hell was she to compete with a twenty-five-year-old who probably had several *Maxim* shoots on her résumé?

Jake shook off the blonde and reclaimed Brighton's hand. He told the other woman, "This is my wife, Brighton."

The woman's glossy pink lips parted in horror. "You're *married*?"

Jake nodded. "It's a recent development."

And all that anguish turned into frustration. "But . . . but I drove all the way from New Hampshire to find you!" She glanced at Brighton, her eyes wild and desperate. "Heart. Bus. Twice."

Brighton went up on tiptoe and whispered to Jake, "It's okay, you know. If you want to go with her."

His brows snapped together. "What?"

"Well, I mean, it was bound to happen."

His shoulders tensed under her fingertips. *"What?"*

"Just because I got pissed at my fiancé and ran off to Vegas doesn't mean I expect you to—"

Jake rested one hand on the nape of her neck and hustled her past the blonde, past the bar, through the stock room, and out the back door of the building.

"What was that about?" Brighton asked as they arrived in the dimly lit alley lined by brick walls and Dumpsters.

He just stared at her, his arms folded, and she finally glimpsed the ruthless, cunning CEO who had built an empire from the ground up. He was using silence as a power play. She knew the appropriate counterstrategy was to stare right back and wait him out.

"You are my wife," he finally said. The planes and angles of his face looked sharper in the shadows.

The grimmer his expression looked, the more nonchalant she felt. Inexplicable but undeniable—kind of like everything else between them. "Yes, I'm your wife—for now—but I'm not your *warden*. If you want to go make out with some heartbreak tourist in need—"

"I don't." He was clearly struggling to keep his temper in check. "While we are married, I am not going to make out with anyone other than my spouse. And, so we're clear, neither are you."

Her eyes widened. "I had no idea you were so old-fashioned."

"Now you do."

They faced off for a moment in the dark, damp alley.

This time, she broke the silence. "I don't understand you at all."

"I don't understand you, either." He took a step toward her. "Why would you want me to go off with another woman?"

"It's not that I *want* you to." She struggled to explain. "I just don't want to tell you that you can't."

He slid his hands around her waist and down to her hips. "I'm with you."

"For now," she murmured.

He leaned down and brushed his lips across hers. "Right now, I am yours and you are mine."

And his tongue was in her mouth and she was tugging up his shirt and a few minutes of making out, neither one of them was in any condition to go back inside and pretend to be having a civilized evening.

"Back to my place?" he murmured as he kissed his way from her earlobe to her collarbone.

She closed her eyes, breathing in his scent and reveling in the feel of his body against hers. "You're very persuasive."

"Say yes," he urged.

She felt so close to him, so swept up in the urgency of the moment, that for a moment she forced herself to detach. This euphoria wasn't going to last. Someone was going to get hurt soon and—*spoiler alert*—it was going to be her.

Because she was getting attached. She was breaking her own rules. And soon, she'd have to pay a steep price for that. Soon . . . but not yet.

"Yes," she whispered in a rush of recklessness. "Yes, yes, yes."

chapter 15

"You still don't have a ring," Jake pointed out as he pressed Brighton's hand between both of his.

She stretched her hand toward the bedroom ceiling and splayed out her fingers in the moonlight filtering through the white wooden shutters. He reached up and traced her ring finger with his index finger.

"Why didn't you pick something out at Lila's?" he asked.

"Because," she said.

He let his fingers trail down her wrist and arm. "I'm waiting for the end of that sentence."

"Well, first of all, given our circumstances, it feels disingenuous to go around wearing a wedding ring." Brighton lowered her hand. "And if I *were* going to wear a wedding ring, I wouldn't just grab the first one I saw. Jewelry should have meaning. It should have a story or a secret that only the owner knows about." She flipped over to rest her head on his bare chest. "Like your watch."

"Don't start with the watch again." He groaned.

"I can't help it! Imagine all the places it must have been with its previous owner." She closed her eyes, envisioning Paris, Geneva, Manhattan, country weekends in the Berkshires and Martha's Vineyard, or maybe Napa and Carmel . . .

He threaded his fingers through her hair. "Refresh my memory: Why do you work in insurance, again?"

"Because I'm a slave to common sense." She turned her face to press her lips against his warm skin. "I wasn't always, though. When I was a kid, I was absolutely convinced I was going to move to New York or LA. I was going to build my grandparents' jewelry business into a luxury brand. I was going to be the second coming of Harry Winston. I had it all planned out."

He stacked his hands under his head, listening. "What happened?"

"My grandparents died and the business went bust." She could feel the steady beat of his heart. "As much as I love making jewelry, I love eating and having a place to live more. The fact is, following dreams has an opportunity cost."

"Not following them has an opportunity cost, too," he countered.

"I notice *you* didn't dedicate your life to following your bliss."

"How do you know?" He tried and failed to sound wounded. "Maybe I grew up dreaming of selling sand and pouring concrete. I love concrete. I'm *emotionally invested* in concrete."

"Uh-huh."

"It's true."

She lifted her head so she could see his eyes. "And you're telling me that you devoted your entire adult life to making boatloads of money, but now you don't care if I try to take a big chunk of it in a divorce?"

He shrugged. "I'll just make more."

"You don't even have a reason to want all this money?" she pressed. "You just do it for the hell of it?"

He nodded.

She nestled back onto his chest and tried to process all this. "Either you're a liar or you're the shallowest person ever."

He laughed. "You should feel sorry for me. I don't have a higher calling."

"Boo hoo. Dry your tears with crisp hundred-dollar bills." She nipped him lightly on the shoulder. "And I call BS that you don't have some secret passion. You have something."

He started rubbing her lower back. "Nope. Nothing."

Brighton closed her eyes and tried to conjure the likely possibilities. "Racing motorcycles? Sailing around the globe? Collecting antique fountain pens?"

His hands stilled. "What about me screams 'antique fountain pens'?"

"I don't know. Isn't that something indolent rich guys collect?"

"Maybe the guy with the mustache from the Monopoly game."

"Well, whatever." She nipped him again. "What's your poison, Sorensen? Confess. I know you have one."

"I don't. I really am this shallow." He shifted under the sheets, propped his back against the padded headboard, and settled her onto his lap. "How did you learn to do metalwork if you never took classes?"

Brighton knew he was deflecting and changing the subject again, but she couldn't resist the opportunity to reminisce. "My grandfather let me hang out and watch him when I was little. I started playing around with whatever scrap metal I could find." She smiled, remembering her earliest attempts at craftsmanship. "Old spoons and stuff. I once made some very avant-garde earrings out of a tangled-up Slinky. I'm pretty sure they gave my sister tetanus, but they looked good."

"One sister?" he asked.

"Yes. It was me, my sister, Cat, and my mother. Anyway, I started experimenting with different shapes and materials. My mom used to say I was like a magpie, stealing all the shiny stuff. I would look at the celebrity tabloids at the grocery store and fantasize that one day, some movie star would have her picture taken wearing an engagement ring that I designed." She was a little embarrassed to admit this out loud. "I used to pray that Cat would grow up to be famous so that my dream would come true."

"Did she?"

"No. She dropped out of college, spent a few years waiting tables and singing in a bar band, and now she's back in school. She's going to be an accountant. I'm proud of her."

"An accountant and an actuary." His voice warmed her from the inside out. "Your family reunions must be out-of-control ragers."

"What's wrong with being an accountant and an actuary?" Brighton demanded. "It's easy to make fun of steady, stable jobs when you're independently wealthy and never have to worry about saving for college or your kids' orthodontia."

"You don't have kids," he pointed out.

"But I will," she assured him. "Someday."

"You don't have a timetable already set? I'm shocked."

She actually had worked out a child-bearing schedule with Colin—they would start trying to conceive six months after their wedding, hopefully timing the baby's birth so as not to coincide with either tax season or cold and flu season—but she didn't feel the need to share that information right now.

"*Anyway*, while I was waiting for my sister to move to Hollywood and become a celebrity, I kept making bracelets and rings and earrings. I didn't really know what I was doing, but I spent hours tinkering with wire and gemstones and a blowtorch."

"Your mom was okay with that?"

"Yeah." Brighton smiled ruefully. "She's always been what you might call a free spirit."

"You sound skeptical."

"She named her daughters Brighton and Catriona—that right there tells you everything you need to know. She's never been a big believer in ten-year plans, or any plans, really." Brighton's tone was still light, but her mood had gone somber. Colin had often remarked upon the same thing. (*Nobody expects you to bail her out anymore, Brighton. She's a grown woman. You're not her safety net.*) But if she didn't step in to help, who would? Her mother needed a safety net, and Brighton didn't mind providing it. Even if that meant always erring on the side of caution.

"Hey." Jake lifted her chin so he could see her face. "Still with me?"

"Yeah." She shook off her pensive mood. "Anyway, that's my sordid confession: My name is Brighton Smith and I was raised by a hippie who let me play with fire in elementary school. Your turn."

He looked down at her. She looked back expectantly. "I just gave you a little piece of my personal history. The way this works is, now you give me a little piece of yours."

"I already offered you the diamond of your choice."

"I don't want a diamond." She rubbed her palms together. "I want *information*. I want you to tell me something about yourself."

He shifted slightly, resettling her against his chest. "Like what?"

"Like . . ." She paused. "What did you want to be when you grew up?"

He looked at her as though she'd lost her mind. "I don't know."

"Yes, you do. Come on! What was your eight-year-old dream job?"

He tipped his head back and confessed to the ceiling, "When I was eight, I wanted to be a park ranger."

She pulled away from him so she could study his expression. "Like the guy up in a tower watching for forest fires?"

"No, like the guy who spends all day by himself in the wilderness, rescuing hikers and making sure all the campfires are extinguished."

"I'm trying to picture you in one of those hats." She ruffled his hair. "I'm pretty sure you could pull it off."

He looked more self-conscious than she had ever seen him. "I had three younger brothers. I just wanted some peace and quiet."

"So why aren't you working at Yellowstone right now?" she demanded.

"Park rangers can't afford beachfront property and corporate jets."

She put both her hands on his shoulders. "You said you didn't care about all that."

"I didn't." His expression changed from wistful to guarded. "But the people I care about did."

"Ah." She thought about her sister's tuition bill. "Are your brothers grown up now?"

"They all finished college," he said with evident pride. "One went on to business school. Two of them work for my overseas division."

"Then you've done your familial duty. It's not too late," she persisted. "You could probably buy your own park at this point. Call Arizona and see if they'll cut you a deal on the Grand Canyon."

He pulled her back into his arms. "A few years ago, I did buy some land in Montana."

"Like a ranch?"

"Like five hundred acres of wilderness."

Her imagination went into overdrive with images of glaciers and bison. "What's it like?"

"There's a mountain and a stream and I'm guessing a whole lot of trees."

"What do you mean, you're guessing?" She shivered against the cool evening air.

He tugged the sheet over her legs. "I haven't actually been out there. One of my advisers said it'd be a good investment, so I bought it."

"What? Why haven't you gone yet? It's your childhood dream come true!"

He kissed the top of her head. "I missed my window for frontier living."

"Oh, come on. You're not even forty yet. You're not even halfway through." She leveled her index finger at him. "You have a long way to go before you peak."

He gazed at her for a long moment, but she couldn't tell what he was thinking.

"The great thing about having all this money is that you have options," she continued. "You could go out there and live your own private version of *Little House on the Prairie*. With fishing and hiking and whittling or whatever."

"I never read *Little House on the Prairie*."

"Oh, you should." She regaled him with tales of maple syrup candy and scarlet fever and Jack the brindle bulldog. "Put that at the top of your frontier reading list."

Across the room, his phone buzzed. He didn't make any move to get out of bed, but his mood changed ever so slightly.

"Do you need to get that?" she asked.

He bent his head and murmured against her temple, "No."

She breathed in, savoring the scent of his skin. He wasn't wearing cologne, but he still managed to smell like the nectar of the gods. *Eau de limerence.*

They stayed like that, quiet and content, both looking out at the clear starry night, until Brighton drifted off to sleep. As her eyes closed and she relaxed against him, she knew that something had changed between them. She felt warm and safe and utterly content. For the first time, she allowed herself to dream about what it might be like to be married—really married—to her husband.

. . .

The next morning, she awakened to find his side of the bed empty. Again.

Brighton snuggled into the white duvet and pillows for a few minutes, trying to hold on to the feelings from last night. All the warmth and emotional connection dissipated in the bright morning light. She rested her palm on the cool expanse of sheet where Jake had slept last night.

She wasn't surprised he'd left, but she *was* surprised at how disappointed she felt.

After a few more minutes, she sat up, slid into a thick white terry cloth robe, and launched into her morning routine. She opened the balcony doors to check the outside temperature and heard a rhythmic clatter on the courtyard cobblestones followed by a splash and a high-pitched wail.

She raced down the back staircase and out the door. A small, stocky boy had fallen into the koi pond; his skateboard lay upended by the pond's edge, the neon yellow wheels still spinning.

As soon as the boy saw her, his eyes went wide and he stopped yelling.

"Here." Brighton leaned over the water and offered her hand. He hesitated for a moment before grabbing on to her.

She braced her bare feet against an outcropping of rock and helped him out of the water. His thick, dark hair dripped and his black oxford shoes squished as he stepped back on dry land.

"Are you okay?" she asked, tightening the sash of her robe.

The child regarded her with huge, solemn brown eyes. "Who are you?"

"I'm, um, I'm Brighton Smith." She tucked her hands into the robe's pockets. "Who are you?"

"Dylan," he replied.

"Dylan!" A shrill voice yelled from the far side of the driveway, and a petite, wiry woman with curly brown hair raced toward them. "What happened?"

"Mom, I was only—"

"He's okay," Brighton assured the frazzled mother. "Took a little spill into the pond, but no harm done."

"You were skateboarding, weren't you?" The mother didn't even wait for a reply. "Look at your shirt. You're going to be late for camp!"

"Hi." Brighton held out her right hand. "I'm Brighton Smith. I'm Jake's, uh . . ."

"Christine Klimes." The woman had a firm handshake. "I'm the head housekeeper."

"So you do exist!" Brighton blurted out before her mental filter kicked in. "I was wondering. I never see anybody actually in the house."

"We try to give Mr. Sorensen his privacy." Christine shot her a speculative look. "And his guests, as well."

Brighton stared at the koi pond.

"You've been here longer than any of his other guests," Dylan chimed in.

"Shh!" his mother hissed. "Stop talking and go change into a fresh uniform before—"

"Good morning." Jake ambled out of the tiny guest cottage adjacent to the garage, his hands full of file folders. He took in the boy's bedraggled state. "You okay, Dylan?"

Now the boy looked suffused with shame. "Yeah."

His mother gave him a none-too-subtle nudge. "Apologize to Jake right now. He just bought you these new shirts."

"Sorry," Dylan mumbled.

Brighton glanced from Dylan to Christine to Jake. She sidled closer to Jake and whispered, "Is he your . . ."

Jake was too busy wringing out the hem of Dylan's shirt to pay attention. "My what?"

"Your—" She lowered her voice even more. "Son?"

All three of them burst out laughing.

"No," Christine said. "He just feels sorry for me because I'm a single mom."

"He's sending me to camp," Dylan informed Brighton. "Bought my backpack and my uniform and everything."

"I don't feel sorry for you," Jake said to Christine.

"Yeah, you do." Christine turned to Brighton. "He does. It's because he had a single mom, so he tries to help me out with my boy."

"He's paying for my school next year, too," Dylan divulged.

Jake and Christine both shushed him at once.

"Christine is tough as nails," Jake told Brighton. "She doesn't need anyone to feel sorry for her."

Christine smiled. "Is that why you got Dylan that puppy when his dad left?" She glanced back at Brighton. "And speaking of dogs—"

"I'll give you a bonus if you stop talking right now," Jake offered.

Christine put one hand on her hip. "How much?"

"Name your price," Jake said.

"Expect my written offer by the end of the day." Christine waved to Brighton as she resumed chastising her son. "Nice meeting you."

Brighton rounded on Jake. "*Innn*teresting. The plot thickens."

He picked up the abandoned skateboard and peered into the pond to check on the fish. "Nothing to see here."

"Oh, I beg to differ." She rolled up the sleeves of the oversize robe. "You're more than just a pretty face who's good in bed."

His head snapped up. "Don't tell anyone."

She gave him a wink and just a hint of smolder. "Your secret's safe with me."

chapter 16

"You know what would go great with that dress?" Jake asked as he squired Brighton into the huge, high-ceilinged hotel ballroom filled with tuxedoed waiters and crystal chandeliers. "Pearls."

"It's a gown, not a dress," Brighton corrected. Lila had schooled her well. "And since *someone* destroyed my pearls in the heat of passion, I had to find a substitute." She pointed out the art-deco-style diamond and emerald earrings she'd fashioned from the gemstones in Lila's store safe. "I made these especially for tonight." She patted her head to ensure her hair was still in place. After reading and rereading Lila's mother's coiffure instructions, Brighton had given up and gone to the Rebound Salon on Main Street, where the stylists had created a soft, elegant updo.

He tucked her hand into the crook of his elbow. "Let's get you something to drink. Champagne?"

She wrinkled her nose. "The last time I drank champagne with you, we ended up in the marital E-ZPass lane."

"We took a long-shot bet and we'll never regret it." He nodded to one of the servers carrying a silver tray of full champagne flutes. "Cheers."

"Remind me again." Brighton accepted the glass the server offered. "What's the occasion and who invited us?"

"It's a local charity benefit, and one of my companies is cosponsoring, so I figured I should make an appearance."

"*One* of your companies," she repeated. "How many companies do you have?"

He shrugged. "Who keeps track of these things?"

Before she had time to press for details, they were deluged with handshakes and hugs. Well, *Jake* was, anyway. Handshakes from the men, and hugs—close, full-body, lingering hugs—from the women.

"This is my wife, Brighton," Jake kept announcing. His female admirers reacted as if he'd spattered them with acid.

Brighton was grateful for her black Chantilly lace dress and diamond and emerald earrings, her armor against the cutting glares from the many, many (*many*) women who had designs on Jake. The moment he got sucked into a cadre of male coworkers who wanted to discuss a logistics issue, the wives and girlfriends clustered around Brighton.

"How'd you do it?" a willowy redhead demanded. "What's your secret?"

Brighton sipped her bubbly. "Pricey booze and no impulse control. Two great tastes that taste great together."

The redhead laughed. "I'm serious."

"So am I."

As news of the nuptials spread across the ballroom, more and more women flocked over to get a glimpse of the newly minted Mrs. Sorensen.

"You must be extraordinary," a reedy-voiced brunette announced, though she looked dubious. "Jake usually won't even bring a date to these things."

"But he always leaves with one," someone else trilled.

"Where's your ring?" Another woman, surprisingly strong for one so petite, practically wrestled the champagne glass away from Brighton in her attempt to inspect her left hand. "I have to see the diamond Jake Sorensen proposed with."

"No ring," Brighton replied. Everyone stared at her. She knew they were waiting for juicy details, but she refused to divulge anything. Yes, her marriage was a sham. Yes, her wedding had been hilarious. Yes, all of this would be great cocktail party conversation. But these experiences were *hers*. Hers and Jake's. Speaking of whom . . .

"Are you behaving yourself over here?" Jake appeared at her side with a charming smile that immediately dispersed all the cattiness.

"Not really." Brighton turned to him with a saucy smile. "I'm starting a bunch of rumors about how you proposed with the worm at the bottle of a tequila bottle."

"It's not a rumor if it's the truth." Jake lifted her hand to his lips, holding her gaze as he kissed her knuckles.

"How gentlemanly of you," she breathed, keenly aware of the audience.

"We are in a ballroom," he pointed out. "And I am in a tux."

She lowered her voice so that only he could hear. "Not for long."

For a moment, it was just the two of them, totally alone. The music and the chatter receded; all she could perceive was his touch and his gaze and the connection between them. Her insides felt as fizzy as the champagne she'd just sipped. He did this to her every time. *Every time.* All he had to do was look her way.

"When can we leave?" she whispered to him.

"Jake!" a jovial male voice boomed. "I've been looking everywhere for you. Come meet the new investors."

"Five minutes." Jake squeezed her fingers, then released them. "Time me."

She nodded, turned around, and nearly ran into a tiny, platinum-haired wisp of a woman. "Oops, sorry." A drop of champagne splashed over the rim of her glass.

The woman waved away the apology, her mouth puckering into a little moue as she admired Brighton's gown. "I absolutely adore what you're wearing. Is it vintage?"

For the first time since she'd walked into the ballroom, Brighton relaxed. "From the fifties, I think."

"Look at that lacework." The woman eyed the Chantilly stretched across the shoulders and bodice. "Divine. And those earrings." She tilted her head, admiring the diamonds and emeralds. "Stunning."

"Thank you." Brighton's smile was genuine this time.

"Harry Winston?" the woman guessed.

"Pardon?"

"The earrings. Are they Harry Winston?"

Brighton's smile brightened into a beam. "Actually, I made them myself."

"You did? Goodness, you do beautiful work."

"Thank you. You have great taste." She hadn't realized how this would sound until she'd already said it. But it was the truth; the other woman wore a stunning statement necklace crafted from peach coral, deep green jade, and black jade. Her hair was pulled back and her black gown was simple—the whole ensemble showcased the unusual piece.

"I know." The woman gave her a conspiratorial grin, then reached out to touch Brighton's earrings. "May I?"

"Of course." Brighton held still while her new acquaintance studied the craftsmanship.

"You're an artist," she declared, stepping back.

Brighton shook her head. "No, I'm an actuary."

"A what?"

"I work in insurance. The jewelry is more of a hobby."

The other woman gasped. "But you're wasting your gift." Before Brighton could respond, she went on. "Do you have your own line? A storefront? A Web site?"

"No, I'm just sort of freelancing for a few weeks at a boutique by the beach."

The woman clicked her tongue and demanded, "Where is your shop? I'd love to commission a piece from you."

"It's in a little town called—"

"Just one moment." The woman whirled and waved to a white-haired gentleman across the room. "Let me get my bag and take down your contact information."

Brighton watched her future client (she supposed "patron" would be more appropriate in this social context) point her out to the white-haired companion. The man whispered something to her, and then pointed across the room.

Brighton glanced behind her to see what they were looking at. Jake was striding toward her. She looked back at the blonde, who was now looking at Jake.

"Hey." Brighton tilted her head toward the blonde as subtly as she could. "See that woman in the black dress and the coral-and-green necklace? Do you know her?"

Jake gave a curt nod. "We're done here." He whisked her out of the ballroom so quickly, she was still holding her champagne glass when they reached the hotel lobby. Brighton noticed a brass elevator so similar to the one in her office building and remembered that, only a week ago, she'd been desperate to escape the humdrum of corporate life.

Her wish had certainly been granted.

Jake led her to the valet stand and handed the uniformed worker a claim ticket and a folded twenty-dollar bill.

"What was that all about?" Brighton asked.

His eyes had gone dark and his whole body was tense. "Nothing."

"Oh, it was definitely something. Is she an ex-girlfriend?"

"No."

"Are you sure?"

He never broke eye contact. "Yes."

"Business associate?" she tried.

"No."

When the valet delivered the truck, Jake opened the door for her, then settled into the driver's seat without a word.

"I'm going to need some answers here," she told him. "Why was everyone looking so intense? You, her, that old guy with the expensive haircut?"

"It's nothing," he repeated. "Nothing important, anyway."

Her jaw dropped as a horrible thought occurred. "Oh God. Is this something I'm not going to be able to testify about because we're legally married?"

"No." He took a slow, measured breath. "Don't worry about it."

She knew she should drop it—the last time she'd had a fight in a car, she'd ended up dumped and disgraced. "When someone looks at me the way that woman looked at me, I have a right to know why."

He glanced over at her, his expression unreadable. "How did she look at you?"

"Like I'd *wronged* her. Like I called her a name and threw a drink in her face." She tapped one finger on the window. "Are you *sure* she's not your ex-girlfriend?"

Jake's laugh was rough and bitter. "That's not what this is about."

"Then what the hell is it about?" she demanded. "Because you have the same look on your face that you had on the night we met." She swallowed, not sure she wanted to hear the answer to her next question. "Is this related to what you said about spending ten years drinking and buying expensive shit and socializing with strangers?"

"Do you really want to talk about this?" he asked. "Or do you want to drive to the Four Seasons in Baltimore, get a suite with a big bathtub, and lay waste to another set of pearls?"

"Don't do that," she said. "Don't try to distract me with the sexy and the shiny."

He blinked. "The what?"

"Every time you don't want to talk about something or answer a question, you start throwing money at the problem." She clenched her molars in frustration. "I just want to know who the hell I'm married to. You swore Google to secrecy, you have an apparently endless stream of money, you do things to people that make them give me death stares across crowded rooms . . ." She waited for him to give her something. Anything. The tiniest scrap of self-disclosure.

He kept his eyes on the road.

"Don't just sit there being inscrutable," she said. "We're having our first official fight."

"I'm not angry," he pointed out.

"That's the problem!" She was suddenly yelling. "You're never angry. You're never angry or sad or frustrated or anything besides sexy and charming. Get angry! Fight with me."

"Brighton." His tone was soothing and reassuring and made her want to start throwing things.

She realized that this was how Colin must have felt when she tried to reason with him during the great zipper-merge debacle. She desperately wanted Jake to engage, to show some sort of emotion, but he remained patient and unflappable. Because he didn't care.

This is how drama queens are born, she warned herself. *Get ahold of yourself.* So she did. She forced herself to stop talking and sit back. To bottle everything up, just like he did.

They spent the rest of the drive home in silence.

When the car pulled into the driveway of Don't Be Koi, Brighton noticed a familiar figure silhouetted against the porch light.

"Oh my God. Is that . . . ?" She covered her mouth with her hand as she recognized the stoop of the shoulders, the downcast profile. "It's Colin."

Jake didn't seem at all surprised. "That's him?"

She nodded. "That's him."

"I figured he'd show up eventually." Jake turned off the truck and took the keys out of the ignition. "I'll handle this."

"No. No, no, no." Brighton's voice shook as she reached for the door handle. "*I'll* handle this. Stay right where you are."

Jake looked half-amused and half-alarmed. "Should I frisk you for weapons?"

"No need. I'll deal with him with my bare hands." Brighton handed him her purse and went to work on the dainty art deco screwbacks. "Here, hold my earrings."

chapter 17

"*N*o," was the first thing Brighton said as she strode up the porch steps to confront her former fiancé.

Colin lifted his head and looked at her face, though he wouldn't meet her gaze. "Brighton, I have to talk to you."

"*No.*" She clenched both hands at her sides.

He held up his palms to ward her off but kept talking. "I made a mistake. A huge mistake." He paused for a moment, his gaze darting over to the pickup truck in the driveway. "I don't know what I was thinking, but I'm hoping that you and I can—"

"*No.*" She pointed imperiously off the porch. "Go."

"Just listen," he begged. "Please."

He seemed so sad and sincere that she relented, keeping one hand on her hip and motioning with the other that he should continue.

"The whole thing with Genevieve was a mistake."

She half sputtered, half laughed. "You don't say."

"We're getting an annulment," he said. "It'll be like the whole thing never happened." He cleared his throat and moved closer. "I could never love her the way I love you."

She stormed to the far side of the porch, yelling over her shoulder. "But it *did* happen, Colin. And you don't love me. If you did, you wouldn't pick a fight and then marry someone you just met. Who does that?"

He hurried after her. "*You* married someone you just met."

"Only because you did it first!"

"Okay, so we both did." He sounded relieved. "We're even."

"We are not even, Colin. Not even close." She kept walking toward the soothing lull of the tide on the other side of the wraparound deck. "But it doesn't matter. We're both married to other people and that's the end of our story."

"It doesn't have to end."

"Yes, it does." She reached the porch railing overlooking the beach. "I never want to see you again."

He trailed up behind her. She crossed her arms and fumed.

"I still love you, Brighton. I always will." He dropped to his knees and grabbed the lace-trimmed hem of her gown.

"Oof." She had to steady herself with both hands on the porch railing.

"I panicked." He let go of her hem and seized her calves. "It was such a relief to find someone who didn't expect anything from me."

She tried to shake him off. "Don't touch me."

"Wait. Please listen," he begged. "I know there's no excuse for what I did, but . . ." He tightened his grip on her legs. "I've spent years trying to be the guy you think I am. The guy who can make decisions, get it all done. But I'm not. You don't know who I really am."

Brighton could see the headlights of Jake's truck through the walls of windows. "Yeah, there's a lot of that going around lately." Her fiery rage tempered down to melancholy regret. "It's over, Colin.

You made the decision for both of us." She managed to free herself and charged back to the other side of the house.

He caught her wrist as she rounded the corner. "You owe me ten minutes."

"I don't owe you anything." She had to laugh at his nerve. "How did you even find me?"

"I drove to town this afternoon and asked around. Everyone I talked to knew exactly who you were and who you were with."

Brighton had to smile. "Of course they did. But how did you get through the gate?"

"Some high schooler told me the code for twenty bucks." Colin seized her arm. "Those pictures you texted me, of the plane and the limo and that guy . . ."

"That guy has a name," she informed him. "It's Jake Sorensen. He's a self-made watch enthusiast who enjoys cooking, nature documentaries, and orange Gatorade."

"You'll never know how much it hurt to see those photos." Colin's voice cracked with emotion. "You looked so . . . You looked like a different person."

"I'm the same person I've always been," she said. "You're the one who's been pretending, apparently."

"No, you're different. I can see it. I can feel it." His hand slipped up her arm to her elbow. "I like it."

She completed her lap around the porch, dragging him along behind her. "It is taking every ounce of self-control I have right now not to punch you in the face. But I won't, because then I could be arrested and prosecuted for assault and battery." She paused, considering. "Although perhaps I could invoke the 'fighting words doctrine,' under which assault is excused because the perpetrator said something to which a reasonable person would be unable to restrain themselves from responding violently. Want to know how I know all that? From helping you study for the *fucking bar exam.*"

He took his hands off her and went back to looking chagrined. "I'm truly sorry, Brighton. Please believe me. Please give me another chance."

"I do believe you. But I'm not giving you another chance." When she turned toward him, he turned away. "What did you expect me to do? Really? When you called me up and told me you married somebody else, what did you expect my response to be?"

"I don't know." He glanced around, taking in the mansion, the ocean, the international man of mystery who had gotten out of the pickup truck and was now watching the proceedings from the driveway. "Not this."

Brighton looked at Jake, hoping he wouldn't intervene. She wanted to have this conversation on her own terms. She'd imagined this scenario countless times over the past seven days—down to the kneeling and begging on Colin's part—but now that it was actually happening, she couldn't muster even the smallest modicum of vengeful glee. No swell of triumph. No urge to say, "I told you so."

Just an overwhelming sense of loss and futility. She and Colin had tried so hard. They had shared everything, but they had nothing left. He was a stranger to her now.

"You're the love of my life." Colin reached out for her. "I thought I was the love of yours."

Brighton pulled back from him as a horrifying realization struck. "Not anymore."

"I'm *in love* with him." Brighton threw her bag down on the leather love seat in Kira's office. "Or, at least, my hormones think I am. It's all unicorns and flowers and sparkly pink hearts in here." She put her hand on her chest. "I can't believe this. How could I be so *stupid*?"

She had texted her old friend early that morning, hoping she might hear back by lunchtime. Instead, Kira had responded immediately, suggesting that they meet at her therapy practice before her morning sessions.

"Have a seat." Kira gestured to the chairs and sofa arranged in a semicircle. Despite the early hour on a Saturday, she looked polished and professional in a blue blouse, a gray and blue patterned skirt, and a pair of blue-framed glasses. "Have some coffee."

"I can't." Brighton compromised on the whole "have a seat" thing by half sitting on the armrest of the couch. "I have to be at the Naked Finger by nine."

"Girl, you're a wreck. You need coffee." Kira handed her insulated travel mug to Brighton. "Here, have mine. I insist. I'll brew more."

Brighton accepted the mug and sipped. Kira glanced at the digital clock on the side table. "Let's cut to the chase. How did it feel? Seeing Colin?"

"I was eerily calm," Brighton recalled. "It was like I was a soap opera character. I felt absolutely nothing for him."

"Uh-huh." Kira looked skeptical.

"What?" Brighton demanded.

"How long were you two together?"

"A while."

"Define 'a while.'"

"Like two years." Brighton flipped the spout of the thermos up and down. "Why? Are you saying it's *not* normal to feel indifferent about a guy I dated, slept with, and planned to marry?"

"Normal is a dryer setting." Kira grinned. "There's a little therapist saying for you."

"Ugh, get out of here with that. And get out of here with Colin, too. I honestly couldn't care less." She passed the thermos to Kira, who took a sip and passed it back. "I'm here to talk to you about Jake."

Kira settled back in her chair and waited.

Brighton hopped off the sofa and started pacing. "Okay. So. For a fraction of a second last night, I really and truly believed I was in love with him. Which is impossible for many reasons, not the least of which is I don't know anything about him except he's rich, good-looking, and great in bed."

"The trifecta." Kira smiled.

"And you were no help with your two-second snap judgment. What happened to leading questions and objective assessment?"

Kira shrugged. "What can I say? The man has charisma."

Brighton clutched the thermos with both hands. "This is crazy. I'm not in love. What I am is a hopped-up junkie, and he is my drug of choice."

"The first step is admitting you have a problem," Kira deadpanned.

"What's going to happen when my two weeks are up? I'm going to have to deal with massive withdrawal."

"And your feelings about Colin," Kira added.

"I just told you, I don't have any feelings about Colin." Brighton flicked her hand in dismissal. "Because I medicated them away with dopamine, courtesy of Jake."

"You said it; I didn't."

"Except, here's the thing. I understand the reality here, with the dopamine and the limerence and all that, on an intellectual level. But . . ."

Kira waited for her to go on.

"But it doesn't *feel* like dopamine. It feels like actual emotion. Like I actually care about him." Brighton smote her own forehead. "And he doesn't care about me at all. The man gives zero damns. How could I let this happen?"

"Hey. Be gentle with yourself," Kira said. "I met him for two seconds, and I got a little dopamine surge myself."

"I'm such an idiot. We all know how this is going to end. I'm not the magical catalyst that's going to transform him from man-whore to good-husband material." She collapsed back onto the sofa. "Real life doesn't work like that."

"Maybe not, but there must be something special about you," Kira said. "He's never married anyone else."

"People keep saying that." Brighton put down the coffee and twisted her hands together. "But I think I was just in the right place at the right time. I don't think it's about me at all. It's about him."

"Getting married is a pretty drastic move. Why now?"

"I'm still trying to piece that together." Brighton glanced around the office. "Do you have any chocolate in here?"

"You know I always keep a secret stash." Kira pulled a Kit Kat out of her desk drawer. "Here. Slow down. Breathe. Let's not go down the rabbit hole of gloom and despair just yet."

"Too late." Brighton shoved a piece of crispy chocolate-coated wafer into her mouth as she thought about the reactions she'd gotten last night at the gala. "God's gift to women has a hidden agenda. Guaranteed."

chapter 18

*B*righton thought she knew what to expect on her first day work-ing solo at the Naked Finger: weepy ex-girlfriends, jaded ex-wives, shell-shocked *Maxim* models who had traveled all the way from New Hampshire to get some fresh perspective and a piece of Jake Sorensen.

But the first customers to stroll into the store were a man and a woman, holding hands and openly groping each other. Despite the PDA, no one would mistake them for soul mates. The woman was a taut, tanned, fading beauty in her forties, and the guy was . . . well, he had to be at least seventy-five. *At least.* She was wearing a short black skirt, a ruffly white halter top, and lipstick so pink it probably glowed in the dark. He was wearing khaki pants, a khaki jacket, and a gray fisherman's hat that was visibly soiled. She called him Puppy. He referred to her as Dumplin'. Brighton greeted them both and tried to remember Lila's rules for compiling an aesthetic "profile." She noticed that Dumplin' was rocking high-heeled mules with interlocked gold Gucci *G*'s on the ankle strap, which coordinated with a matching logo'd handbag.

"Are you looking for something special?" she asked, heading straight for the display case containing the high-end designer bling. "We have some lovely Tiffany and Cartier pieces."

"I want a Rolex," Dumplin' announced with absolute authority. She reached over and took her companion's hand. "Look, Puppy, they have one in rose gold."

Her companion shook his head, wheezing so hard the brim of his floppy gray hat fluttered. "No."

"*No?!*" Dumplin's voice got so shrill that Brighton couldn't suppress a wince. "What do you mean, 'no'?"

Puppy cleared his throat in a loud, phlegmy display of displeasure. "I just bought you that ruby ring last week."

"That was *two* weeks ago. And I don't have anything nice to wear on my wrists." Dumplin' held up her bare arms, a martyr in a miniskirt. She batted her eyelashes; she pulled down her halter top. She simpered and smooched her companion while Brighton busied herself with paperwork and pretended to be blind and deaf.

Then, just when it seemed she was out of ammo, Dumplin' slapped Puppy on the shoulder and pointed toward the door. "Give me your credit card and go take a nap."

Without a word of protest he handed over his wallet and shuffled toward the door, pausing only to cough up another bit of phlegm on the way.

"Thanks, babe. Meet you back at the hotel!" Dumplin' turned to Brighton with an air of brisk efficiency. "Now, where were we? Ah, yes, the rose gold Rolex. What's the diameter of the face?"

"Thirty-seven millimeters." Brighton unlocked the case and took out the watch. "This is a lovely piece, probably from the midnineties. The dial and the casing are both original and in excellent shape."

"It's nice, but it needs more sparkle." Dumplin' draped the watch over her wrist and studied the effect. "Can you put little diamonds all around the face?"

"Of course," Brighton said. "It'll take a few days, but we can do that." She inventoried the contents of the safe and sketched a few different design options. After the client selected her favorite, they discussed the precise quality and placement of the diamonds.

"Great. We'll be in town until Friday." Dumplin' pressed the credit card into her hand. "I'll give you my number. Just call me when it's ready."

"Okay." Brighton hesitated before processing the credit card. "Should we maybe call your, uh . . ."

"Friend," Dumplin' supplied.

"Maybe we should call your friend and make sure he's cool with your spending twenty-three thousand dollars."

"He's fine with it." Dumplin' scribbled her phone number on a gum wrapper, checked her cleavage and her teeth in the mirror next to the cash register, and strutted back out to the sidewalk.

Just as Dumplin' walked out, a clean-cut, middle-aged man walked in. With his sandy-colored hair, glasses, neatly pressed shirt, and very visible wedding ring, he looked like the type of guy who would help make dinner and attend every parent-teacher conference.

"I'm looking for a gift." He smiled, which only added to the J.Crew Dad effect. "For my wife."

"You've come to the right place." Brighton returned the smile. "Tell me about your wife. What does she do for work? What type of jewelry does she normally wear?"

"I already know what I want." The guy pulled out his smart-phone and consulted his notes. "Diamond stud earrings, no less than half a carat each, I color or better."

"Well, that does narrow it down." Brighton led him to the ear-ring display, which featured several pairs of well-matched studs. She displayed each pair, extolling their beauty. She didn't mention that almost all of the diamonds had been the center stones of engagement rings in a previous life. Some people got superstitious about the whole bad-karma thing. Which Brighton had never understood—even the most extravagant ring was nothing more than rock, metal, and clever advertising. The raw materials meant nothing without sentiment. Monetary value could never trump the emotional value of a gift selected with care and consideration.

And that's why I don't have a wedding ring.

"So, what do you think?" She glanced up when she finished her spiel, trying to determine whether he wanted to make the final selection himself or would prefer to delegate to her.

"Those are nice." He pointed out a pair of sparkling studs. Then he nodded at another set featuring brilliant blue sapphires. "But those are nice, too."

Brighton pulled out the second pair. "These are amazing. Three carats total weight. And look at the cut." She encouraged him to hold them up to the overhead light. "Phenomenal."

He paused for a moment, then shrugged. "What the hell—I'll take them both. Wrap them up."

"Lucky lady." Brighton accepted his credit card and boxed up the earrings in velvet cases with bows.

As she tucked the receipt in the bag and sent him on his way, she experienced a pang of jealousy for a woman she'd never even met. She wanted what her customer's wife would have when she opened the jewelry box: the feeling that she was cherished. The knowledge that the man she loved had been thinking of her and planning ahead.

She snapped to attention as the phone rang and answered with brisk professionalism: "Naked Finger. This is Brighton."

"Do you make deliveries?" asked a suave male voice. "I need the nicest diamond necklace you have."

. . .

"It was testosterone day at the jewelry store," Brighton told Jake as they shared a glass of red wine in Don't Be Koi's huge, airy kitchen. "Steady parade of guys from open to close."

"Did you move a lot of product?"

"Yeah, including a twenty-three-thousand-dollar Rolex that I'm customizing with pavé diamonds."

"Nice. I hope Lila's paying you commission."

"Oh, I don't care about the commission." Brighton froze, her wooden spoon midway to the pot simmering on the stove. "Did I just say those words? What's happening to me?"

"It's part of the screw-up summer," Jake said. "Go with it."

"I don't even know who I am anymore." She put down the spoon, reeling. "Eight days in a mansion with housekeepers, groundskeepers, and an endless supply of twelve-dollar strawberries, and I'm ruined."

"The term is 'spoiled.'"

"Even worse." Her hand flew to her mouth. "That makes me sound like a kept woman."

He laughed. "No one would ever accuse you of being a kept woman."

She went from horrified to defensive in a split second. "What is that supposed to mean?"

"It means you're not trophy wife material." Before she could respond, he added, "That's a compliment."

"And yet somehow, I'm not feeling very complimented. I mean, I get that our society wants me to spend all my time and money trying to look perfect, but you know what? I have shit to do. Sometimes finishing a report comes before touching up my pedicure. I apologize for nothing."

"For the record, you're beautiful." He picked up the spoon she'd put down and resumed cooking. "And I like a woman who can get shit done."

"Is that why you married me?" She held her breath, watching his expression.

"In part."

She folded her arms. "I'm waiting for the other part."

A clatter in the front hallway shattered the tense silence. Brighton and Jake rushed to the doorway to see Dylan speeding along the custom hardwood floor on a filthy skateboard. When he reached the end of the corridor, he used an upended antique side table as a makeshift ramp.

Brighton glanced up at Jake, who looked more upset than she'd ever seen him. She touched his arm and opened her mouth to tell him to go easy on the young boy.

"Put on a helmet!" Jake yelled, returning to the stove. "Concussions are serious business."

The clattering stopped and Brighton heard the pounding of sneakers against wood as Dylan raced for the garage. Two minutes later, the skateboarding resumed.

"If I've told that kid once, I've told him a thousand times," Jake muttered as he sprinkled sea salt into the sauce.

"But what about the coffee table?" Brighton flinched as she heard breaking glass.

Jake shrugged. "What about it?"

She tilted her head. "I'm guessing it was expensive."

"Everything in this house is expensive. But that hall is perfect for skateboarding. I can always refinish the floors."

Brighton gave him a long assessing look. "You've done it, haven't you? You've gone skateboarding in the hall."

"If I did, I wore a helmet." He winked at her. "You want to borrow my board later?"

"I kind of do," she confessed.

"It's a date," he said. "We'll do it after dinner when it gets dark, with mood lighting and the audio system turned all the way up."

She shook her head. "Can't. I'm booked after dinner. Which reminds me, where's the Gull's Point country club?"

"Out by the preserve on the other side of town," Jake said. "I'll have to look up the exact address."

"Really? I thought you'd be all over the country club scene."

"I hate golfing." He grimaced. "What do you have to do over there?"

"I told one of the guys who called today that I'd meet him at the country club restaurant to surprise his wife with a necklace." She glanced at the clock. "I should probably start getting ready. What should I even wear for something like that?"

Jake gave her a look. "A flak jacket."

"What? Why? It's a romantic dinner. A special occasion."

He leaned back against the counter. "You said he called? Meaning he didn't pick the necklace out himself?"

"Well, no." Brighton tried to recall the conversation. "Maybe he knows he has bad taste in jewelry and opted to leave the selection process to a professional. Maybe he's a man who knows his limits."

"So he dialed a phone and threw some money at the problem?"

She frowned. "Well, when you put it that way, it sounds so . . ."

"That necklace is a guilt gift," Jake proclaimed. "He's trying to placate his wife with dinner and jewelry."

"You know," Brighton mused, "that thought did cross my mind. But I was hoping that I was just a bitter cynic."

Jake turned off the stove burner with a definitive click. "Let me ask you one question: Did the guy negotiate?"

Brighton nibbled her lip. "Well . . ."

"He didn't, did he? He asked for a necklace, you named your price, and he rolled over."

"Yeah," she had to admit. "How did you know?"

"I told you, I know how this works. One of these days, you'll start to believe me."

"Oh, I believe you." Brighton grabbed the spare paring knife and started hacking away at a carrot with great vigor. "How many diamond guilt gifts have you given away in your time?"

"Zero." He looked offended at the question. "I don't get myself into those situations. If the guy is at the point where he needs a fancy dinner and an emergency call to a jeweler, he seriously screwed up his strategy somewhere along the way."

Brighton abandoned all pretense of cooking. "What exactly are you saying? Are you saying he shouldn't have cheated on his wife or he shouldn't have gotten caught? Or are you saying he never should have gotten into a real relationship at all?"

"Why are you mad at me?" Jake looked genuinely puzzled. "I didn't do anything. I'm not involved in any way."

That's why I'm mad. "I'm not mad at you," Brighton lied. "I'm mad at that guy for being a tool; I'm mad at myself for selling him the guilt gift like a sucker. I'm just mad."

"You're not a sucker; you're a good businessperson." Jake took the knife away and pulled her into his arms. "This is no different than the guy who needed the replacement ring on short notice."

"Ah, yes. Another example of screwed-up male strategy."

"That's your customer base," he informed her. "Accept it. Work with it. Maximize it."

Brighton rested her head against his shoulder. "Lila opened this shop as a safe haven for wronged women, not one-stop shopping for wayward husbands."

"You can't give every potential client a screening questionnaire and then sit in judgment. That's bad business. Not to mention illegal." He pulled his T-shirt over his head. "Come on, I'll go with you. Give me five minutes to shower and shave. We'll complete our mission at the country club and then go buy you a skateboard."

She kind of stopped listening when he took off his shirt. But his mouth was still moving and she managed to tune back in just as he finished up with, "It'll be fun."

"I don't know. The guy didn't say I could bring any witnesses along."

"He didn't say you couldn't. Go wrap the guilt gift," he ordered. "Leave everything else to me. I'll show you a good time."

"You always do." And there it was again: a little rush of limerence that felt a lot like love.

chapter 19

"*You* were definitely right about the guilt gift," Brighton said as she and Jake hurried out of the country club restaurant. "That woman is *pissed*. Slightly less so since you gave her the Jake Sorensen routine, but still pissed."

"You sound sad." He placed his hand on her back.

"I am. It feels disgusting to be bailing out cheaters."

"Don't worry, you didn't bail that guy out," Jake said. "You saw the look on his wife's face. He's not talking his way out of anything." He held the door for her as they headed out to the parking lot filled with late-model European cars and one gray Ford pickup. "And I'm sure that you sell plenty of things to couples who are hopelessly in love."

"That's true." She recounted the story of the man who had bought the two pairs of earrings.

Jake listened, looking as though he were fighting back a smirk.

"What?" Brighton demanded. "What now?"

"Nothing."

"Just say whatever it is you have to say."

"I don't want to ruin your romantic illusions."

"I don't have romantic illusions." Brighton bristled at the mere suggestion. "I'm practical to a fault, remember?"

"You say that, but I'm not seeing a lot of evidence."

She "accidentally" elbowed him as they walked through the parking lot.

Jake responded by slinging one arm around her shoulder and stealing a kiss. He held the passenger-side door for her and said, "I'd bet half my business holdings that one pair is for his wife and the other for his girlfriend."

She gasped. "You're crazy. And/or high. And/or just mean."

"As long as I'm being mean, I bet he's giving the more expensive pair to the girlfriend."

"What is wrong with you?" Brighton reached across the front seat and swatted his shoulder as he got into the driver's seat. "Why is it so hard to believe that a husband could want to give two pairs of earrings to his wife? Just because *you* can't imagine loving a woman enough to make that kind of grand gesture—"

"You're making my point for me." He started the truck. "If the guy loved his wife enough to be faithful and show up every day, he wouldn't need to make these grand gestures."

Brighton considered this. "Hmm."

"Verdict: *I'm* a better husband than that guy, and I'm not even a real husband." He nodded at her. "Believe it."

She half laughed, half sighed. "If only I could."

Brighton woke up the next morning at nine a.m. She hadn't slept this late in years, but skateboarding had proved to be a very challenging cardio workout. Her leg muscles ached, her knees were bruised, and her lips were swollen from all the post-wipeout kissing. As she looked around the huge bedroom suite with floor-to-ceiling views of the Atlantic and empty Gatorade bottles strewn across the rug, she realized that she could be content living like this forever. Doing her dream job. Sleeping in. Skateboarding at midnight with the lost Hemsworth brother.

Speaking of which, where was he? Every night she drifted off to sleep curled up next to Jake, and every morning she woke up alone. She was never sure when he left or where he went, but she didn't want to ask him. That would be too needy, too relationship-y.

So she didn't ask. But she did wonder.

She hurried to shower and dress, then went downstairs to find that the huge house was empty—and the hardwood floor was marred with black streaks from the skateboard wheels. As she crouched down to inspect the damage, she heard Jake's voice from the porch.

Then she heard a deep, booming bark.

She opened the side door to find Jake, his dark hark still tousled from last night, placing a stainless steel dish on the weathered wooden boards of the deck. A gigantic brown dog with short floppy ears wolfed down the kibble—well, "dog" was an understatement, really. This beast appeared to be part mastiff, part pony.

When Brighton stepped onto the porch, Jake straightened up with a stricken expression, as if he'd been caught doing something truly nefarious.

"Who's this?" Brighton approached the dog, who stared up at Jake with soulful golden eyes, clearly hoping for seconds. "I didn't know you had a dog."

"I don't." Jake sounded a touch defensive. "He's a stray."

Brighton noticed a clean black nylon collar around the dog's neck. "Uh-huh."

"He made friends with the construction crew when we started

building the houses here. They left, he hung around, I let him."
Jake couldn't look her in the eye. "That's it."

"So he lives here. Which makes him your dog."

"He's *a* dog, but he's not *my* dog." Jake attempted to distract her
with the Sorensen Smolder, but she would not be distracted.

She glimpsed a huge sack of dog chow in the storage bench next
to the door. "And yet you have dog food and designated dishes."

"You can't prove that's for him."

"And you let him sit on your foot."

Jake glanced down at the drooling brown behemoth who
beseeched him with the eyes of a starving orphan. "How could I
stop him?"

Brighton grinned. "Admit it: He's totally your dog."

"He is not my dog; he's a squatter with four legs and fur. That
happens to live in my guesthouse."

"Classic denial." Brighton sighed. "Tragic but common in these
situations. Look at the two of you together; you have something
really special."

The Sorensen Smolder started to sputter out. "I don't even live
here most of the time. I'm in New York, D.C., Mexico, Saudi Arabia. My lifestyle is not conducive to pet ownership."

"Uh-huh."

"I swear to you, we barely know each other." He tried to nudge
the colossal canine off his feet. The dog didn't budge. A speck
of drool fell from his muzzle onto Jake's bare foot. "There's no
license, no paperwork in place. We just hang out here sometimes.
It's casual."

"So you never take him anywhere with you?" Brighton went
into prosecutor mode. *Thanks, bar exam study guides.* "You leave
him for months at a time and hope Christina and Dylan remember
to feed him?"

"I don't have to answer these questions. I have the right to an attorney."

Brighton laughed. "I think it's sweet. Remember that documentary you were watching? It's like you have your own radioactive wolf. Look at his head! It's like an anvil." Disarmed by the floppy ears and mournful eyes, Brighton reached over to pet the dog. "Hey, buddy. Where have you been hiding all this time?"

"It's possible I took him to work with me," Jake muttered. "Once or twice."

"Who's a good puppy? You're a good puppy." Brighton baby-talked to the giant beast, heedless of the drool and the shedding.

Jake watched them for a minute. "Remember when you asked me to tell you something I'd never told any other woman?"

"Mm-hmm. I also remember you deflecting that question and seducing me into silence."

"You're the only woman who's met Rorschach."

Brighton frowned. "Rorschach?"

Jake pointed out a black patch of fur on the dog's haunches. "Looks like an inkblot."

"You *named* him? Oh, come on. You one hundred percent have a dog," she concluded. To the dog, she crooned, "You're too sweet and cuddly for a name like that. I'll call you Rory for short."

The dog thumped his tail against the porch, then got up, moved from Jake to Brighton, and sat back down on her feet.

"He likes you," Jake said.

"Of course he does. Because I don't call him a squatter and make him live in the guesthouse." Brighton scratched Rory behind the ears. "But don't get too attached, buddy. I'll only be here for a little while."

Rory started panting, his tongue lolling out of the side of his cavernous maw.

Brighton glanced up at Jake. "Should we talk about that, by the way? My inevitable departure date."

"Nope." He strode across the porch and opened the door. "Let's go have breakfast."

"We need to start getting things in place for when I leave." She hated the sound of her own voice—so chilly and impersonal. "Paperwork, divorce decree, all that stuff."

He lifted his chin, indicating she should proceed through the door. "Sounds fun."

"Divorce isn't supposed to be fun. But we still have to deal with it." She walked inside, then stopped. "Wait." She glanced back toward the porch. "What about Rory?"

"Rorschach," he corrected. "He won't come in. He only likes the guesthouse." Jake called to the dog, who responded by walking in the other direction. Seconds later, Brighton heard splashing as Rory took a drink from the koi pond.

Something clicked into place in her brain. "Is that where you've been going at the crack of dawn every morning? The guesthouse?"

"Look at this place." He gestured to the soaring ceilings, the ocean vista, the handcrafted textiles and furnishings. "Why would I hang out in the guesthouse when I have all of this?"

"Because you consider this a glorified skate park." Brighton gave him a little kiss on his cheek. "And because you love your dog. Don't worry—your secret's safe with me."

"For the last time, he's not my dog." Jake rested his forehead against hers. "Don't file for divorce just yet. Stay a few more weeks."

She inhaled, buzzed on the blended scent of laundry detergent, sea salt, and pheromones. After another kiss, she had no interest in filing for divorce or doing anything else that didn't involve taking off his pants.

"Stay," he urged.

"I can't."

He backed her up against the wall. When she reached for him, he caught her wrists and pinned her arms above her head. He kissed her again, tender and unhurried. "Stay."

"For a little while," she relented, closing her eyes.

He brushed his lips across her eyelids, his voice like a caress. "Forever."

chapter 20

"So, how was the weekend?" Lila returned to the Naked Finger on Monday morning wearing a wine-colored leather blazer adorned with silver studs.

"Very productive." Brighton sat down with her sketch pad and an old pair of chunky turquoise earrings that badly needed updating. "I love that jacket."

"Thanks. My mom picked it out for me in Paris."

"Cool mom."

"Yeah, she's much cooler than me. She's pretty much cooler than everyone in Black Dog Bay, which is why she ran off to Paris." Lila smiled. "Speaking of which, how did everything go with the gown she sent you? Were you the belle of the ball?"

"Mm-hmm." Brighton nodded and kept her head down.

"I'm waiting for details," Lila prompted.

"Let's just say that there's never a dull moment when you're married to Jake Sorensen." Brighton handed her preliminary sketch to Lila. "What do you think of this type of setting for the turquoise? In yellow gold?"

"You're so good at this." Lila looked at the drawing. "Admit it: This is your calling."

Brighton thought of her mother. "I don't have a 'calling.' Which is why I don't have bill collectors calling."

"Ice-cold," Lila accused.

"But financially solvent," Brighton finished. "The only reason I can hang out here wasting the rest of the month is the fact that I can afford to pay my mortgage even if I take a few weeks off from my soulless corporate job."

"Oh, so now you're staying through the end of the month?"

"Um. It's possible."

"I had a feeling Jake would persuade you. He's hard to say no to." Lila ended this statement on upward inflection, inviting Brighton to provide details.

"Yes, he is. And he . . ." Brighton smiled as she thought about Rorschach. "He has sides to him that I didn't expect."

While Lila waited for Brighton to divulge more details, she thumbed through the handwritten receipts. "Wow, you sold the rose gold Rolex?" She kept reading, her eyes widening. "And the diamond rivière necklace? *And* that pair of diamond studs?"

"Don't forget the sapphire studs. They basically sold themselves. All I did was nod and take the money. You know what I've learned after one week in the jewelry business?"

Lila was still poring over the receipts. "What?"

"People are weird. Relationships are weird. And that guy who quote-unquote 'lost' his wedding band and wanted a replacement made on the sly?"

"Yeah?"

"Tip of the iceberg." Brighton flipped to a new page of her sketch pad and started doodling. "People do horrible things to their partners all the time, apparently. People are cheaters and liars and gold diggers."

"*Some* people," Lila corrected. "Not all."

As if on cue, a starry-eyed couple walked in, no older than twenty-two and all over each other.

"Hi." Lila smiled. "May I help you?"

"We're looking for an engagement ring," the young man proclaimed. "The best diamond you have."

"The best diamond under five hundred dollars," the young woman stipulated. "We're kind of on a budget."

"Eight hundred," the man countered. "You can upgrade later. As soon as I start making real money."

"Baby, this is the ring you proposed with. I'm never going to change it."

Brighton and Lila absolutely melted, exchanging a flurry of glances as they led the lovebirds over to the ring display.

"They're like the cutest kitten video on all of YouTube," Lila whispered to Brighton. To the clients, she said, "What kind of design were you thinking about? We have lots of different settings and stones."

"I'd be happy to custom design something for you," Brighton offered, even though there was no way an eight-hundred-dollar budget would cover those services. She kept forgetting that she got paid to do this—for now, anyway.

"I don't need anything fancy." The young woman, clad in a threadbare concert T-shirt and jeans, gazed down at the sparkling diamonds. "A simple gold band is fine."

"No way." Her scruffy-haired suitor shook his head and addressed Lila directly. "She needs a diamond."

Lila and Brighton offered up several options, and the young woman selected a thin white gold band featuring a tiny embedded diamond—more of a chip than a stone.

"Perfect fit." She held up her hand. The diamond glinted under the bright overhead lights. "Like it was made for me."

"It's beautiful on you," Brighton said, and she meant it. The young woman's style was minimalist and casual, and the ring complemented her slim hand.

The woman turned to her fiancé, her eyes sparkling like the diamond on her hand. "I love you so much, baby."

"I love you more." He kissed her on the lips.

"No, I love you more."

This escalated into a full PDA situation, during which Lila and Brighton discreetly excused themselves to the other side of the showroom.

"Aw, that's sweet." Lila looked away as the guy picked up his bride-to-be and sat her on the glass counter. "We have Windex in the back, right?"

"Full bottle," Brighton confirmed. When the couple came up for air, she cleared her throat and suggested, "Would you like me to engrave something on the inside of the ring?"

"Like what?"

"Whatever you want. You're the only ones who'll know it's there."

The guy looked at the girl. "'At first sight.'"

Lila, Brighton, and the bride-to-be all *aww*ed in unison, which sparked another intense make-out session, during which Lila and Brighton discussed lunch plans and the latest fashion trends coming out of Paris and New York. As the topic turned to TV series worthy of binge watching, the happy couple finally disentangled themselves, straightened their shirts, and handed over a wad of crumpled fifty-dollar bills.

"We'll come back later for the engraving," the young woman said. "I want to wear this right now." Another passionate kiss. "I'm going to wear it when I sleep, when I shower, at the gym . . ."

"You can bring it in anytime for a cleaning," Lila offered. "We have a special machine."

"It's real now." The woman splayed out her fingers, admiring her bejeweled hand. "It's really real."

"We're official," her intended agreed. They strolled back out to the sidewalk, their hands in each other's back pockets.

"There you go." Lila closed the door with a flourish. "The living, breathing cure for cynicism."

Brighton peered out the window, watching the couple walk toward the beach. "The two of them against the world." She sighed. "I hope she's still wearing that ring at their fiftieth anniversary."

Maybe it wasn't so crazy to believe in love at first sight. Maybe passion really could prevail over practicality. Maybe she should leave work early, track down her husband, and take a few laps around the hallways on the skateboard.

And that's just what she did.

When she pulled her safety-conscious white Subaru into the driveway, she noticed a sleek silver roadster parked in her usual spot. At first she assumed it was Jake's—he probably had a different car in each bay of the garage next to the house. Then she noticed someone standing on the porch and realized they had company.

For a moment, she feared Colin had returned for another round of begging, pleading, and hem hugging. But no—this visitor was petite. A gorgeous, fine-boned blonde turned as Brighton bounded up the porch steps.

"Hi." Brighton stopped at the top step and waited for the woman to introduce herself. There was something familiar about her, but Brighton couldn't quite place her.

"Hello, Brighton." The woman looked her over for a moment, registered the conservative clothes and sensible footwear, then glanced away.

I've just been dismissed, Brighton realized. A month ago, she would have let that go. She would have stepped back and made her peace with the fact that some people—especially people who'd been genetically blessed to an almost freakish degree—weren't going to deem her glamorous or beautiful enough to talk to.

But a lot had changed in the last few weeks.

"What can I do for you?" She rested her hand on the railing, making no move to invite the stranger inside.

The blonde's smile was a bit apologetic. "I'm Genevieve."

Brighton sucked in her breath. "Genevieve?"

"Yes."

"Colin's Genevieve?"

The woman blinked, obviously confused. "Who's Colin?"

Brighton pushed her hair back, more confused than ever. "Um . . ."

"I'm Jake's Genevieve. Would you kindly let him know I'm here?"

chapter 21

"*E*xcuse me, I'll be back in one moment." Brighton kept her tone and her smile fixed as she opened the door and stepped into the house. She suppressed the urge to slam the door behind her and race down the hall. Until she found Jake and figured out what the hell was going on, she would show no weakness. She would show no fear.

"Jake?" She checked the kitchen, the living room, the massive study on the first floor. No sign of her husband.

"Jake?" Her pace quickened as she climbed the steps to the second story. By the time she started down the hall to the master suite, she was sprinting.

The bedroom was empty.

Panting a bit from the exertion, she braced herself against the doorjamb and dialed her cell phone with a mounting sense of dread.

I knew this was too good to last.

"Hey." Jake sounded so relaxed, so confident. Part of her—the part that wasn't whipped into a frenzy—couldn't help responding to the deep, strong timbre of his voice.

"Hey." She tried and failed to match his casual tone. "Where are you right now?"

"Working."

"At your office?" She had no idea where that was.

"I'm in the guesthouse."

"Okay, well, can I come out to the guesthouse for a second?"

"Absolutely." His voice dropped even lower. "Bring some Gatorade."

"Yeah, no. This isn't about that."

He finally picked up on the undercurrent of tension in her tone. "What's it about?"

She said a quick good-bye and hung up. No way was she going to give him a heads-up; she wanted to watch his face and his eyes when she broke the news.

Plus, she didn't want to get dumped over the phone—again. Losing her boyfriend of two years over a staticky cell conversation had been bad, but losing her husband of two weeks would be worse.

Brighton darted out of the mansion via the back porch to avoid Genevieve on her way to the guesthouse. When she reached the tiny cottage, she debated knocking but opted to barge right in. Which proved impossible to do—the second she set foot inside, Rory greeted her with a leap of joy that knocked her to the floor.

"Oof!" Before Brighton could get to her feet, the massive brown beast draped himself across her lap and rested his giant, drooled-drenched jowls on her black pants.

Jake, who was sprawled out on an oversize couch with a laptop, sat up and snapped his fingers. Rory reluctantly got up, but not before licking Brighton's cheek.

Under other circumstances, Brighton would have demanded a grand tour of the tiny cottage where Jake actually spent most of his working hours: a modest, sparsely furnished little bungalow barely big enough for a sofa, a dog bed, and a whole lot of tech gear to Skype with Saudi Arabia. Right now, she had more pressing concerns than decor.

She did, however, notice the honey-hued rectangular coffee table by the sofa. "Hey. Is that from IKEA?"

He nodded. "How'd you know?"

"Because I have the exact same one in my condo." She'd bought in on sale and spent an entire Sunday swearing and sweating while trying to assemble it. "Why do you have furniture from IKEA?"

"I like IKEA. It's fun putting everything together. They give you those little Allen wrenches . . ." He trailed off when he saw her expression.

"You're sick and depraved." She narrowed her eyes as she glimpsed a few images on his laptop screen. "Hang on. Are you looking at the stock market?"

He shut the laptop as if he had been caught perusing the filthiest pornography. "No."

"Stop lying. Your secret's out," she informed him. "Deep in your soul, you're a die-hard workaholic, just like me. Speaking of which . . ." She stepped closer. "There's someone at the door for you. Someone named Genevieve."

His expression flickered. Just for a fraction of a second. He tried to hide it, but she saw it.

She saw it, and she knew.

"Brighton, wait." Jake put aside his laptop and stood up.

She remained perfectly still, trying to prepare herself for whatever he was going to say next.

"Okay. I'm waiting," she said. "And so is she. She says she's *your* Genevieve."

He opened his mouth to reply, but his gaze wasn't focused on her. He was looking toward the main house.

Suddenly, Brighton realized where she'd seen the beautiful blonde before, why she looked so familiar. Pull that hair back into an updo, put on some red lipstick and a black ball gown and some fancy jewelry . . .

"She's the woman I met at the charity ball, isn't she?"

"She's still here?" he asked.

Rory glanced from Brighton to Jake and started whining.

"As far as I know." She couldn't hide the hurt in her voice. Because Jake had looked at her with desire and passion, but he'd never looked at her the way he was looking at the door right now.

All traces of charm and charisma had vanished. He looked determined and intense and . . . vulnerable?

Brighton didn't know any of the history between Jake and "his" Genevieve, but she understood that she would never inspire this depth of emotion in him. She would never strip away all his defenses like this.

She turned on her heel and strode out to the sand.

When he called her name, she didn't turn around. She heard the tread of his footsteps on the gravel, heading away from her. Heading toward the main house.

Toward the woman he'd sworn meant nothing to him.

chapter 22

"Thank God you picked up," Brighton whispered into her phone. "I was terrified you'd screen me."

"I'd never screen you. Why are we whispering?" Kira whispered.

Brighton tried to figure out how to explain. She felt so overwhelmed with panic and suspicion and anticipation and, underneath all of that, a stubborn sense of hope that this would turn out to be some crazy misunderstanding. "It's Genevieve."

Kira gasped. "Colin's Genevieve?"

"No. Jake has a Genevieve, too." Brighton sagged against the side of the house as she summarized the porch ambush. "What should I do?"

"Come over," Kira instructed. "Right now."

"I can't." Brighton rubbed her eyes with the back of her hand. "She's still here."

"Can you see her? I thought you said you were hiding out."

"I am, but I would have heard her car on the gravel if she'd left."
Brighton's breath came in quick, shallows gulps. "Kira, you should
have seen his face." A sharp physical pain shot through her at the
memory. "He looked . . . I can't even explain it. He looked *hurt*." She
inched closer to the corner of the house, straining to hear anything
over the pounding of the surf. "I can't even eavesdrop because this
house is too gigantic and the ocean is too loud." She startled as she
heard heavy panting behind her. "And the dog just busted me."

"What dog?" Kira asked.

"Jake's illegitimate dog. I'll explain later." Brighton paused, trying to catch any sound beyond the steady pull of the tide and the
canine panting. "I'm going to try to get closer. Call you back in a few."

"Try to be optimistic," Kira said. "Maybe it's nothing. Maybe
she's just an old friend."

Brighton wanted so badly to believe this. "Men aren't just friends
with women who look like that." She squared her shoulders and prepared to face reality. "I better go."

"Good luck. I hope it turns out the way you want."

"Thanks." She considered going into stealth mode, but it was
impossible to go into stealth mode while being trailed by a pony-
size dog who sounded like a bulldozer when he breathed. So she
strode back around the house and prepared to join the conversation.

Genevieve had her back to Brighton, so she couldn't see the
woman's face, but she could see Jake's, and he no longer looked hurt
or vulnerable.

He looked angry.

She marched up the steps with her head held high.

"Brighton." The blonde offered her a warm smile this time. "How
lovely to see you again."

"Go inside," Jake said to Brighton. He rested one hand on the
doorknob and the other on Brighton's back.

Genevieve watched this with what appeared to be genuine

sympathy. She regarded Jake with reproach in her big blue eyes. "You didn't tell her yet, did you?"

"Go inside," Jake repeated. It was an order, an employer addressing his subordinate.

Brighton shook off his hand and stared back at Genevieve. "Tell me what?"

Genevieve backed off, retreating to the edge of the steps. "I'm so sorry. I shouldn't have come—I thought you knew."

Brighton could sense the power dynamics shifting, and she didn't want to give up any advantage, so she remained silent.

Genevieve's voice was soft. "There's no easy way to say this. I'm his first wife."

Brighton turned to Jake. "I thought you said you'd never been married before."

His expression had gone neutral, his eyes flat and cold.

"Jake? What's going on?"

He opened the door, guided her inside, and stepped back out to the porch.

"One minute," he said. "I will handle this."

"But—"

He closed the door and went back to his wife.

chapter 23

*B*righton stood in the foyer, arms crossed tightly over her chest, and waited for what felt like an eternity.

When Jake entered, he looked grim and detached. "Let's talk."

She looked out at the blurred blue line where the ocean and the sky came together. "Let's."

"But first, let's have a drink." He led the way to the living room and pulled two highball glasses out of the cabinet by the wet bar. "Scotch?"

"You know my feelings about scotch." Brighton sat down on the couch, then stood up again. "Am I going to need it for the conversation we're about to have?"

"You should probably have a double." He poured amber liquid into her glass. She took care not to brush her fingers against his when she accepted the glass.

"Is she gone?" Brighton asked. She couldn't bring herself to say Genevieve's name aloud.

He took a sip of his scotch. "For now."

"What does that mean?"

"She'll be back." Jake tilted his chin toward her glass. "Drink."

She did, expecting to retch at the taste of the smoky liquid. But the dark burning gave way to a hint of sweetness as she swallowed. "Was she telling the truth when she said she used to be your wife?"

He sat down on the sleek black sofa that offered a floor-to-ceiling view of the sea. Whitecaps were rolling in, crashing on the sand, but the insulation in this house was excellent; Brighton couldn't hear anything from outside. All she could hear was her own breathing and the clink of the ice cubes against glass.

"Depends on your definition of 'wife,'" he said.

Brighton put her drink down on the gleaming wood side table with no coaster. "This is not a difficult question. Did you get married or not?"

"We signed a marriage license. Fourth of July weekend. I was twenty-one; she was nineteen."

"But you told me you'd never been married before." She racked her brain, trying to remember the details of that flight to Vegas. "Didn't you?"

"The marriage was annulled by Halloween. From a legal standpoint, it never happened."

She picked up her drink again. "It doesn't matter what the legalities are," she said softly. "That was a real marriage, wasn't it? You were in love."

"I was twenty-one." His expression hardened. "I was an idiot."

Not a denial. "Where did you meet her?"

"How is that relevant?"

"Jake."

He gazed out at the horizon. "We met at the beach. The private beach by one of her family's hotels. I was working there for the summer."

Brighton looked at him. He looked back at her.

"And?" she finally prompted.

"And there was a marriage, an annulment, and a whole bunch of adolescent drama. The end."

She forced down another sip of scotch. "You skipped a few details. What does she mean to you? Why is she showing up at your door introducing herself as 'Jake's Genevieve'?"

He gave a harsh laugh. "She was married to me, but she was never mine."

"You still love her," Brighton breathed.

"No."

"Then tell me what happened."

"Here's the short version: When we met, I was poor; she was not. Her last name is Van Petten." He looked at her expectantly.

"Genevieve Van Petten," Brighton marveled. "Sounds like a character from *Melrose Place*. Not that I have any room to talk, but still."

"Her family is like the Kennedys of Delaware."

"Why did you decide to get married?"

"Why do twenty-one-year-olds do anything?" he countered. "She did it to piss off her parents. Mission accomplished."

"Why didn't her parents want her marrying you?"

"I was dirt poor, Brighton. I didn't have any of this." He gestured to the house, the ocean, the art and antiques. Then he gestured to his face and his body. "All I had was this. I was a novelty for her. She had a huge fight with her parents one day and we ran down to the courthouse to get married."

Genevieve married him for spite, Brighton realized. *Just like I did.*

"When she moved into my apartment, she said it was like camping."

Brighton blinked. "Camping?"

"I was renting a room right by the highway with no kitchen and iffy plumbing. After a few weeks, she got tired of eating cold

SpaghettiOs for every meal and her parents threatened to cut off her trust fund if she didn't go back to college." He looked pointedly at Brighton. "She had to get back to her real life."

Before Brighton could reply, he continued. "She moved out and petitioned for an annulment."

"On what grounds?" Her actuary brain kicked in. "Isn't it pretty difficult to be granted an annulment?"

"Not if you're the Kennedys of Delaware. Her father made one phone call to a judge and it was like the whole thing never happened."

"And now you still have that." She indicated his body and face. "Plus you have this." She indicated the luxury goods. "I bet she's kicking herself for letting you go."

He shook his head and swirled the scotch in his glass. "No."

Brighton raised her eyebrow and waited him out.

"I saw her again when I'd just made my first million. I thought I was hot shit. I thought I had everything she wanted."

Brighton cringed. "I'm guessing this story doesn't end well."

He refused to reveal anything more. He refused to even look at her.

"She must be amazing," Brighton went on. "To be worth that kind of devotion. To be worth making a million dollars for."

His smile was sardonic. "I'm guessing you've never been a smoker."

She glanced at him, surprised. "You guess correctly."

"I used to smoke."

"You did?" She sat down on the far edge of the sofa. "I can't see it."

"I started right after the annulment." He scrubbed the side of his face with his palm. "Smoked for a year and a half."

"But not anymore." She'd kissed him enough to say this with certainty.

"One day I woke up, decided I was sick of my taste buds not working, and quit."

"Just like that?"

"Yeah. I had half a pack left, but I tossed it." He draped one arm along the back of the sofa. "Never had another cigarette."

"That's amazing," Brighton said. "The odds were very much against you. Did you know that only twenty percent of smokers who attempt to quit will be successful over the course of their lifetimes?"

He regarded her with a trace of a smile. "Do you memorize these stats just to impress me?"

"Maybe."

"I'm impressed." His eyes warmed, and just for a moment, she wished she hadn't left work early and met Genevieve on the porch. She wished she didn't have to find out how very flawed and damaged and human he was beneath the fantasy she'd projected onto him. "And I'm surprised that it's twenty percent. That seems high."

"Twenty percent lifetime success rate seems high to you?"

"Clearly, you've never tried to quit smoking. The withdrawal was hell. It's been fifteen years and I still crave cigarettes sometimes." He turned away from her again. "As hard as it was to quit smoking, it was easy compared to quitting Genevieve."

She waited for him to follow this up with a quip or a qualifier, but he had gone still. He was sitting with her, but his mind was with a woman who'd left him long ago. He'd forgotten to keep his guard up, and she finally glimpsed what was underneath all that captivating charm and wit and physical beauty.

Regret. Doubt. Loneliness.

"Have you ever wanted somebody like that?" he asked her. Even his voice sounded distant. "Like a drug? Like you'd do anything for one last hit?"

She blinked. "Well, actually . . ."

He straightened up, his vulnerability vanishing. "Of course you haven't. You're too smart for that. You'd never fall in love with someone who's the equivalent of an addictive carcinogen."

Brighton didn't trust herself to say anything.

"And now she's back," he concluded. "The timing is interesting. I hadn't heard from her in years, then she made contact last week."

Brighton froze. "Before or after you met me?"

His gaze shuttered. "What?"

"Before or after I met you at the Whinery?"

He put down his drink. "It was that day. A few hours before we met."

"I knew it." Brighton got to her feet. "I knew there had to be a reason. I knew a man like you would never marry a woman like me unless . . ."

"Stop." He sounded tired and defensive.

"You used me." She wrapped her arms around herself. "You heard she was back and you used me as a human shield to protect yourself."

"You used me to get back at your boyfriend," he pointed out.

"I was completely honest with you from the first moment we met! I told you who I was, what I was doing, and why. And you . . . did not."

"It wouldn't have made any difference," he said flatly.

"How can you say that?" she exclaimed.

"What would you have said if I had told you about Genevieve the night we met? Would you have called it off?"

"It wouldn't have made any difference," she had to concede. "On the night we met."

"Then why does it make a difference now? You can use me as a human shield, but I can't use you?"

She knew he was right. He'd done nothing to her that she hadn't done to him. Both of them had gotten onto that plane to Vegas with selfish, misguided motives. Both of them had been completely focused on themselves. Both of them had been running away from mistakes that they knew would catch up with them eventually.

The only difference was, he had played the game better. He had followed the ground rules they established.

And she hadn't.

"Brighton."

"What?"

"I'm sorry." The words were so simple; his voice was so stark. He got to his feet and offered her his hand. "Tell me what you want."

She had no idea—what to do, what to say.

"Anything." A deeper note of regret crept into his voice. "You deserve better than this."

And in that moment, she realized she might as well be in this big, fancy house alone, because he was gone. Whatever tenuous connection they'd shared had been severed.

He would do whatever she asked because he wanted her to feel a certain way, while he felt nothing at all. He would give her anything she wanted, but he would never want her the way she wanted him.

He would never want her the way he wanted Genevieve.

"I want a divorce," she said softly.

He nodded. "Done."

chapter 24

"*D*one." Brighton brought her left hand down on the Whinery's glossy black bar top. "Good thing we never bought a ring."

"You just called the whole thing off?" Kira sipped a frosty glass of chardonnay.

"I had to." Brighton stared down at her naked finger. "His ex showed up at the front door."

"Your ex showed up at the front door, too," Kira pointed out.

"Yes, and when my ex showed up, I told him to get off the porch and never darken my door again. Jake, on the other hand . . ." She heaved a mighty sigh. "I'm just another bimbo from the bar to him, Kira. He would've married any hysterical dumpee who'd walked in the door."

Kira offered Brighton a sip of chardonnay.

"I'm sure that's not true."

"Yes, it is." Brighton tasted the crisp, chilled white wine. "And look, I know I don't have any moral high ground here, given that I pretty much live-tweeted our drive-through ceremony to rub it in Colin's face, but at least I was honest." She crumpled up a napkin. "I hate to admit this, but I wouldn't have married anyone else that night. It's *him*. There's something about him."

"Oh, I agree." Kira fanned her face.

"I lo—" Brighton hastened to correct herself. "I *like* him. A lot. He took me midnight skateboarding in his downstairs hall."

Kira squinted at her. "Is some sort of euphemism?"

"I wanted to believe that I was special to him, but no. I was just a preemptive strike against Genevieve."

"Genevieve," Kira spat out. "I haven't even met her, but I already hate her."

"Thank you. You're a good friend." Brighton passed the wineglass back. "Here's a question for you: He told me he'd never been married before, when in fact he'd had an annulment. Is that a lie or not a lie?"

"Hmm." Kira rested her chin in her hand. "I'd call it a gray area. But here's a better question: Did you learn anything from all this?"

"Yes," Brighton answered immediately. "I learned that until two weeks ago, I had no clue how good sex could actually be."

Kira's eyes widened. "Really?"

"There are no words." She suppressed a little shiver just thinking about it. "I should have gotten one last hit before I cut off my supply."

"We're back to the drug analogies?"

"It's fitting," Brighton assured her. "In fact, Jake himself—"

"Hey, ladies." Lila appeared next to Brighton. "Mind if I join you?"

"Not at all." Brighton introduced Kira to Lila, then added, "I was just telling Kira here that Jake and I are officially over."

"What?" Lila cried.

"What?!" Jenna the bartender, who had been standing all the way on the other side of the bar, swooped in to get the details. "Why?"

Brighton smoothed her hair. "It just isn't working out. We're two very different people."

"So what?" Jenna gaped at her.

"We're going to have an amicable divorce and I'm sure we'll always be friends," Brighton tried.

"Try that one more time, with ninety percent less BS. What happened?" Lila demanded.

"Yeah, why would you want to be *friends* with Jake Sorensen?" Jenna demanded. "Have you *looked* at him?"

Brighton finally cracked. "We had a fight."

"About what?" Jenna and Lila chorused.

"That's not relevant," Brighton murmured. "But I got caught up in the heat of the moment and said things I didn't mean. Well, I did mean them, but I should have waited to say them."

"The good thing about Jake is, he's very reasonable," Lila said. "No drama."

"I don't think I've ever seen him get mad at anyone," Jenna added.

"That's because he doesn't actually care about anyone." *Except his first wife, apparently.* Brighton took a morose swig of water.

Kira jumped into the conversation. "I think their point is, regardless of what you said in the heat of the moment, he's not going to hold a grudge."

As Brighton glanced out the window at the town square, a skateboarder sped by, picking up speed as he headed for the pier.

She knew a sign from the universe when she saw one. "So what you're saying here is that I don't have to go cold turkey just yet. I could go back to his house and, you know. Get some 'closure.'" She used her fingers to make air quotes.

"Do it," Jenna advised. "I would."

"Are you sure that's a good idea?" Kira asked.

"No." But Brighton felt a surge of relief and anticipation at the very thought. "It's totally stupid. The smart thing to do would be to get in my car, drive back to New Jersey, and send him some divorce papers via courier."

Lila looked traumatized. "What? No! You can't do that! I need you to keep working with me for the rest of the summer."

"I wish I could," Brighton said. "But we always knew I was a short-term employee."

"I was so sure you would get sucked into the whole beach-town scene." She grinned and clarified, "By which I mean the whole Jake Sorensen scene."

"He's a hard man to leave," Brighton mused. "But I will leave him."

Another sip of water.

"Tomorrow."

Kira pressed her lips together in an obvious effort not to comment.

"I just want one more time. And why not, really? I've made so many bad decisions lately, why stop now?"

"And you never know," Lila said. "Maybe you'll go back to his place and you'll talk and laugh and bond . . ."

"Or maybe I'll go back there and he'll already have some woman sweating all over the sheets in the master suite." She exchanged a look with Kira. "A blond, blue-blooded socialite, perhaps."

"No!" Lila cried. "He wouldn't!"

There was a long, loaded pause.

"Would he?"

Brighton got to her feet and slung her purse strap over her shoulder. "Only one way to find out."

As soon as she pulled into the driveway at Don't Be Koi, the front door opened and Jake appeared on the porch. "You came back."

She could tell from his voice that he'd kept drinking scotch after she'd left. He started toward her and she started up the stairs. They crossed paths in the middle, Brighton standing two steps above Jake so that they were eye to eye. She rested her hand on his chest, feeling the warmth of his body through his soft cotton T-shirt.

He kissed her before she could say a word and she leaned into him, relieved to skip all the arguments that would ultimately resolve nothing.

"I'm not staying," she murmured as she wrapped her arms around his neck.

He slid his hands down to her hips and picked her up.

"This doesn't mean anything." She wrapped her legs around his waist.

He kept kissing her. He tasted like scotch.

"We're still getting divorced." She tilted her head back so he could kiss her neck.

He carried her up the stairs, turned around, and kicked the door open with his heel.

She tried to savor all the sensations—the high, the thrill, the certainty that she'd never experience this kind of intensity again.

He put her on her feet and she pulled off his shirt, then her shirt.

As they made their way to the bedroom, she promised herself that this would be the last time, that this would be enough.

That this moment of weakness would give her the strength to let go.

"You are so beautiful." Jake's voice was rough, but his hands were gentle, stroking Brighton's hair back from her forehead.

She turned her face to one side. "Don't say that."

He gazed down at her. "You are."

"I know you've been with women who are way more glamorous than I am."

"Yeah," he admitted. "I have. But they weren't you."

She had yearned to hear these words from him, but now that he was saying them, she didn't believe him. He was so good at telling her what she wanted to hear, but so guarded with his true intentions.

The curtains rustled as a breeze blew in through the balcony doors.

"Gatorade?"

Brighton shifted against him, sated and a bit sweaty. "Mmmm. I really should go."

"Don't move." The mattress dipped as he sat up. "I just bought a six-pack. Orange. It's in the fridge downstairs."

Well. She *was* thirsty after all that exertion. "Okay, but can I ask you one thing first?" She placed her palm between his shoulder blades. "What did she say?"

He didn't have to ask what she was referring to. "She said a lot of things. Bottom line, her grandfather died and her father lost most of the family fortune."

"I know how that feels." Brighton thought about the sick, nervous feeling she got in her stomach when she saw her mother's name on her phone.

"She still has the Van Petten name, but the money's gone." He stood up, keeping his back to her.

Brighton propped herself up on her elbows. The sheets felt soft and smooth against her skin. "Did she tell you that?"

"No, but it's a small state. I know what's going on."

"And now she wants your help?" Brighton prompted.

"She wants my money." He raked his fingers through his hair. "She's willing to deal with me as a means to an end."

Brighton sat up straighter. "She said that?"

"No. She said things like 'nostalgia' and 'mistake' and 'first love.'"

"Well, what did you say?" Brighton held her breath, her eyes wide in the darkness.

"I told her I'm already married to someone else."

Ah yes, his little human shield.

Before Brighton could start on her long list of follow-up questions, his cell phone buzzed on the nightstand. He glanced at it, frowning. Then he picked it up.

"You're going to *answer* it?" She was too incredulous to be mad.

"If this guy is calling me at this hour, it must be important." Jake picked up the phone. "Life or death." He answered the call with a terse, "Sorensen."

Brighton buttoned her shirt as Jake's frown deepened.

"Who is it?" she whispered. "The developer from Mexico?"

"No." He listened intently for a moment, then passed the phone to Brighton. "It's for you."

chapter 25

"*T*hanks for meeting me so early." Malcolm Toth, Jake's cybersecurity consultant and Lila's boyfriend, was waiting by the front door of the Naked Finger shortly after dawn the next morning.

"No problem." Brighton tried to think caffeinated thoughts. "Lila mentioned you do, like, supersecret spy stuff."

The former marine, who seconds ago had appeared stony faced and imposing, laughed with surprising warmth. "Lila exaggerates."

"Are you sure? You look pretty badass to me."

"My badass days are behind me," he assured her. "But I do need your help with a covert mission. You can't tell anyone."

"Okay." Brighton unlocked the door and ushered him into the showroom.

"Especially Lila."

She glanced back at him, confused. "Why not? Aren't you guys pretty close?"

"Yeah, but I want her to be surprised when I propose."

Brighton whirled around, banging her wrist against the corner of a glass case in the process. "Tell me *everything*."

And with that, the last traces of flinty-eyed brusqueness vanished. "You have to keep this on lockdown."

"Lockdown. Absolutely." Brighton cradled her injured wrist in her other hand. "But how long do I have to live with this secret eating away at me?"

"Depends how soon I can get the ring."

"Then let's get to work." Brighton snatched up her sketch pad and a pen. "What are you thinking?"

"No idea," he confessed. "I want to give her a ring she'll love, and jewelry isn't my thing."

Brighton sat down and performed a jewelry-style profile on Lila. "She usually wears classic pieces with a whimsical twist."

"Whimsical?" Malcolm's forehead had started to perspire ever so slightly, despite the chill from the air conditioner. "Okay. Let's go with that."

Brighton tried to remember the pieces Lila had admired over the past two weeks. "I know she likes Asscher-cut diamonds. We can use one of those for the center stone, flanked by . . . what?"

The marine broke as though Brighton had been interrogating him for hours. "I don't know. I love her, but I don't know a damn thing about jewelry."

"Calm down," Brighton advised. "Deep breaths."

"I'll pay you whatever you want." Malcolm brandished his wallet. "Just help me."

Brighton waved this away. "You're not paying me anything. I'm happy to help. Everything's going to be fine."

Malcolm took a minute to pull himself together. "Could we put some red in there somewhere?"

Brighton nodded encouragingly. "Could you be just a tiny bit more specific?"

"We have . . . a history with the color red. Red dresses." He cleared his throat. "That sort of thing."

"How about ruby baguettes?" Brighton suggested. "We have a pair of matched ruby earrings. I could take them out of the settings and put one on either side of the center diamond."

"Sounds good." He paused, gave her an assessing look, and started to say something several times.

"Spit it out," she advised. "I'll keep it in the vault. Literally. We have three fireproof, bulletproof safes in the back room."

"Is there any way we could include a, uh, needle in the design?"

Brighton strove to maintain a poker face. "What kind of needle?"

"Regular, run-of-the-mill needle." Was the burly marine *blushing*?

"Like a sewing needle?"

"Sure, go with that."

Brighton sat back, mulling her design options. "Well. I guess I could solder a needle along one side of the shank. No one else will be able to tell what it is, though."

"That's the point."

"Consider it done. It's going to look fantastic."

"And you won't say anything to Lila?"

"I'm the soul of discretion. I'll tell her we sold the ruby studs," Brighton said. "I'll write up a receipt for them and you can pay cash. And good news, I'm giving you a screaming deal on them."

"Then we're done here." He visibly relaxed. "That was easier than I thought."

She smiled. "And here I thought ring selection was the easy part of marriage."

"Not for men," Malcolm said. "It's a toss-up between a jewelry store and a war zone."

"But you're here anyway," she pointed out. "You got it done."

He stood up and crossed his arms, reverting to macho masculinity. "I'd do anything for her."

Brighton managed to make it to the back room before she started crying.

"What are you doing here?" Lila looked bewildered when she arrived at the Naked Finger twenty minutes later to find Brighton weeping her way through a box of tissues. "What's wrong?"

"Nothing." Brighton plucked the last tissue from the box.

Lila put down her purse and waited.

"Nothing!" Brighton broke into hiccups. "Just allergies."

"Do you want to take the morning off?"

"No." Brighton drew a ragged breath. "Just give me a minute to splash some cold water on my face and, um, take my allergy meds."

"Go home," Lila ordered.

But Brighton didn't have a home here. She certainly couldn't go back to Jake's house. "I need to work. I need to be productive."

"Then you're in luck. I have a design job for you." Lila looked excited, then chagrined. "But this isn't the right time."

"Yes, it is. Please, give me a job to do." Brighton pushed aside the tissue box and reached for her sketch pad.

"You're sure?"

"Positive. Hit me."

Lila's big brown eyes sparkled as she confided, "I want you to help me with a man's ring. I'm going to ask Malcolm to marry me."

Brighton froze, her pencil suspended in midair. "You . . . what? Why?"

"Don't look so scandalized." Lila laughed. "This isn't 1850, you know. Malcolm and I haven't had a conventional courtship. From the very beginning, I broke protocol." She ticked off her acts of dating defiance on her fingers. "I called him first; I asked him out. I was a shameless hussy, and let me tell you, it is paying off in spades.

So I'm thinking the next logical step will be proposing. I'll take him by surprise. I know he'll say yes."

Brighton stopped sniffling. "I'm sure he will. But—"

"I want a simple platinum band, no frills, nothing fancy. That part I can take care of by myself." Lila's eyes got even sparklier. "But I want you to engrave the inside. One word: *Proliferation*." She grinned. "Don't ask."

"Oh, I wasn't going to."

"Can you do that?"

"Sure, engraving is simple enough. Just pick a band and I'll get on it. But—"

Before she could finish her sentence, the shop door swung open and Dumplin' strutted in. Once again, the busty blonde's skirt was short, her hair was high, and her entire wardrobe—from hoop earrings to handbag to high heels—was emblazoned with designer logos.

"Oh good, you're here." She made a beeline for Brighton, ignoring Lila completely. "I was telling my friend how much I love my new watch."

Brighton glanced at Dumplin's companion, then had to do a double take. She recognized the tall, willowy redhead from a slew of romantic comedies . . . and, more recently, from the tabloid covers at the grocery checkout. Clea Cole had dated her way through Hollywood's A-list before settling down with Carson St. Giles, an actor who contributed to children's charities when he wasn't starring in summer action flicks.

But now, after several years of photo-op bliss, Clea and Carson were divorcing.

Lila had mentioned that celebrities occasionally retreated to Black Dog Bay after breaking up with their boyfriends or husbands, but Brighton was still a bit starstruck. She did her best not to stare. "I'm glad you like it."

"I look like a rap star. That's a good thing," Dumplin' said.

Brighton glanced around. "How's your . . . gentleman friend doing?"

"Who?" Dumplin' seemed genuinely mystified for a moment. "Oh, you mean Hiram? We broke up right after I picked up the watch." Dumplin' punctuated this with an exasperated sigh and an eye roll.

"I'm sorry to hear that," Brighton murmured.

"Don't be." Dumplin' laughed. "He had truckloads of money, but not enough to pay me to go bass fishing with him all day."

"Oh," Brighton said weakly. "Well, that's . . ."

"I guess if I were a lady, I'd return all the jewelry he bought me, but I figure I've earned it." Dumplin' let loose with a raucous laugh.

"You are so crass." Clea Cole finally spoke up. Her voice was as rich and cultured in person as it was on camera.

"Which is why you've been my best friend since middle school," Dumplin' concluded cheerfully. "Anyway, I want you to make something for my friend here. She's having a tough summer and she needs some cheering up."

"Pleased to meet you; I'm Brighton." Brighton extended her right hand and tried to forget the fact that she'd read all about this woman's split from her husband during her last visit to the dentist. The actress didn't appear to be suffering—she looked fantastic even in jeans and a white T-shirt, and the article about her breakup (titled "A Perfectly Pleasant Parting") had included interviews with her and her ex, both of whom raved about how much they still adored and respected each other. ("We've evolved past petty and bitter," Clea had been quoted as saying. "I'm so grateful Carson has shared this portion of my journey.")

"I'm Clea." She leaned in and bestowed a double air-kiss on Brighton. "I'm not quite sure what I'm looking for. Something one of a kind. Amber says you do excellent design work."

Note to self: Dumplin' has a name, and it's Amber.

Brighton looked down and demurred. "Oh, I'd love to, but I'm not going to be working here much longer."

"What?" Clea and Dumplin'—*Amber*—both looked outraged. Not to mention Lila. "Why?"

"I'm here on a temporary basis, and my time is up, I'm afraid." Brighton nodded across the counter. "But this is the store owner, Lila, and she has lots of fantastic designers she works with—"

"No." Amber slammed her hand down. "We want *you*."

Brighton communed with the countertop. "I'm so flattered, but I really—"

"Ooh, what is that?" Clea drifted over to the other side of the showroom.

"What is what?" Brighton joined Lila to see which piece Clea was pointing out.

Lila pulled out the white leather case and handed Clea the massive silver ring. "That's a poison ring."

"A poison ring?" Clea sounded delighted. "Is that a real thing?"

"Apparently. I'd never heard of it, either, until Brighton filled me in." Lila and Clea turned to Brighton, who summarized the history and purpose of poison rings.

The sweet-faced starlet with the voice of an angel broke into a diabolical smirk. "So you could actually kill someone with this?"

"I guess theoretically you could." Brighton didn't like the way Clea's smile broadened. She hastened to add, "*If* you put actual poison in the chamber, which of course we don't recommend."

"Yes," Lila chimed in. "We don't endorse homicide here at the Naked Finger."

The two-time Oscar nominee rubbed her palms together. "Of course not."

"They're purely decorative." Lila sounded a bit panicky.

"A poison ring—I love it. I love everything about it." Clea examined the stones. "Everything except the actual ring, that is. It's so big and clunky." She held the ring aloft and turned it from side to side, considering her options. "Can you make a smaller one? Dainty and feminine, with diamonds and platinum?"

"I could," Brighton said. "If I were staying through the end of summer. But since I'm leaving and I have a bit of a backlog—"

"What backlog?" Lila demanded.

"Don't worry about it," Brighton said.

"I want it." Clea addressed Lila. "Make this happen. Make her stay and do this."

Lila turned to Brighton. "Stay and do this."

"I'll draw one sketch," Brighton relented. "But after that—"

"Actually, I want three," Clea decided. "One for me; two for my friends who are getting divorced. We'll put lovely designs on the outside—flowers or hearts or something—and our exes' names on the inside." She turned to her BFF from middle school. "What do you think? I need something original, meaningful, and still cute."

"How about a black dog?" Amber suggested. "We're in Black Dog Bay."

"Perfect!" Clea exclaimed. "Yes, I want little black dogs on the lids of the poison chambers. Like the dog on the sign at the town border. Can you do that?"

"Sure." Brighton started sketching. "I could do a little Labrador silhouette in onyx against yellow or white gold. The black dog is kind of a big deal around here. It's magic."

Clea leaned in, intrigued. "Magic?"

"Yes." Brighton tried to recount the snippets she'd heard from the locals. "Supposedly, there's a phantom dog that appears to you when you're starting to heal from heartbreak." She turned to Lila for clarification. "Right?"

"Right. The black dog symbolizes hope and new beginnings. It's good luck." Lila glanced down, smiling to herself. "Not really appropriate for a poison ring."

"That black dog will still mean good luck," Clea promised. "Good luck for my ex that his lying, cheating ass is still alive."

Brighton blinked. "What happened to 'A Perfectly Pleasant Parting'? I thought you and your husband were having some sort of Zen divorce?"

Clea snorted. "I hate that narcissist with undying passion. Everyone warned me about on-set romances, but would I listen? No. I was convinced he was *different*. I fell in love with the role he was playing, and by the time the mask came off, it was too late—our wedding pictures were on the cover of *People*."

"I know just how you feel," Brighton murmured. "Minus the *People* cover."

"And riddle me this: If he's so damn Zen, why is he fighting me for the Malibu beach house?"

This is how it ends, Brighton realized. *This is what happens when you don't really know the person you marry.*

Clea shook her fist. "I need that engraved poison ring and I need it now. And you can do the two for my friends in onyx, but I want my dog made out of black diamonds. With a little green collar made of emeralds."

"But . . ."

"Shut your mouth and sketch," Lila hissed.

"We can do pavé with black diamonds," Brighton muttered as she put pen to paper. A few minutes later, she tore off the sketch and showed it to her audience.

"Exquisite," Clea declared.

"Masterful," Lila pronounced.

"Fuckin' fabulous," Amber exclaimed. "Cute and cuddly on the outside, lethal on the inside. Just like Clea."

"I'll call my bench jeweler and see how soon he can get started once we source materials," Lila said.

"You do that," Brighton told Lila. "Meanwhile, I have to track down some intel."

Lila lowered her voice. "What kind of intel?"

"Intel about the man I married."

Lila hesitated for a second, then scribbled a name and number on the back of a business card. "Here. You're helping me; I'll help you. But use this wisely—remember, you can never unhear what this woman is going to tell you."

chapter 26

"*You* want intel on Jake Sorensen?" Summer Benson leaned over the bar and poured herself a glass of pinot grigio. With her wind-blown platinum pixie cut, cat-eye sunglasses, and devil-may-care attitude, Summer didn't exactly fit the stereotype of a mayor's wife, but Brighton was instantly drawn to her. "I'll tell you what I know, but it's really not much. Congratulations, by the way." Her glance lingered on Brighton's ringless left hand, but she didn't comment.

"Excuse me," Jenna huffed. "*I'm* the bartender. *I* pour the drinks."

"I'll try to remember that next time." Summer added a few ice cubes to the white wine, eliciting a horrified gasp from Jenna. Then she winked at Brighton. "Never gets old."

Brighton took a sip of Jenna's special-edition, limited-time-only sun tea. "Lila told me you were his best—and only—female friend."

"I guess that depends on how you define 'friends.' We hang out every now and then, but we don't have some deep emotional bond." Summer sipped her wine. "Mmmm. The ice makes it extra good."

Jenna let out a strangled growl.

"So you two don't talk about anything of substance?" Brighton asked.

At this, Summer laughed. "Look at me. Look at Jake. Do we strike you as people of substance?"

"Well, what *do* you talk about?" Brighton pressed.

Summer shrugged. "I don't know. Nothing."

"You talk about *something*," Jenna insisted. "I see your mouths moving."

Time for some leading questions. "Do you talk about his business deals?" Brighton asked.

Summer made a face. "No."

"What about his childhood?" Brighton continued. "Have you met his brothers?"

Summer seemed genuinely surprised. "Jake has brothers?"

"Hold the phone." Jenna twisted her pink dish towel into a cloth pretzel. "He has *brothers*? Where are they? Do they all look like him?"

Brighton settled back against the wrought iron seat, simmering with frustration. "Why is it so hard to get any kind of straight answer when it comes to Jake?"

"Because he's emotionally crippled." Summer put down her wineglass. "And he's managed to work it to his advantage."

"It's part of the Jake Sorensen mystique," Jenna agreed.

"Let's think about this. What do you do with your friends? You have fun, you laugh, you go out on the town now and then." Summer ticked these off on her fingers. "Jake and I do all that stuff. But real friends talk to each other about, you know, life. Real things like work and family and relationships. We don't get into all that." She tapped her lower lip, considering. "Actually, now that I think about it, I tell him stuff about my life and he's a good listener. He gives good advice. But he doesn't reciprocate at all."

Brighton waited until Jenna bustled into the back room, then confided, "As I said on the phone, his first wife showed up out of the blue yesterday. I was really hoping for answers. You don't have any insights at all?"

"Insights, no. Answers, yes." Summer placed a manila folder on the bar top with the air of a seasoned PI who'd struck pay dirt. "Genevieve Van Petten. Married Jake fourteen years ago in Dewey Beach. Marriage was annulled, reason cited as 'fraud.' Records are sealed."

Brighton glanced through the paperwork with astonishment. "How did you get this?"

Summer adjusted her sunglasses and smiled enigmatically. "I have my ways."

"Fraud?" Brighton frowned down at the grainy photocopied sheets of paper. "What does that mean?"

"I have no idea," Summer said. "But I know who might. We're going to have to hit up Black Dog Bay's most reliable source for old-money, high-society scandal." With a grim expression on her face, she yelled to Jenna, "We're taking two shots of vodka! Each!"

Brighton blinked. "Isn't it a little early to be hitting the hard stuff?"

"Normally, yes. But these are special circumstances." Summer downed her shot and pointed to the sprawling purple mansion barely visible around the curving shoreline of the bay. "We're going to the Purple Palace."

"Why is this house painted purple?" Brighton asked Summer as they walked down the cobblestone driveway toward the massive marble steps.

"Because the owner is petty, spiteful, and can hold a grudge for all eternity." Summer unwrapped a stick of gum and popped it into her mouth. "Oh, and she also happens to be my employer."

Brighton stopped in her tracks. "You talk about your employer that way?"

"She likes it." Summer snapped her gum. "She's the original gangster around here, and she's proud of her reputation."

"But if you work for her, she must have a soft side, right?"

"Not really." Summer rang the doorbell.

"Then why do you look so happy to be here?"

"Because hard-to-handle harpies like to hang out together?" She blew a huge pink bubble while the chimes resounded inside the house. When the bubble popped, she grinned at Brighton. "Introducing Miss Hattie Huntington, harpy at large."

The door swung inward. Before Brighton could even glimpse the face on the other side of the threshold, she heard a cold, commanding voice. "How many times do I have to tell you that chewing gum is vulgar? Vulgar beyond the telling."

Summer obligingly leaned down toward the planted shrub next to the door.

"If you spit that chewing gum onto my myrtle, you will wish you had never been born." The voice was so chilling, Brighton physically shuddered.

"Hey, girl. I missed you, too." Summer bounded into the foyer and threw her arms around a woman Brighton still couldn't see.

Brighton stayed right where she was on the steps until Summer waved one arm to beckon her in. "Don't be scared. Come on in and meet Hattie."

"For the last time, you will address me as Miss Huntington." A tiny, white-haired old woman with piercing blue eyes and a huge emerald cocktail ring spared Brighton a dismissive glance. "How many times must I tell you, it's unspeakably rude to show up on my doorstep with no warning."

"One woman's unspeakably rude is another woman's way to show how much she cares." Summer wandered around the entry hall, stopping to sniff a floral arrangement and snag a truffle from a beribboned white box. "Ooh, these are delicious."

Miss Huntington balled up her bony fists. "Don't talk with your mouth full."

Summer returned to the doorway, yanked Brighton over the threshold, and shoved a truffle in her face. "You have to try this."

Miss Huntington snatched the box away from Summer. Brighton cringed.

"Stop showing fear," Summer advised. "You're just making things worse."

"Don't you dare speak about me like that, Ms. Benson," Miss Huntington said. "I am an impeccable hostess. You are just so . . . so . . ."

"So!" Summer helped herself to another truffle. "Have you given any more thought to that online dating profile?"

"No. Why are you here, Ms. Benson?"

Brighton, gaze cast downward, edged back toward the door.

Summer gave up tormenting the old woman and got down to business. "We need some insider info on a bunch of snobs, and I figured we'd go straight to the source."

"Well, I never." Hattie sniffed. "The nerve! The very implication that I would engage in such talk."

Summer leaned against a marble column and waited.

After five seconds of silence, Hattie cracked. "Who is it?"

"What do you know about the Van Petten family?" Summer asked. "Genevieve Van Petten, in particular."

Hattie opened her mouth to reply, then turned to Brighton with dark suspicion. "I don't believe we've been properly introduced."

"Oh, this is Brighton Smith," Summer said. "She's cool."

"Are you a tourist?" Hattie demanded.

Before Brighton could reply, Summer forged ahead: "She tried to be, but you know how things go around here. She just married Jake Sorensen, so she'll be in town for a bit."

Hattie's pinched expression finally relaxed as shock set in. "Jake Sorensen got married? Surely not!"

Brighton nodded. "That seems to be the universal reaction."

"Hattie, come on," Summer chided. "You hadn't heard about that? Get with the program."

Hattie took a moment to digest the news, then narrowed her eyes and took a step toward Brighton. "Why on earth would a man like Jake Sorensen marry a woman like you?"

Brighton backed away until she banged her hip on a decorative table, almost upending a porcelain vase. While she tried to steady the wobbling vase, Summer rounded on Hattie: "Dude. That is so uncouth."

"We've been over this, Ms. Benson. I do not respond to 'dude.' Not in this lifetime nor the next."

"Brighton's very accomplished." Summer threw an arm around Brighton's shoulders. "She's working with Lila Alders at the jewelry store, and she's also an insurance . . . Uh, she does something with numbers."

"I'm an actuary," Brighton informed the ceiling.

"Right." Summer nodded. "She's not just some pretty face."

"My point exactly," Hattie said. "Jake Sorensen doesn't dally with smart, capable women. And while I suppose she might be considered passably pretty—"

"Ouch," Brighton whispered to Summer.

"—don't his predilections run more toward the peroxide blond pinup type?"

"Hey," Summer said, fluffing her platinum hair. "You say that like it's a bad thing."

Miss Huntington turned on her polished pump heel and led the way to a sumptuously appointed sitting room overlooking the ocean. "*You're* much more his type than Miss Smith is."

"Yeah, and look who I ended up with," Summer argued. "Dutch isn't my usual type, but he's perfect for me."

"What's your usual type?" Brighton asked as they trailed after Hattie.

"Narcissists with cool cars and no conscience," Summer replied. "And, Hattie, how do you know all this about Jake? I didn't realize you took such an interest in him."

Hattie quickened her pace. "I've been to the Whinery a time or two. I make it a point to keep abreast of the goings-on in my town."

"Your town." Summer rolled her eyes. "Like you own the place. Which . . . I guess you kind of do."

"Yes." Hattie's smile was sinister. "You'd both do well to remember that."

"Don't mind her," Summer told Brighton. "She's just trying to distract us from the fact that she's got a schoolgirl crush on your husband."

Hattie whipped around again, and Brighton threw up her hands in a reflex of self-defense. The heated pink hue spreading through Hattie's cheeks was faint but unmistakable.

"Oh my God." Summer burst out laughing. "You totally do. You cougar, you!"

"Silence." Hattie settled into a pink and green striped settee and crossed her dainty ankles. "I do not fancy Jake Sorensen in the way you're implying."

Brighton perched on the tufted pink chair next to Hattie.

"I have to ask." Summer sprawled out next to Hattie and gave the old lady a little nudge with her elbow. "Did you guys ever hook up? Maybe you had one too many glasses of cabernet at the Whinery? It's okay—you can tell us."

Hattie stood up and moved to a chair across the room. "How dare you even imply such a thing!"

"*Anyway.*" Brighton scrambled to redirect the conversation. "We have reason to believe he was once married to a woman named Genevieve Van Petten. Do you know anything about her?"

"Married?" Hattie sat perfectly still for a moment. "Astonishing. That little tidbit explains quite a lot, actually."

Summer and Brighton exchanged glances. "It does? Like what?"

Hattie waved one hand, dismissing them. "If you'll excuse me, I have to make a phone call."

"To whom?" Summer asked.

"If you want me to find out more about Jake Sorensen and Genevieve Van Petten, you're going to have to stop asking questions and be patient."

"Can we at least wait in the kitchen?" Summer asked. To Brighton, she said, "Her chef makes the most delicious lemon frosted cookies." She led the way through the dining room to a cavernous kitchen so white and gleaming with stainless steel accessories that it could double as an operating room.

While Summer rummaged through the pantry in search of cookies, her cell phone rang.

"Well, well, well. Speak of the devil." Summer held up her phone so Brighton could read the name on the screen: SORENSEN. "Why's he calling me and not you?"

"Oh, I turned my phone off." Brighton's stomach felt fluttery. "I don't want to talk to him right now."

"Well, I do." Summer answered the phone with, "This better be good." She cast her gaze up and listened for a moment, then said, "Tell it to Brighton, buddy. We're at the Purple Palace getting the lowdown on your sordid past . . . Yeah, I'd hurry if I were you." She ended the call with a click and a smile. "He'll be right over."

Brighton blinked. "He's coming over here? Now?"

"Mm-hmm. Lila told him she sent you to me, and I guess he wants a sit-down." Summer opened the massive refrigerator and started rifling through the shelves.

Brighton sank down on a carved hardwood stool. "I can't believe this."

"Which part?" Summer asked.

"All of it." Brighton tried to pinpoint where, exactly, things had gone wrong. "'Let's get married,' we said. 'It'll be fun,' we said." She lowered her head into her hands. "And now I'm making black diamond poison rings and asking scary old ladies for gossip and trying to wean myself off my sexual addiction to my drive-through husband and relapsing in the middle of the night."

"Well, it could be worse," Summer soothed. "You could still be normal."

chapter 27

"*L*et me ask you, Miss Smith." Hattie arranged herself in a white wicker settee on her vast veranda as her butler (or "manservant," as Summer insisted on calling him) served iced lemonade garnished with sprigs of fresh lavender. "Have you ever read *The Great Gatsby*?"

"Yes." Brighton tried to remember the details. "Junior year of high school, I think."

"Well, according to my sources, Jake Sorensen and Genevieve Van Petten are the contemporary equivalent of Gatsby and Daisy. When they met, he was poor and uneducated. But very attractive. He amused her for a summer; then she left to finish her schooling."

"That's not *The Great Gatsby*; that's *Dirty Dancing*," Summer said.

"When you say he amused her, you mean he married her," Brighton clarified.

"Yes," Hattie replied. "They lived together for a month or two, which had the intended effect of scandalizing her mother's social circle. But then her father put his foot down, and that was that."

Brighton cast her mind back to the older man who'd been frowning at Genevieve at the ball. "Is her father tall and lanky? Lots of white hair like he stuck his finger in a socket?"

Hattie smiled. "Yes, that sounds like Russell. At any rate, Jake is very successful now."

"Understatement," Summer declared. "The man bleeds green. He probably has more money than you do."

"He might," Hattie allowed. "But I have social cachet and connections far beyond his reach."

Summer laughed. "I seriously doubt he cares about social cachet."

"Oh, but he does." Hattie sat back, very pleased with herself and her birthright. "The people I spoke to don't know that Genevieve actually married him. Her parents kept that very quiet. I've only heard there was a dalliance, and that he adored her."

The phrase had an almost physical impact on Brighton.

"He would have done anything for her," Hattie continued. "Everything he did, everything he became, he did to be worthy of her."

"No way." Summer rolled her eyes. "Jake Sorensen is nobody's puppy dog."

"Indeed, he is. Shortly after Genevieve left him, he started his first company. He amassed what he considered to be a sizable fortune and arranged to run into her at an auction house, where he bought an antique watch to show off his money."

Brighton froze. "What kind of watch?"

Hattie waved one wrinkled hand dismissively. "What does it matter? He approached her in front of her family and friends and declared his love."

"What happened?" Summer asked.

"She laughed at him. She made it clear she would never marry beneath her again. Later that evening, she announced her engagement to one of her childhood friends." Hattie inclined her head. "He made a fool of himself because he didn't understand that it's not enough to have means if one doesn't have the right breeding."

"We're talking about people here, not horses, right?" Summer stuck out her tongue. "You and your sources are insufferable. And Genevieve sounds like a bitch."

But Hattie sided with her fellow socialite. "What else could she do? He'd put her in a very awkward position."

"Uh, she could be a decent human being," Summer suggested.

"She should have shown more grace, but she did the right thing," Hattie said firmly. "The kind thing. If she'd acquiesced to his advances, she would have succumbed to his considerable charms—"

Summer winked at Brighton. "You *love* him. Admit it. Late at night, when you're not plotting evil deeds, you're fantasizing about his abs and his pecs and his—"

"If she had acquiesced, she would have had to break his heart again eventually. She had her family to think about."

"He was so young then," Brighton murmured. "He must have felt—"

"Don't waste your sympathy on him. He got over it," Hattie assured her. "He went home from that auction with two young women, spent the next few years doubling his fortune many times over, and now he can have any woman he wants." She regarded Brighton with a slight curl to her lip.

Brighton couldn't get the image of that battered old watch out of her head. He had been wearing it on the night she met him. The night Genevieve had gotten back in touch. That couldn't be a coincidence—he'd been wearing that watch as a reminder of . . . what? How much he still loved Genevieve, or how badly he'd felt when she left him?

"How do you know all this?" Summer demanded of Hattie. "Aren't you too rich and rarefied to talk on the phone like the commoners? Don't you have to send handwritten letters on engraved stationery?"

"Go ahead and mock me," Hattie said. "I know I'm right. I have power and connections that you will never have."

"And you'll never get tired of lording that over me," Summer shot back.

"No, I don't imagine I will." Hattie reached over and rested her cool, papery hand atop Brighton's. "Miss Smith, let me give you some advice. If a man prefers another woman over you, let him have her. You don't want to endure a lifetime of trying to live up to standards set by someone else."

"Yeah, look at the bright side and take this for what it was," Summer urged. "A really hot summer fling. You got to live the fantasy of half the women in this town."

"That's true. I got exactly what I wanted," Brighton said. But somehow, it wasn't enough.

"Focus on that. Don't overreach." Summer took a sip of lemonade. "I can't believe I'm saying this, but I agree with Hattie: There's no such thing as happily ever after with a guy like Jake. Speaking of whom . . ." She shot to her feet, grabbed Hattie's elbow, and tried to hustle the old lady off the porch.

"How dare you?" Hattie cried. "Unhand me immediately."

And then Brighton heard the footsteps on the porch steps. She knew before she turned around that she was about to get another hit of her drug of choice.

"What up, Sorensen?" Summer continued wrestling with Hattie. "We'll just wait in the parlor while you and Brighton catch up."

"Jake. How lovely to see you again!" Hattie's sour expression vanished. She looked almost giddy. "May I offer you something to drink?"

"No, thank you." Jake nodded at Brighton. "I've been looking for you."

Hattie smiled sweetly and placed her fingertips on Jake's forearm.

"Are you sure I can't tempt you? We've been having the most refreshing lemonade with fresh lavender."

Summer mumbled something that sounded a lot like, "Get a room."

Hattie kept her hand on Jake's arm. Jake kept his gaze focused on Brighton, and Brighton kept her gaze focused on the sunlight glinting off the ocean waves.

"Okay, then." Summer cleared her throat. "We'll give you two crazy kids some privacy."

Hattie sighed and acquiesced. "Yes, and if you need anything at all . . ."

"It's fine." Brighton forced herself to face Jake. "The whole town's already talking, so you might as well say whatever you have to say in front of Hattie and Summer." She refused to back down or back away even an inch. "Do you still want her?"

She could hear Summer suck in her breath.

Jake didn't react. "What's going on between me and Genevieve has nothing to do with you."

"I'm well aware." She lifted her chin. "Please answer my question. Do you still want her?"

"No." But he couldn't meet her eyes.

"Then what is she doing here?"

"She wants things from me." He waited a beat. "Just like you."

"What are you talking about?"

"You married me because you wanted something from me." He gave her a moment to refute this, but she couldn't. "That's what relationships are: Each person has something the other person wants. It's a transaction."

"I don't believe that," Brighton said. "And I don't believe you do, either."

"Believe what you want," he said flatly.

"Then why me?" Brighton knew how hurt and vulnerable she

sounded, but she didn't care. "You could have used any single woman at that bar as your last line of defense again Genevieve."

"That's true," Summer chimed in. "Jenna will never get over the fact that you didn't pick her."

"I didn't show up at the Whinery planning to get married," Jake said.

"Neither did I," Brighton shot back. "So why me? What did I bring to the transaction?"

He looked at her for a long moment, his gaze softening. "Ten-year plans, a balanced portfolio, and a thorough understanding of small aircraft safety records."

"You're mocking me."

He shook his head. "You dress like a CEO and you're sexy as hell."

Summer practically melted into a puddle. "Aww."

Brighton gave her the side eye of death. "Don't fall for this. He's deflecting the real question."

"You're different from Genevieve in every way," Jake finished.

"So you wanted me for what I'm *not*? It had nothing to do with who I *am*?" Brighton watched him, hoping that he might deny this. Hoping that he might fight for her. "I refuse to be a pawn in whatever game you and Genevieve are playing. I'm done. I give up. You win."

His gaze shuttered as he stepped back, calm and impassive. "I'll set up an appointment with an attorney tomorrow."

chapter 28

"*T*his is a little unusual," the attorney said after Brighton and Jake had settled into matching leather wing chairs. "Typically, my clients don't come to my office with the spouse they're going to divorce."

"That's par for the course for us." Brighton nodded. "We did everything backward, upside down, inside out, and out of order."

"We're very amicable," Jake said.

Amicable. The word, so harmless and neutral, made Brighton suck in her breath. Of all the terms she would use to characterize the past few weeks with Jake, "amicable" wouldn't even make the top hundred. She stared down, twisted her hands in her lap, and tried not to reveal any trace of her feelings.

"That's a welcome change." The attorney shuffled some papers and waited for Brighton to glance up again. "And it will make the dissolution process much smoother. Let me ask a few questions and we'll start the filing procedures. First, though, I have to advise you that, legally and ethically, I cannot represent both of you. The way it usually works with a collaborative divorce is, each party retains an attorney or selects a mediator to hammer out the details."

"We don't need a mediator," Jake said firmly. "I'll agree to whatever terms she wants."

"Gosh." Brighton's voice was faint. "How very *amicable* of you."

Jake shot her a strange look, then turned back to the lawyer. "If you can only legally represent one of us, represent her. Draft up the paperwork and I'll sign it."

Brighton rearranged herself in her chair and touched her hammered gold link bracelet. "But what are we going to put in the paperwork?"

Jake had pulled out his phone. "Whatever you want."

The lawyer looked alarmed. "Mr. Sorensen, I strongly advise you not to make any agreements, verbal or otherwise, before you—"

"I don't want a settlement from you," Brighton said.

Jake remained focused on the e-mail he was reading. "You're angry."

"I'm not angry; I just don't want anything of yours."

The attorney threw himself into the emotional cross fire. "If I may, I need to ask a few questions before we get into any details concerning the division of assets."

"Fine." Brighton looked straight ahead. "Shoot."

The attorney picked up a pen. "When and where did the marriage take place?"

Jake gave the lawyer a knowing look. "You live in this town. You've heard about this by now."

"Rumors and gossip don't hold up in courts of law. When and where did the marriage take place?"

"About two weeks ago." Brighton had to pull up the digital calendar on her smartphone to cite the exact date. "We flew to Vegas for the ceremony."

"Are you both current residents of Delaware?"

"I'm a part-time resident," Jake said.

"I'm from New Jersey," Brighton said.

"But you currently reside here with your husband?"

"Well, yes." *I guess.* "Technically."

"Do you have a copy of the marriage license?"

"Yes." Brighton crossed her legs and folded her hands on her knee. "But I should probably tell you that we were drunk at the time. Which they're normally very strict about."

The attorney put down the pen. "You were drunk? Then how . . . ?"

"I bribed the official," Jake said.

The lawyer put down his pen, picked it up, then put it down again. "I'll need to make some inquiries." He spoke to them in the same tone an elementary school principal might use to shame spitball-wielding third graders.

Brighton had to suppress the sudden and inappropriate urge to laugh.

"Not to worry—we'll get everything sorted out," the attorney continued. "And we can start the clock on your mandated separation period."

Brighton started making notes of her own. "There's a mandated separation period?"

"Thirty days."

"So what happens? We file for divorce, wait thirty days, and then a judge finalizes it?"

"In theory. I'll have to check about the residency issues. But the inebriation issues have the potential to complicate matters." He thinned his lips. "As do the bribery issues."

Brighton got the church giggles again, which the attorney pretended not to notice.

"The fact that you two are sharing a living space also complicates matters," he said.

"I'll move out," Jake and Brighton said at exactly the same time. She turned to him. "Don't be ridiculous. It's your house."

He shook his head. "I don't want to make your life any harder than I already have."

She glimpsed a mix of pity and regret in his eyes. *Pity.* Just when she thought she couldn't feel any more inadequate.

"No." She crossed her arms.

"I insist." He shrugged. "It's not like I don't have anywhere else to go."

"I've got somewhere else you can go," she muttered under her breath.

"Brighton . . . ," he started.

She addressed the lawyer. "When can we start the paperwork?"

He glanced from Brighton to Jake and back again. "Ms. Smith is my client, then?"

"Yes," Jake confirmed. "But I'll pay your retainer on the way out."

Brighton stood up and snatched the strap of her handbag. "That won't be necessary. I'm perfectly capable of paying my own retainer."

Jake got to his feet, towering over her. "I know you're capable, but I want to do this for you."

"Well, I don't want you to do this for me."

They squared off, separated by the matching wing chairs.

"I'll go find some coffee." The lawyer practically ran out to the hall and closed the door behind him.

"Do not do this," Brighton warned before Jake could say another word.

"I am doing this." He set his jaw. "The least I can do is be a gentleman and pay the retainer."

"Because that's what gentlemen do? Bankroll quickie divorces to random women they met in a bar when the long-lost loves of their lives showed up?"

"Yes." His jaw muscle twitched again. "That's what gentlemen do."

Her whole body tensed, just like the night she first saw him. "For the last time: I do not want your money."

"Why not?" He took a step toward her. "Be practical, Brighton."

"I cannot be practical about this." She could be practical about everything else in her life, but not him.

"It's just money."

"Exactly." Her voice quavered. "It doesn't mean anything to you, so you throw it around to make all of life's little inconveniences disappear. Like me."

He sighed and rubbed one side of his cheek. "Yeah, about that . . ."

Brighton fell silent.

"I know it's too late. All this stuff with Genevieve . . . But I'm sorry, Brighton. I am." Another step and he was close enough to raise his hand to touch her face.

She held her breath, waiting for . . . she didn't know what, exactly.

He dropped his hand to his side. "The least I can do is make this marriage worth your while. We never got around to drafting that post-nup you wanted."

She held up both palms. "Please stop talking."

"I don't want you to leave with nothing," he said.

"Jake." She turned away from him, studying the framed oil painting on the far wall. "I married you for spite and sent pictures of your private jet and your perfectly sculpted cheekbones to my ex on our wedding night. Nothing is *exactly* what I deserve."

"I'm giving you a settlement. You've earned it."

She whirled back around. *"Excuse me?"*

His smartphone buzzed and he pulled it out of his pocket to check his message while he told her, "Name your price."

Brighton literally couldn't breathe for a moment. She clutched the back of a chair for support.

"Hell, I'll give you the beach house if you want it."

She waited for him to look up from the phone screen again. Seconds ticked by.

Finally, she gave up on getting his full attention. "You're willing to walk away from Don't Be Koi if it means a nice, easy divorce?"

"Sure." He still hadn't glanced back at her. "It's just a house."

"What about the furniture?" she pressed. "The artwork? The boat?" She hadn't actually seen a boat, but she was willing to bet he had one stashed away somewhere.

"Sure." He inclined his head. "Whatever you want."

"What I want is not to be treated like a prostitute."

His head snapped up.

"Yes," she assured him before he could protest. "I see what you're doing. You're treating me like a business decision."

He put his phone away and crossed his arms, waiting.

"But the fact is, I'm not a business decision. I'm your wife." She glanced around the empty room and lowered her voice. "I did things with you that I've never done with anybody else. I *skateboarded* with you."

His expression flickered for a split second, and then he recovered his composure. "That's why I'm trying to make this easy."

"And that's why I'm upset. It makes me sad to think that you could write a check or sign over a deed and forget about me." She paused as she remembered who she was talking to. "Wait—let me try to explain. 'Sad' is a feeling people get when—"

"Don't." His voice deepened. "It's not like that."

"It kind of is." She wasn't sure if he could hear her. "I was planning to stay, Jake. And now I can't."

He finally betrayed a hint of frustration. "I have no idea what you want right now."

She wanted him to love her—to *adore* her—too much to let her go, but she couldn't say that. So she went up on tiptoe, wrapped her arms around his neck, and brushed her lips against his. She knew she shouldn't, but she didn't care. He kissed her, she kissed him, and then they were making out in the middle of the attorney's office. Swapping spit at a billable rate of hundreds of dollars per hour.

There was a lot of muffled thumping and laughing as they moved from the bookcase to the chair to the rug. They ended up sweaty and intertwined, staring up at the underside of the massive mahogany desk.

At which point rational thought staged a comeback.

"I'm glad I married you, Brighton." He gazed down at her, his brown eyes at once so bright and so dark.

"Me, too." She rested her cheek against his bare arm. "I wish it didn't have to end like this, even though I knew it would." She could hear a phone ringing in the office next door and traffic passing by outside the window. "What's going to happen with you and Genevieve?"

He turned away from her and rolled onto his back. "I'm good at a lot of things, Brighton."

She looked around at the office furniture they'd just defiled. "Yes, yes you are."

"When I set out to accomplish something, I do it. I do not quit. I do not fail. But when I married Genevieve, I showed horrific judgment." He sat up and put his shirt on. "I had a huge blind spot. I made terrible decisions. I failed."

She sat up, too, combing her fingers through her hair. "What are you talking about? You're the ultimate success story."

"Put it this way: If you were phenomenal at every other sport—football, baseball, hockey, lacrosse—but terrible at basketball, why would you keep trying to play basketball?"

Brighton furrowed her brow, trying to follow. "Jake. We're not talking about sports. We're talking about relationships. Everyone gets their heart broken when they're young."

But he reached for his jeans and refused to say anything more.

"Jake, come on. Talk to me."

He stood up and pulled on the jeans. "Let me ask you something: Would you have married me that night if I weren't rich? Would you still have decided to run off in the middle of the night to Vegas with me if I were an average-looking guy with an average bank account?"

Brighton tried to envision this. "Well . . ."

"You wouldn't," he answered for her. "Because you say the money doesn't matter, but it does. If I didn't have what I have and look the way I look, you wouldn't have done what you did."

"That's not true!" She located her shoes and looked around for her blouse. "I wasn't thinking about any of that. I was focused on your watch."

"A watch that I wouldn't have if I weren't rich," he pointed out. "A beat-up Patek Philippe is still a Patek Philippe. Or so I used to think."

"You love that watch," Brighton said. "Otherwise you wouldn't still have it."

"I bought it because I liked it. I kept it to remind myself not to make the same mistake twice."

"And that mistake would be . . . ?"

Instead of answering her question directly, he said, "I gave her my grandmother's ring. She never wore it. Not once. It was too small for her finger. She kept saying she would get it resized, but she never did. It embarrassed her. But when she left, she took it with her. I never knew why."

Brighton's throat felt dry and tight. "And you still love her."

"Love is a feeling. I'm more about action." He reached behind the desk and located her blouse. "Here. Let me find your bra."

. . .

A mere ten minutes after Brighton straggled out of the attorney's office with messy hair, smeared lip gloss, and tattered dignity, Jenna intercepted her in the middle of Main Street.

"So! I hear you and Jake just got into some very *heated* negotiations at the family law office."

Brighton gaped at the bartender. "How on earth did you hear that? It's been like five minutes!"

Jenna shrugged one shoulder. "Welcome to Black Dog Bay."

"No, seriously. Did the legal secretary send out a mass e-mail the minute I walked out the door?"

"I cannot reveal my sources." Jenna led the way to the Whinery and held the door open. "I can, however, offer you a refreshing glass of sangria. Made it this morning with fresh peaches from the farmers' market."

"How can I say no to that?" Brighton took a seat at the bar. She glanced around at all the pink and silver fripperies and sighed. "And to think this is where this whole, champagne-drenched mess began."

Jenna pulled an icy pitcher of sangria from the refrigerator beneath the bar. "Would you do things differently? If you could go back to the night you met him?"

Brighton nibbled her lower lip, considering. "I should have run out the door the second he smoldered in my direction."

"Why? You said yourself it's been fun."

"Yeah, but he's not a good match for me. He was a spur-of-the-moment, seat-of-my-pants, double-dog-dare marriage of convenience. Like a Regency romance meets Mad Libs."

Jenna smiled. "Sometimes, that's just what a woman needs."

The Whinery's front door swung open and Genevieve Van Petten swept in, looking like European royalty with her dark sunglasses, ivory sheath dress, and lean, sculpted legs.

"Look who's here," Brighton muttered. "Daisy Buchanan." She held her ground and sipped her sangria. Eyes front, back straight, ankles crossed. *Show no weakness, give no quarter.*

Genevieve approached and cleared her throat—but not a normal, phlegmy, plebian throat clearing. No. Genevieve's *ahem* had been cultivated in the poshest finishing schools in New England. "Hello, Brighton. I hoped I might find you here." She rested her hand on the back of the nearest barstool. "Is this seat taken?"

chapter 29

I'm too sober for this. Brighton signaled Jenna to top off her sangria, then acknowledged the other woman with a curt nod. She could smell the faint trace of Genevieve's light, floral perfume.

"May I sit down?" Genevieve asked.

Brighton kept her expression perfectly pleasant as she inwardly dry heaved. "I can't stop you, but I should give you fair warning that I'm not feeling very chatty at the moment."

"That's fine; I just need you to listen." Genevieve arranged herself on the stool with the effortless grace of a ballerina. "I heard that you and Jacob . . ." Her self-assurance finally faltered. "I heard you decided to divorce."

Brighton refused to confirm this. She remained still and silent until Genevieve tried again.

"I know it must have been a surprise, seeing me on his porch like that. Again, I can't tell you how truly sorry I am." The perfect high-society blonde tucked a strand of perfect hair behind her perfect ear.

Brighton couldn't tamp down her disappointment and anger any longer. She put down her glass and swiveled her stool to confront Genevieve. "Sorry for what, exactly?"

"That you found yourself caught in the middle of this. I know how hard it is to let go of him." The other woman's smile was calm and compassionate. "It's been fifteen years since we first met. And not a day goes by that I don't think about him."

"I heard that you only got together with him to piss off your parents," Brighton remarked. "Is that true?"

Genevieve took this as an invitation to relay her version of the story. "I didn't marry him to upset my parents. I married him because I couldn't bear not to. It was the first time in my life I wanted something enough to defy my mother and father. He was different from anyone I'd ever met. So brash and smart; completely unafraid. He made me feel brave, too. When he went down on one knee and asked me to marry him, what could I say?"

Brighton couldn't imagine Jake making such an old-world display of gallantry. Proposing on bended knee wasn't his style.

Then again, who was she to say what was and wasn't his style? She was just the human shield he used to ward off this ethereal, blue-blooded siren.

"From the moment I said yes, I knew it was temporary." Genevieve sighed. Even in the harsh afternoon sunlight, her complexion appeared smooth and poreless. "But I thought that if I could escape my family's expectations for a summer, I might be able to change the rest of my life."

"Did you?" Brighton asked.

Genevieve shook her head. "After we ended things, I went back to my ordinary life. I was exactly the same, at least on the outside."

Brighton thought about the corporate office waiting for her back in the city. The closet full of dark suits, the dental appointments and gym memberships, the gray, overcast skies and the bumper-to-bumper commutes.

"But inside, in my heart and soul, I've never been the same." Genevieve sounded wistful. "And even though I couldn't manage to change my life, he changed his. Jacob had nothing when we got married." She paused to let this sink in. "*Nothing.* Not even a credit card. We lived in a rented studio. I had to eat ramen noodles and SpaghettiOs for the first time in my life." She shuddered, then waited for Brighton to commiserate.

"I love SpaghettiOs." Brighton hadn't eaten them in years, but suddenly she was starving. "But then, I grew up poor, so . . ."

"I married him even though he couldn't afford a proper engagement ring." Another dramatic pause. "All we had was a hand-me-down from his grandmother."

"Wow," Brighton murmured. "How you've suffered."

"I'll admit it: I was ashamed to wear it. I was afraid of what my friends would say. I was cowardly and vain." Genevieve's demeanor changed ever so slightly. Her tone and expression shifted as she sized up Brighton. "But I kept it all these years. I still have it."

Brighton shook her head. "You didn't give his family heirloom back after your family got the marriage annulled?"

"It meant something to me."

"It meant something to him, too," Brighton pointed out.

Genevieve glanced at Brighton's left hand. "What did you do with your ring from Jacob?"

Brighton reached for her sangria. "Don't have one. As I'm sure you've heard, we had kind of a spontaneous wedding."

"And he wouldn't even buy you a ring?" Genevieve looked horrified and a little smug. "That's awful. When *I* married him, he was determined to give me everything I wanted."

"I said that he *didn't* buy me a ring, not that he *wouldn't*," Brighton snapped.

Genevieve looked confused. "Oh. Well, it's none of my business, I suppose."

"No, it's not." Brighton smiled sweetly and let the silence expand.

Finally, the exquisite blonde rallied with, "I came here to apologize. I can't imagine how you must be feeling about all this. But I also came to explain that Jacob and I have a long, complicated history, and it's not over. It will never be over."

"Mmmm." Brighton ran her fingertip along the rim of her glass. "Because after he made a bunch of money, you still rejected him. In front of a roomful of people."

"That was . . ." Genevieve's flawless complexion flushed. "That was complicated. I had already promised to marry another man."

Brighton glanced at the socialite's bare fingers. "And how did that work out?"

"It was the worst mistake of my life. I married a man I didn't love and I paid for it every single day." Her blue eyes brimmed with tears.

"I'm confused; break this down for me again." Brighton rested her chin in her hand. "Why did you get that annulment?"

"My parents were going to cut me off."

"From what?"

"My trust fund. The family investments. What was I supposed to do?" Genevieve shed a single dainty tear. "Be penniless? Drop out of college?"

"You didn't have to drop out of college. You could have applied for student loans and done work-study."

Genevieve stared at Brighton as though she had started speaking in tongues.

"And why did you marry that other guy after Jake came back with a million dollars?"

Genevieve looked stricken. "I know how this is going to sound. I know. But . . . a million dollars isn't really all that much. And a good marriage is about more than money. My family and his family had known each other for years."

"And yet it didn't work out."

"It didn't." Another ladylike tear ran down her cheek. "As I said, I suffered for my sins."

Brighton rolled her eyes. "That's a bit dramatic, don't you think?"

"You wouldn't say that if you'd been in my marriage."

"Okay, but be honest: Why are you showing up now?" Brighton asked. "He'll never be up to your lofty standards. He's moved on. He's married someone else. Why don't you give back his grandmother's ring and let him be?"

"I tried. I've been trying for years." Genevieve rested her fragile, spindly wrists on the edge of the bar. "But as I said, there's something about him that makes him impossible to forget. Which is why I wanted to talk to you, woman to woman."

Brighton snorted. "'Woman to woman'?" She pushed her stool back. "We're done here."

Genevieve rested one hand lightly on Brighton's shoulder. "If he didn't want me, I'd leave. I'd go away and never come back. But the truth is, we're not done with each other, and I'm not sure we ever will be."

Brighton shook off Genevieve's hand. "He is done with you. He married me."

"After fifteen years of being single. On the day I contacted him. Isn't it possible that he married you to send me a message?"

"Yes, and I don't think the message was: 'Please show up at my house at your earliest opportunity.' If you're so insistent on chatting 'woman to woman,' let me ask you something." Brighton tried to remain emotionless, but she wasn't as good at this game as Genevieve was. "Why *did* you contact him? Why now, after all this time? What do you want from him?"

"Who says I want anything from him?"

"I do." Brighton thought back to what Hattie Huntington had said about the Van Petten family's financial distress. "Call it woman's intuition."

Genevieve looked a bit discomfited. "I don't expect you to understand our history."

"Good. Because I don't. What I do understand is that you didn't want him enough to stay with him when he was poor, you didn't want him when he 'only' had a million dollars, but now that your trust fund dried up, suddenly he's the long-lost love of your life." She had to stop to catch her breath.

Genevieve's expression froze. "Who said anything about my trust fund?"

Brighton leveled her gaze. "I heard that the Van Pettens are having a cash-flow problem. I heard that all you have left is social currency, and that doesn't pay the bills."

Genevieve's lip trembled. "That's just vicious gossip."

"So you're saying that you'd be here throwing yourself at him if he were still making minimum wage and eating SpaghettiOs?" God, she was hungry.

Genevieve pulled herself together and sat up straight. "You don't need Jacob. I do."

I don't need him, but I want him.

"Stop calling him Jacob," Brighton said.

"But that's his name."

"His name is Jake. Jacob is annoying and pretentious."

"You're only saying that because you don't like me."

"Fair point."

"I married Jacob—Jake"—Genevieve looked pained as she forced herself to say the nickname—"for the right reasons. We were desperately in love. Both of us."

"No, you weren't." Brighton said this instantly, almost as a reflex. But maybe she was wrong. Jake hadn't married Genevieve because he was drunk and bored and reckless. He'd married her because . . . well, maybe he *had* loved her. Maybe once upon a time, Jacob Sorensen had been capable of a deep, genuine connection.

"He loved me more than anyone else has ever loved me before or since." Genevieve sounded stronger with every syllable. "I didn't appreciate it at the time because I was so young, but he would have done anything for me." She inhaled slowly. "You need to let him go, Brighton."

"Why? Because you want another chance? Sorry, life doesn't work that way. You don't get unlimited chances with a guy like Jake. One per customer, lady. You had your turn."

Rather than argue, Genevieve changed the subject. "I wish we'd met under different circumstances. I feel as though we could have been friends."

"I doubt you'd want to be friends with someone like me," Brighton said. "I'm very ordinary."

"You're talented. I was sincere when I asked you about commissioning a piece of jewelry."

"If you're looking for someone to design your next engagement ring from Jake, you're going to have to keep looking." Brighton took another big gulp of sangria. Overwhelmed with loss and frustration, she turned to the only healthy outlet left to her. "Which reminds me, I should get going. I've got a few designs to finish up before Monday."

"What are you working on?" Genevieve asked.

"Rings." Brighton thought about Lila and Malcolm and their starry-eyed devotion. "For a couple that actually stands a chance in hell of making their marriage last." She pushed her half-empty glass aside and flagged down Jenna. "Check, please."

chapter 30

*B*righton worked for hours in the back room of the Naked Finger. The hot light and the dull ache in her shoulders as she hunched over the workbench served as welcome distractions. At closing time, she locked the doors and continued to polish a thin platinum band, taking the occasional break for junk food she'd bought in a fit of despair.

At eight o'clock, Jenna popped over from the Whinery to make sure she was okay.

At nine, Kira texted to check in.

At ten, Lila called to ask why on earth she was still at the store.

Brighton assured everyone she was fine and declined to leave the premises. She had made a commitment to deliver these rings before she left town. Besides, it wasn't like she could sleep right now anyway. She kept thinking of the mixture of hope and despair she'd seen in Genevieve's big blue eyes.

Brighton prayed that *she* wouldn't still be getting over him a decade and a half later.

At ten thirty, she heard the metallic scrape of a key in the lock. She stashed the ring in a drawer and glanced up, expecting to see Lila.

Jake walked in, rumpled and unshaven and clearly exhausted. Her body responded instantly. She tried to look blasé as she picked up her plastic spoon and took a leisurely bite of Chef Boyardee's finest.

"What are you doing?" he demanded.

"Is this a trick question?" Brighton glanced down at her tank top, navy skirt, and bare feet. "I'm working and having a midnight snack. What are *you* doing here?"

"Lila gave me the keys."

"Of course she did. You're so charming and persuasive. But how'd you know I was here?"

He shifted his weight. "Genevieve mentioned you'd said you were going to work late."

"Ah, yes. Genevieve." Brighton pulled the ring back out of the drawer. "She and I had quite a conversation today."

"She told me."

Brighton studied the surface of the smooth platinum band for imperfections.

"Let's go back to the house." He took a step toward the door, expecting her to follow him.

She stayed right where she was.

He exhaled as he turned around to face her. "You know you're more than welcome to stay there as long as you want."

"I know. You made it very clear that you'd sign the deed to that house over to me right now if I asked."

He nodded at her with evident relief. "You could stay here and work with Lila indefinitely. If you want, I'll—"

"For the last time, Jake, I don't want anything from you." She peered through a magnifying lens at a tiny divot in the platinum. "I'm perfectly capable of providing for myself."

"Eating SpaghettiOs out of a can?" He sounded angry, and she realized that this must be a sore spot. A throwback to the days when he was poor and struggling to be worthy of his bride.

Too bad. "I'd rather eat SpaghettiOs out of a can for the rest of my life than spend one more day eating twelve-dollar strawberries with you." She spooned up another bite of pasta with an air of defiance.

A scratch at the door and a plaintive canine whine interrupted his reply. "Hang on." He opened the door so that Rory, who'd been waiting outside, could come in. The giant brown dog padded over to Brighton, greeted her with drool-drenched kisses, and sprawled out across her bare toes.

Brighton reached down to pat his side. "Who needs fuzzy slippers when I've got you around?"

Rory's tail thumped against the floor.

"Hey." Jake frowned. "That's my dog."

Brighton patted Rory again. "Actually, he's not your dog. He's *a* dog. You said so yourself, remember?"

For once, Jake Sorensen had nothing to say.

Brighton cupped a hand to her ear. "Yes?"

"Maybe he's not officially my dog, but he's not yours, either."

"Jake, I'm not going to argue with you about dog ownership. I'm too busy eating empty calories and working on what is probably the best piece of jewelry I've ever made in my life. So if you're done—" She slipped on her safety goggles and flipped on her polishing machine. The humming noise drowned out further attempts at conversation.

He leaned over her shoulder until his cheek rested against hers. "Show me."

She could feel, rather than hear, his voice. "No."

He placed his fingers atop hers, his touch light but steady. "Brighton."

"Ugh. Fine." She switched off the polisher, put down Malcolm's wedding band, and handed over the wax model of Clea Cole's black diamond dog ring. "Behold, genius in the making."

He studied her handiwork in silence.

"It's a poison ring," she informed him. "See the lid right there? There'll be a tiny chamber under there that one could use to conceal poison that one might pour into one's ex's Gatorade. If one were so inclined."

He peered at the intricate ridges and curves in the blue wax, the hollows that would be filled with precious metals. "It's beautiful."

"Not really. It's just stone and metalwork."

He kept studying the wax, and she knew that he could visualize the finished product based on the negative space. He could see what would be there based on what wasn't there.

"The divorcée who commissioned it ordered three. One for her, two more for her friends. Because, you know, lots of marriages end in divorce." Brighton used the spoon to gesture between them. "We're not special. Now, if you'll excuse me, I have a lot of work to do. With my trusty sidekick." She leaned down to pet Rory again. "I'm not afraid to file some paperwork and make it official."

"You're bluffing." But he didn't sound certain.

"We'll see." She prepared to resume polishing.

He rested his hand on her shoulder. "I don't want Genevieve. Not anymore." He started stroking her back, his hand warm and comforting.

She hadn't realized how tense she was until she relaxed against him. "Then why is she still in town? If you don't want her, tell her to go."

"It's not that simple." His hand stilled on her back. "I can't just turn her away."

"Why not?"

He sat down next to Rory and scratched the dog's ears. When he spoke, he sounded drained. Defeated. "I don't love her. But I did. I won't deny it."

"She didn't love you," Brighton pointed out. "Nothing you did was ever good enough for her—until she got divorced and lost her trust fund."

He acknowledged this with a wry smile.

"She doesn't want you. She just wants to take the easy way out—again—by running back to you."

"Yes." He nodded.

"Doesn't that bother you? To know she just wants to use you?"

"Yes."

"But . . . ?"

"She can't do it, Brighton. She can't earn her own money. She can't survive without a safety net."

Brighton just looked at him.

"I know you don't understand."

"You're right—I don't. Getting a job and shopping at Target is not some Greek tragedy. Everybody starts over sometime. Everybody has to struggle."

"No. You do. I do. But Genevieve can't. She doesn't know how. I can't walk away from her when she's begging for help."

"Because you still have feelings for her."

"We have a history."

Genevieve had said the same thing. She had a history with Jake and Brighton didn't. No matter how she felt or what she did, she couldn't alter that fact.

When Jake saw Brighton's expression, he added, "If you called me fifteen years from now, I would help you, too."

"I would never do that," Brighton said softly.

He regarded her with a mix of affection and respect. "I know you wouldn't."

"So what are you going to do?"

"I don't know. I can't throw money at this problem. If I give her money, no matter how much, she'll run through it, and then she'll be back."

"Well, then, I guess that's that. I can live without you and she can't." For a moment, Brighton cursed her own strength, the stubborn practicality that wouldn't allow her to plead with him the way Genevieve would. She was too proud to compromise her principles, too independent to surrender her goals, and so she would lose out to a softer, suppliant woman. Again.

"I don't want Genevieve," he murmured, so close she could feel his breath on her cheek. "I want you."

She could feel her anger melting away. It would be so easy to turn around and indulge in one more night. One more that she would convince herself would be the last. Even as she reached back to cover his hand with hers, she said, "Then tell her to go."

He stilled. "I can't."

Brighton flinched at the raw regret in his voice, and she understood what he could not tell her: He had failed again. He knew that he had hurt her, but he could not heal her. Just as she could not heal him. "Then I don't have anything else to say."

He left without another word. Rory remained at Brighton's feet, snoring softly. Brighton swiveled around in her chair and stared at the door, but all she could see was the glare of the fluorescent light reflected back in the gleaming plate glass.

Let him go. Work through it. She tucked her hair behind her ear and went back to polishing the platinum band.

Five minutes later, her resolve crumbled. She snatched up her phone and dialed. "Hey, it's me. I changed my mind. Can I come over?"

chapter 31

"*Thanks* so much for taking me in." Brighton stood under the porch light along with her massive furry sidekick. "Sorry I woke you up."

"No problem." Kira, squinty eyed and wild haired in her pajamas, waved Brighton into her apartment. "You're always welcome. Who's your friend?"

"This is Rory. He's a sweetie but he does shed, so I understand if you don't want him in your house." Brighton glanced back at her car, wondering where else she could take him at this hour of the night.

"Don't be silly. Bring him in." Kira led the way to the small, cozy kitchen, where she prepared a glass of warm milk for Brighton and a bowl of water for Rory. "So, what's going on?"

"I need you to arm me with the verbal equivalent of a nuclear bomb."

"Yeah, I try to use my powers for good." After she handed out beverages, Kira directed Brighton and Rory to an oversize sofa, then handed out blankets and pillows.

Brighton kicked off her shoes and curled up on the couch. "I'm trying to quit Jake, but willpower alone doesn't seem to be working. At all. Logic's not working, drinking's not working, and work's not working."

Kira wrapped a soft blue afghan around her shoulders. "Work's not working?"

"No. And work *always* works for me. This is officially a crisis."

Kira stifled a yawn. "I hate to sound simplistic—"

"Go ahead," Brighton urged. "The simplest solutions are usually the best."

"—but have you tried just *talking* to him?"

"Yes. It made things worse."

"Oh."

"There's something wrong with me, Kira. I'm too structured, too cautious. Men just keep walking away from me."

"Be kind to yourself." Kira reached over to pat Brighton's foot. "Whatever's going on with Jake has nothing to do with what happened with Colin."

Colin. Brighton was shocked to realize that she hadn't thought about her fiancé in days. Her mind and heart and body had been completely consumed with Jake. She'd been determined to forget all about her ex, and she'd succeeded.

And now she had all new problems.

"Here's my deal," she announced. "I want to cut ties with Jake. Scratch that—*want* has nothing to do with it. I *need* to cut ties with him."

Kira's expression remained totally neutral. "Okay."

"Take your therapist face somewhere else." Brighton scowled. "Just be my friend."

"I am your friend."

"Then as my friend, you have to admit that I'm stuck in a hellish cycle of futility with this guy."

Kira leaned over to grab a box of cookies from the coffee table. "You mean your husband?"

"Don't rub it in." Brighton accepted a gingersnap from her friend. "The man is so emotionally unavailable—"

"Are *you* emotionally available?"

"That's not relevant; we're talking about him. He uses sex as a smokescreen, he uses money as a placeholder for love, he's still hung up on some chick from fifteen years ago . . . and I stand for it. I not only stand for it—I keep going back for more!"

Kira nodded. "I heard about the attorney's office."

"You and everyone else. It would be easier, actually, if he hated me, but he doesn't. He likes me and he wants to spend time with me, but only when it's convenient for him. If some gorgeous ex-wife shows up at the door, party's over. Until he wants to hang out again. And then we have sex and he decamps for the guesthouse. Rinse and repeat until I've lost all sanity and self-respect."

"Is he still really into his ex from fifteen years ago?"

"He says he isn't, but *something's* going on." She tried to explain about Genevieve. "He refuses to let her tough it out in the cold, cruel world on her own. And she still has his grandmother's ring after all these years, even though she was too embarrassed to ever actually wear it because it wasn't five flawless carats from Tiffany. How could he fall in love with someone like that?" Brighton looked at Kira. "Here's the part where you say something deep and meaningful."

Kira patted the patch of sofa next to her and Rory climbed up. "The person we choose as a partner says a lot about how we feel about ourselves."

"We both set ourselves up for failure," Brighton realized. "I'm always going to be too much for him, and he's never going to be enough for me."

"Well then . . ."

"That's it!" Brighton snapped her fingers. "I know exactly what to do to make a clean break forever. You're a great therapist."

"But I didn't even say anything," Kira pointed out.

"If you're this good off duty, I can only imagine how awesome you must be in your office."

Kira nibbled another gingersnap. "Glad I could help."

"It's obvious," Brighton mused. "I *am* emotionally unavailable, and that's just the way he likes it. When I push him away, he pulls me back in. But I know how to end this once and for all."

"You do?" Kira asked in a tone that conveyed she was kind of afraid to ask.

Brighton raised her glass in triumph. "How do you solve a problem like Jake Sorensen? Three little words for the win."

The next morning, Brighton and Kira slept in, took Rory for a romp in the park, and then strolled down to Main Street for brunch at the Jilted Café. The clear skies and calm water imbued Brighton with renewed optimism.

They had to wait five minutes for a table, during which at least a dozen locals approached and said hello to Kira. Many of these strangers politely introduced themselves to Brighton, but they all had a knowing look in their eyes.

As the hostess led them to a table by the front window, Brighton said, "Every single person in here knows about what happened at the attorney's office yesterday, don't they?"

"Yep." Kira settled into the booth and picked up her menu. "But don't worry—there'll be a fresh new scandal to take the heat off you soon enough. Give it a day or two."

"Doesn't matter." Brighton scanned the breakfast offerings. "I'm leaving tomorrow."

"I feel like I've heard that before," Kira teased.

Before Brighton could insist that she really meant it this time, Jenna slid onto the booth with them. "Sorry to interrupt, but I have a question. You deal with lots of engagement rings, right?"

"Yes," Brighton confirmed.

Jenna turned to Kira. "And you deal with lots of relationship problems, right?"

"Yes."

"Then let me ask you guys a hypothetical question."

"Oh boy," Brighton and Kira chorused.

"Let's just say that—hypothetically—you had a customer come in and ask for advice about surprising her boyfriend for a special occasion. But then, a few days later, you overhear the boyfriend talking to one of his buddies about trying to surprise his girlfriend in a similar fashion."

"I'd say that these people are mind-melded freaks of nature," Kira replied.

Brighton gave her a look. "That's helpful."

Kira laughed and reached for her coffee cup. "I can't say more than that without knowing more details."

"I can." Brighton grabbed her purse and nodded at Jenna. "Shall we adjourn to the ladies' room?"

After triple-checking that the restroom stalls were eavesdropper-free, Brighton leaned back against the sink and asked, "Are you by any chance referring to a couple whose initials are L and M?"

Jenna's eyes widened. "Yes. How did you know?"

"Because I'm designing the rings that they're hell-bent on keeping secret from each other."

"Oh, thank God we can talk about this. It's killing me. The pressure! The suspense!" Jenna slumped back against the white tile wall. "Those two have to do everything the hard way."

"It's a quick-draw proposal," Brighton said.

"Well, what should we do? Should we tell one of them to back off?"

Brighton crossed her arms, deliberating. "Which one? And what would our line of reasoning be?" They pondered this for a moment; then Brighton concluded, "We're better off not trying to interfere."

"You're just going to hand over the rings to whoever asks about them first and let the chips fall where they may?"

"That doesn't seem fair, either." More pondering and listening to the faucet drip. "Okay, what about this?" Brighton said. "I'll get the rings ready. You rustle up a bottle of the finest champagne this side of Paris."

"And then?"

"We give them a time and place and let them shoot it out. Battle of the bling. Winner take all."

"Great news." Brighton announced when she joined Lila at the Naked Finger that afternoon. "I finished all the drawings for the poison ring and the bench jeweler said it should be done in a few days. We'll FedEx it to Clea the second the platinum cools." She smiled slyly and reached into her bag. "And more importantly, the ring for Malcolm is done."

"Ooh, gimme!" Lila snatched the box out of Brighton's hand and pried open the lid to examine the strong, simple platinum band. "It's just what I was hoping for. Understated and perfect proportions." She checked the inside of the band for the engraving. "Brighton, this is why you can never leave."

"We're not having that conversation again," Brighton said. "Let's talk about something more uplifting. Namely, the details of your big proposal. How are you going to ask him?"

"You know, I've been thinking about that." Lila nibbled her lower lip. "I kind of wanted to go back to where we had our first date, out by the cliff where we used to have bonfires in high school. The problem is it doesn't exist anymore. A bunch of developers got together, bulldozed it, and threw up a bunch of mansions for rich people."

Brighton made a face. "Boo."

"Yeah." Lila raised one eyebrow. "And guess who lives in the house right where the bonfire pit used to be?"

Brighton took a seat and hooked one arm over the back of the chair. "Could it be . . . the man who ruins everything?"

"Why, yes, it could. Don't Be Koi is sitting smack-dab on the site of our first date."

"Eight thousand square feet of wasted resources," Brighton said. "Do you know he hardly spends any time in that house?"

"Really?"

"Yeah. It's criminal. Have you seen the inside?"

"I waited in the foyer once while Malcolm had to drop something off," Lila said. "It was very *Architectural Digest*."

"The whole house is like that." Brighton got agitated just thinking about it. "Italian linens and custom upholstery and artwork from the trendiest galleries in SoHo."

"Refresh my memory: You're moving out *why*?"

Brighton ignored this. "And he doesn't even appreciate it. He sleeps, works, and hangs out in the guesthouse—which is smaller than the closet in the master suite, by the way—with his dog."

"Jake doesn't have a dog."

"Oh yes, he does. It's some kind of mastiff mix. His name is Rory."

Lila looked supremely skeptical. "*I've* never seen him with a dog."

"Yes, well, that's why his dog is slowly becoming my dog." Brighton smiled as she thought about Rory, who was deeply attached to the fleecy square dog bed she'd bought to save Kira's couch from his nonstop drooling. "*I'm* not afraid of commitment."

"Ooh, a canine love triangle," Lila said. "Good luck with that."

"If you're done mocking me, can we get back to your proposal now?"

"I guess. So the first-date site is out because I don't want to propose to Malcolm in Jake's living room."

"I'm sure Jake would be happy to let you do that. It's not like he's using it."

Lila leaned back against the watch display case. "I'm not asking him to marry me in his boss's living room."

"When you put it that way . . . ," Brighton conceded.

"I want to keep it simple and romantic."

Brighton pretended to rack her brain for ideas. "Maybe you could meet him at the Whinery, have Jenna bring you guys a really nice bottle of champagne, and pop the question. Done."

Lila considered this. "We have had some good times at the Whinery. The night I first got back into town, he got sweat on my sweater."

"Sounds hot."

"You know, it kinda was." Lila fanned her face.

"Talk to Jenna about reserving the place tonight for an hour or two. I'm sure she'd be happy to oblige."

Lila's eyebrows shot up. "Tonight?"

"No time like the present."

"Yeah, but . . ." Lila tilted her head to one side, then the other. "You don't think a proposal at a restaurant with champagne is cheesy? Clichéd?"

"It's classic," Brighton assured her. "Like a little black dress or a strand of pearls."

"Classic," Lila echoed. "Maybe you're right."

"I'm definitely right," Brighton said. "Ask him tonight. No stress, no drama, no agonizing wait."

But Lila couldn't seem to shake the last vestiges of hesitation. "Should I be worried that this all seems too easy?"

"I'm no expert." Brighton sighed. "But I'm pretty sure that this part of love—the falling in love and deciding to get married—is supposed to be easy."

"You're right." Lila brightened and clasped her hands. "I love him so much, Brighton. I hope he says yes."

Brighton gave her a look. "Are you really worried about that?"

"No." Lila flipped her hair. "How could he resist me? He can't. We're meant to be."

"I'm sure you're going to be very happy together. Now, if you'll excuse me, I have to return a client call." She stepped outside and dialed Malcolm's number. "Good news—the ring is ready and it looks beautiful. I took a few photos and I'm texting them to you right now."

"You think she'll like it?" he asked.

"She'll *love* it," Brighton assured him. "The metalwork is perfect and the diamond is gorgeous."

"I hope she says yes."

"How could she resist you? You two are meant to be."

"When can I pick it up?" he asked.

"Yes, about that . . ." Brighton tried to sound brisk and businesslike as she implemented phase two of the plan. "I can't keep it in the safe here, obviously, because I don't want Lila to see it. So I've asked Jenna at the Whinery to keep it in her office safe."

"That's great," Malcolm said. "Because I was planning to propose at the Whinery."

"What a coincidence! This is definitely fate. Tell you what—we'll coordinate our schedules and this will all come together flawlessly."

chapter 32

$\mathcal{B}$righton ran through the dark alley, jumping over puddles and banging her shoulder against the corner of the Dumpster in her haste.

"Ow." She clutched her shoulder, then checked her watch and rapped on the unmarked metal door.

The door opened two inches. A voice whispered, "Did you bring the goods?"

"Yes." Brighton clutched the velvet box in her jacket pocket. "Are the targets en route?"

"They should be here in about five minutes. I've got a bottle of Veuve Clicquot on ice."

"Excellent." Brighton slipped into the Whinery's storeroom, but before the door closed behind her, she heard another voice from the alley: "Hold the door!"

Brighton glanced at Jenna, who looked sheepish.

"Who's that?" Brighton asked.

Summer Benson slipped through the doorway, her eyes gleaming and her cheeks pink with excitement. "Did I miss it? Did I miss it?"

"No." Jenna motioned her inside. "You got here just in time."

"What is she doing here?" Brighton demanded. "No offense."

"None taken," Summer assured her. "I'm here to be a general nuisance and looky-loo." She bounced up and down on the balls of her feet. "What can I say? I'm a sucker for a great love story."

Brighton heard a soft knock at the door, then another voice asking, "Did I miss it?"

"Come on in—you're just in time!" Summer threw one arm around a tall, gangly teenager in an NYU T-shirt. "Brighton, this is Ingrid."

Brighton looked at Jenna. "I thought this operation was top secret."

"It is." Jenna shrugged. "I only told one person—Summer."

"And I only told Ingrid," Summer said.

Everyone looked at Ingrid.

"I didn't tell anyone," the teenager vowed. "Except Lila's mom." She held up her cell phone, which she was using to FaceTime with a brunette who looked like a slightly older, even prettier version of Lila. "She wanted to see this."

"*Bonjour* from Paris, *mes chéries!*" The brunette waved.

Brighton looked around in dismay. "This is not what we planned."

"So we'll move on to Plan B," Jenna said. "Total chaos."

Brighton swallowed all her protests about the need for order and control. She stood back, let the chaos wash over her, and tried to embrace the vibrant, vivacious community that surrounded her.

Summer peeked out into the bar area and hissed, "You guys, you guys, they're here! Shh!"

"Shh!"

"*Shh!*"

The squeals and pleasantries dissolved into everyone shushing one another with maximum lung power. The storeroom sounded like a nest of vipers.

"Now what?" Ingrid whispered. Everyone turned to Brighton. She produced the ring box. "Now we pour the champagne."

With a smooth, practiced efficiency ("I used to be a flight attendant, you know"), Summer filled two champagne flutes and handed them off to Jenna.

"And . . . action." Jenna headed out to the barroom.

The rubberneckers in the back room clustered around the tiny round window in the door, delivering a play-by-play for those who couldn't see:

"She just saw the ring in her glass!"

"He just saw the ring in his."

"They're both shocked . . . they're laughing . . . they're kissing . . ."

"Hold up the phone!" Lila's mother cried via AT&T. "I can't see!"

"Wow. They're still kissing."

"I'd say they're beyond kissing. This is more making out territory."

"Necking?"

"Heavy petting?"

"They're stopping. They're . . . Oh shit, I think they saw us."

Commence giggling and a new round of *shh*-ing.

Lila's voice rang out, loud and clear: "How many people are back there?"

Summer gave everyone a stern look, pressed her finger to her lips, and cracked open the door. "One?"

Brighton had tears in her eyes from trying to suppress her laughter.

"Well, we appreciate the support, but show's over," Lila called. "Skedaddle."

Malcolm was much louder and more direct. "Get out."

Summer yelled back, "Don't you want us to stay and have a celebratory glass of champagne with you guys?"

"*No!*" Malcolm and Lila screamed in unison.

"All right, all right, we can take a hint." Jenna pitched her voice loud enough for everyone to hear. "But before we go, let's set the record straight: Who proposed to who?"

"'Whom,'" Ingrid corrected.

"Is it 'whom'?" Brighton asked. "I can never remember—"

"*Get! Out!*" the newly engaged couple roared.

The looky-loos obliged, filing back into the alley, all atwitter and aglow.

"They're so happy," Ingrid murmured.

"Their kids are going to be gorgeous," Summer predicted.

"I'll have to find something spectacular to wear to the wedding," Lila's mother declared via FaceTime.

Jenna turned to Brighton with a triumphant smile. "We did it. They both got what they wanted, and they're going to live happily ever after."

Brighton tried to smile back. "Does that actually happen in real life?"

"Of course it does."

"Hmm."

"It happens," Jenna assured her. "This town is magical that way."

"I don't believe in magic," Brighton said.

"Stick around." Summer gave her an enigmatic smile. "You will."

Late that night, Brighton tossed and turned on Kira's couch while Rory snored on the floor next to her. Even as her body grew more fatigued, her mind raced with thoughts about what would happen tomorrow when she got into her car and drove back to New Jersey.

She'd been gone for only a few weeks but she couldn't imagine walking back into her office. She couldn't imagine battling morning traffic and stressing over Excel spreadsheets and jogging on a treadmill instead of skateboarding down a hallway.

Jake Sorensen had ruined her for real life.

And she had to leave, but she'd been lying when she told him she had nothing else to say to him.

Her phone rang just as she started to dial his number. The bright, cheery chime and the sight of his name on the screen unleashed a fresh flood of dopamine.

She swallowed hard as she held the phone to her ear. "I have something to tell you."

"I have something to tell you, too," he said. "Genevieve's gone."

Her breath hitched, so loud that she was sure he heard it. "What happened? Did you give her the beach house?"

"No. I thought about what you said and I gave her a job."

Brighton dug her nails into her palm. "So she'll be working with you?"

"She'll be working with Javier," Jake corrected. "In Mexico. She's on the corporate jet right now."

"She's willing to move to Mexico?" Brighton furrowed her brow. "She's willing to *get a job*? What kind of job?"

"That's Javier's call. I told him who she is and what she needs, and he said to send her down. He's taking care of it from this point forward. I'm not involved."

"But how . . . ?" So many missing pieces in this story.

"I get things done." His tone indicated he had concluded that portion of the discussion. "Come over."

I'm leaving town in less than twenty-four hours. What's one more night, give or take?

Despite the distance between them, she felt as though he were right next to her, murmuring into her ear. Before she could protest, she was already up, slipping into her shoes, reaching for her hairbrush so she would look pretty for him. "We said last time was the last time."

He paused. "I never said that."

"I did."

"Come over. I'll do anything you want."

"Anything?" she pressed.

"Anything."

And just like that, she was hoping again. Hoping that this time would be different. But they were still holding back, hedging their bets. Both so afraid of getting hurt that they were hurting each other.

The time had come to go nuclear.

"You want me? You got me." She headed for the bathroom, lipstick in hand. "I'll be there in ten minutes."

chapter 33

"I have to tell you something." Two hours later, Brighton sprawled in the middle of Jake's big white bed, her bare skin bathed in moonlight.

She waited for him to reply, then realized he'd fallen asleep. For a moment, she considered curling up next to him and drifting off, too. Maybe tonight would be the magical moment when everything changed. Maybe tomorrow morning he'd still be here when she woke up.

Or maybe not. She nudged his arm. "Hey."

He stirred and reached for her. "Hmm?"

"I have to tell you something."

He yawned and pulled her back down against him. "Shoot."

She turned her face away from him and took a deep breath. "I love you."

The room went suddenly, totally still. He didn't move. She didn't look at him. The moon shone down with steady, pale light, but the room seemed to go darker.

She said it again, louder this time. "I know it's against our code of conduct to say it, but it's true: I love you. I need you. I can't live without you."

He'd gone so still and silent, she couldn't even tell if he was breathing.

Wait for it . . . Wait for it . . .

There was a chasm between them as black and endless as the ocean stretching out under the clouds. Finally, she couldn't stand the tension any longer. She gave him an easy out. "Could you go grab me some Gatorade, please?"

He left without a word, his steps slow and measured.

And he didn't come back.

Brighton located her phone and kept track of the minutes ticking by. After five minutes passed without any sound from downstairs, she put on her clothes and crept into his closet to retrieve one last item from their time together.

As she tiptoed toward the door, she heard a footfall on the step. She froze, her pulse pounding as she strained to hear.

Another footstep. He was coming up the back staircase.

He was coming back.

Brighton snatched up her shoes and her bag and fled down the front staircase.

chapter 34

"...And so I ran away in the dead of night," Brighton concluded as she poured another glass of orange juice at Kira's house the next morning. "The end."

"Wait, what?" Kira asked. "That's not the end—that's a cliffhanger. To be continued!"

Brighton put down the pitcher and dusted off her palms. "Saying 'I love you' was the equivalent of giving him an invisibility cloak. It was like a Harry Potter novel up in there."

Kira nibbled her bagel. "But he was coming back up."

Brighton studied the countertop. "He was down there freaking out for a long time."

"Maybe he wasn't freaking out," Kira suggested. "Maybe he was just . . . gathering his thoughts."

Brighton's head snapped up. "Why are you defending him?"

"I'm not," Kira swore. "I'm just saying, you've both been through a lot these last few weeks. And then you love bomb him when he least expects it."

"You should have seen him, Kira." Brighton closed her eyes against the memory. "He looked like I'd punched him in the face."

"Maybe he was coming back up to tell you that he loves you, too. Maybe he wanted to have a long, heartfelt chat about his innermost feelings."

Brighton scoffed. "Maybe he was planning to put me on a private jet to Mexico, just like he did with Genevieve."

Kira shrugged. "We'll never know now, since you fled the premises. Why did you do that?"

"I was scared."

"Of what?"

Brighton didn't reply. She didn't want to tell her friend the truth: Of course it would be awful if Jake told her he didn't love her—but it would be truly terrifying if he told her he *did* love her. "Look, it was great, okay? It was . . ." She paused, trying to find the right term for what she had shared with Jake. "A whirlwind romance. The kind I never thought I'd have."

"Aww."

"But it was temporary. It had to end and I ended it." She waved one hand around, indicating the whole town of Black Dog Bay. "None of this is really who I am."

"Except the jewelry-designer part," Kira said.

"I'm an actuary," Brighton said firmly. "That's my real job in my real life, which I will be returning to this afternoon. In fact"—she glanced at the clock on the microwave—"I should get on the road."

"Have you told Lila you're going?"

"Yes. She keeps claiming I'll never actually leave, but she's going to have to make her peace with it. Because I can't stay here without backsliding every time my phone rings. I have to make a clean break." Brighton got out of her chair and carried her dishes to the sink. "Although, um, I took something of his before I left."

Kira's jaw dropped. "You're keeping souvenirs like a serial killer?"

"I'm a junkie, not a serial killer," Brighton corrected. "And I'm not keeping it." She showed Kira the antique watch she'd liberated from Jake's closet the night before. "I'm going to finish restoring it. Then I'll send it back to him."

Kira just looked at her.

"Fine, I'm a *codependent* junkie. I can't stand to think of it moldering away in a drawer for another decade. I can fix timepieces, unlike people, with my love and attention." Brighton got to her feet and collected her bag. "I'm going. Here I go."

Kira walked her to the door. "Drive safe."

"I always do."

They hugged and headed out to the white Subaru. Rory followed them and plunked himself down next to the driver's-side door.

"What do you want me to do about him?" Kira asked.

"I guess I should take him back to the guesthouse where he doesn't officially live." Brighton kissed that giant, furry head, then unlocked the car door. Rory leaped in and somehow managed to wriggle over the console into the backseat. He stared at Brighton, tongue lolling and tail wagging.

"I think he wants to go with you," Kira said.

"I want him to go with me, too." Brighton nibbled her lower lip. "But I can't kidnap Jake's dog. That's unconscionable."

"I wouldn't exactly call this kidnapping," Kira said. "He's clearly a willing volunteer."

They both regarded the slobbering beast with the golden eyes of an angel.

"Jake did say I could have anything I wanted," Brighton mused.

"I think if you want the dog that much, he'd want you to have him," Kira said. "And he *did* refer to him as a squatter."

Brighton slipped into the driver's seat and turned on the car's ignition. "I'll text him to let him know Rory's joining me. Once I'm safely across state lines."

She closed her eyes and held on to the warm steering wheel, hoping that if she could just hold her breath and wait long enough, the pain would recede.

Kira rapped on the window. "Everything okay?"

"Everything's fine." Brighton opened her eyes, glanced at the gas gauge, checked her mirrors, and started back to the land of corporate meetings and ten-year plans. As she merged onto the highway, abiding by all traffic signs and speed limits, she waited for a rush of relief that never came.

chapter 35

An envelope from Black Dog Bay arrived four weeks later.

Brighton rushed into her building at seven thirty on Friday evening, her feet blistered from a new pair of pumps, her stomach growling from a workday so busy that she hadn't eaten lunch, and her eyes itchy and dry from hours of staring at a computer monitor. She was desperate to go to the bathroom, eat something, and make sure that the dog walker had taken Rory for the extra afternoon outing she'd requested.

But first she had to get the mail. That was her daily routine, the one she was trying so hard to resume. If she could get her body and brain back into her old schedule, her heart would follow. Eventually. Hopefully. Frazzled and impatient, she stopped at the bank of little brass doors in her building's lobby and twisted her key in the lock. Amid a stack of bills and credit card offers, she found a lavender envelope sealed with purple wax and bearing a Delaware postmark.

She didn't recognize the shaky, spindly handwriting. Someone in

Black Dog Bay was reaching out, but not the person she most wanted to hear from. A month after she'd left the town limits, little pieces of her screw-up summer were still drifting back, reminding her of everything she'd left undone.

Jake hadn't contacted her since she'd sent the text informing him she'd absconded with Rory. His silence could be interpreted in a million different ways. Maybe he was angry. Maybe he was mounting a high-powered legal defense team to reclaim his dog. Maybe he'd already moved on to the next woman at the Whinery.

Most likely, he'd taken the next logical step and followed up with the divorce attorney. Every day, she expected a process server to arrive at her office with the separation papers, but nothing so far.

He didn't file and she didn't file, and so they remained in marital limbo. Not together, not apart, with no resolution in sight.

As always, Rory greeted her at the door with frantic, slobbery enthusiasm. While he shed all over her suit and sat on her briefcase, Brighton kicked off her shoes and prepped a high-protein dinner of chicken and goat cheese vinaigrette. After she brought her dishes to the sink, she grabbed the lavender envelope, settled into the sofa, and kicked her feet up on her IKEA coffee table. She broke through the wax seal and pulled out a clipping from a publication called the *Wilmington Social Record*. The paper was thick and rich and featured a black-and-white photograph of a dark, handsome groom and a beautiful blond bride on a beach.

"A Whirlwind Romance," the caption read. "Ms. Genevieve Van Petten, daughter of Russell and Jacqueline Van Petten, married Javier Mendoza of Mexico City after a brief courtship. The couple met when the bride, a philanthropist with a degree in art history, agreed to consult with Mr. Mendoza's resort development firm. 'As soon as we locked eyes at the airport,' the bride gushed, 'we just knew.' The couple plan to move to Manhattan, where they will host a reception for family and friends."

After rereading the announcement five times, Brighton snatched up her phone, dialed Kira, and relayed the story to her friend. "She went down there four weeks ago and they're already married!"

"Seems to be a lot of that going around," Kira observed.

Brighton rolled her eyes. "When *I* do it, it's different."

"Oh, okay."

Brighton squinted down at the photo, trying to discern the details. "She has a veil and a bouquet and a diamond ring that could plug the hole in the ozone layer. This was not some drunken night in Vegas. Someone coordinated this whole thing with military precision."

"She moves fast," Kira said. "Guess she'd rather marry the guy than work for him."

"Hasn't she heard the expression 'Marry for money, earn every penny'?" Brighton tsk-tsked.

"I'm going to go out on a limb and say she doesn't care. But I do wonder what the guy was thinking. He's a friend of Jake's, right?"

Brighton had an immediate physical reaction to the mere mention of his name. She closed her eyes against a wave of loss and longing. "He did mention that Javier was hell-bent on breaking into East Coast society. And now he's married to a Van Petten who will get him into every polo tournament and yacht club. He got the society connections he wanted, she got the cash flow she needed. A win-win transaction."

Kira's tone softened. "So how's your reentry to the real world?"

"Everything's just the way I left it: a slow, gray march toward death fueled by coffee and fluorescent lighting." Brighton heaved a melodramatic sigh, then laughed. "No, it's fine. It's nice to see my work friends again, and I'm up for promotion. How's everything in Black Dog Bay?"

"Everything's just the way you left it. Small-town scandal galore."

Brighton's smile faded. "I miss it."

"Come back anytime," Kira offered. "My house is your house."

"I can't. I'll relapse." Brighton knew she shouldn't ask the next question, but she couldn't seem to stop herself. "Do you ever see him?"

Kira paused. "Who?"

"Who do you think? Jake Sorensen, my legally wedded husband."

"I see him around from time to time."

Brighton put her feet on the floor and sat up straight. "And?"

"I have to go, Brighton. My next client's here."

"Yeah, okay. Bye." Brighton hung up, but she couldn't seem to put the phone down. She wanted to call him; she wanted to hear his voice. Her chest literally ached from missing him.

But nothing had changed. He still couldn't love her and she still couldn't trust herself not to love him.

She put the phone in the kitchen so she wouldn't be tempted, then retreated to her bedroom and pulled the antique Patek Philippe watch out of her nightstand drawer. Every night before she went to bed, she cleaned and calibrated, but it still wasn't perfect. The stainless steel case had a chip on one edge of the dial casing; the piece would never look brand-new again. But it was still beautiful. She'd poured her heart and soul into the project, attending to every detail and using the polished steel as an outlet for all the words she couldn't bring herself to say.

The time had come to let go and give this piece of his past back to him. She would return his priceless antique Swiss watch—the Jake Sorensen equivalent of returning a T-shirt and photos after a breakup.

She packed the watch carefully in layers of tissue and cardboard and Bubble Wrap, then addressed the package to Don't Be Koi. She hoped he would wear it and appreciate it.

She hoped that he would remember the good when he saw it, even though it meant good-bye.

chapter 36

After she mailed the package the next day, Brighton took Rory to the dog park. Even though it was a bright Saturday morning with a crisp hint of autumn in the air, she planned to spend the afternoon in her home office putting the finishing touches on a presentation on insurance premium trends. She checked her e-mails on her phone while Rory galumphed around on the grass, drooling and trying to play with a boisterous little terrier.

"Okay, boy, let's go." After Rory climbed into the car, Brighton buckled him into his canine safety harness. The massive dog submitted with world-weary patience while she snapped the straps into place. "I know you hate these, buddy, but rules are rules. Safety first."

Her phone dinged and she glanced at the screen, expecting another e-mail about upcoming client meetings and conference calls. Instead, she saw a text from Lila:

Go look at the cover of the new issue of People magazine.
CALL ME!!!

Brighton stopped at the nearest drugstore, hurried in . . . and almost fainted when she saw the cover. The headline read, STARTING OVER WITH STYLE, and the photo featured a gorgeous, glossy close-up of Clea Cole resting her chin on her hand . . . which was adorned with the diamond-encrusted poison ring.

So this is what it feels like to have a childhood dream come true. She couldn't process all the emotions coursing through her, and there was only one person she wanted to talk to right now.

But she couldn't call him.

So instead, after buying a copy of the magazine, rushing back to the parking lot, and doing a wild, flailing car-dance while Rory whined with concern, she dialed Lila.

"Oh my God," was how Lila answered the phone. "Did you see? Did you see?"

"I saw!" Brighton launched into another bout of car-dancing.

"Did you read the article?" Lila pressed.

"No." Brighton opened the magazine with such enthusiasm, she tore the cover in half. "What's it say?"

"She talks about Black Dog Bay and why she decided to put the diamond dog on the ring. She mentions the Naked Finger by name!"

"Oh my . . . That is . . . I can't even . . ."

"*I know!*" Lila was practically hyperventilating. "I'm already getting calls for new orders. Poison rings are going to be the new A-list breakup accessory."

Brighton skimmed the article, her smile widening with every paragraph. "I'm so thrilled for you."

"Be happy for yourself," Lila said. "Like I said, the phone is ringing off the hook. I need you back here right now."

"Oh, Lila." Brighton was surprised at the depth of her regret. "I can't. I wish I could, but I can't." Her throat tightened and she didn't trust herself to say more.

"Will you at least help me find a new designer?" Lila asked. "I need someone with an eye for quality and really high standards."

"Of course."

"Great!" Lila responded with such speed and enthusiasm, Brighton had to wonder if she'd just walked into some sort of trap. But Lila would never do that. Lila was too sweet for any kind of ambush or trickery . . . right?

"I'm going to make some calls and ask for recommendations," Lila continued. "I should be able to set up a few interviews this week. Will you sit in on them and give your opinion?"

Brighton thought about how it would feel to drive back down to the shore. The white clapboard sign with the black Labrador welcoming her to Black Dog Bay. The shops on Main Street. The smell of the ocean.

That huge, empty mansion by the beach.

"I'm really busy at work," she said.

"Don't give me that. You're coming," Lila declared. "And after we take care of business, we're going to celebrate our soon-to-be fame and fortune at the Whinery, so wear something fun."

Brighton looked down ruefully at her conservative outfit. "How about a button-down blouse and a knee-length skirt?"

"Let's not get crazy," Lila teased. "I don't want to get arrested."

Brighton smiled. "Hey, did you by any chance send me a clipping?"

"Like, a newspaper clipping?" Lila sounded genuinely bewildered. "No. Why?"

"Someone sent me an announcement from some fancy publication called the *Wilmington Social Record*."

"Never heard of it, but it sounds like something one of the summer residents would read," Lila suggested. "The only local who's into that kind of thing is Hattie Huntington."

"Ah."

"What did it say?"

Brighton recounted the epic love story of Genevieve and Javier.

"She'd rather marry a stranger than get a job?" Lila marveled. "That's dedication."

"The woman knows what she wants and she's not afraid to go after it." Brighton dabbed Rory's jowls with a tissue in an effort to salvage the leather seats. "There's something to be said for that."

"So Friday, two p.m." Lila sounded threatening.

"I have a meeting on Friday morning," Brighton protested.

"Skip it. If you're not here, I'm sending my bounty hunter, aka Malcolm."

Brighton hesitated. "Wait. Before you go, there's something I have to ask you. Is, um, is Jake still in town?"

"I'm not sure. I haven't seen him since you left. He stopped going to the Whinery altogether. Jenna is in mourning."

Brighton said her good-byes, then started reading the magazine article again. Before she made it to the second page, her phone chimed again. This time the text was from her mother:

GREAT NEWS, sweetie! So proud. Call me.

Brighton dialed right away. As soon as she heard her mother's "Hello?" she launched into a breathless rush of words: "Did you read it, Mom?"

"Read what?" her mother asked.

Brighton deflated a bit. "The magazine article."

"What magazine? What are you talking about?"

"I thought that . . ." Brighton frowned. "Isn't that the great news you just texted me about?"

"No." Now it was her mother's turn to get excited. "The great news is, I got a new job."

Again? Brighton braced herself. "That is great. Where is it?"

"Right here in town. I'm the set designer for the college's production of *Pippen*."

"Really?" Brighton decided this was not the time to point out that her mother had zero experience in theater.

"They heard about me from one of my old students." Her mother sounded so thrilled. "They practically begged me to interview. See? See what happens when you follow your passion?"

Brighton tucked the magazine under her arm and watched the traffic zoom by. "I hope they're paying you what you're worth."

"Oh, honey, money doesn't matter when you're an artist. Speaking of which, I just got a letter from the IRS and I can't make heads or tails of it."

Brighton froze. "The IRS?"

"Something about my tax return from last year." There was a rustling of papers on her mother's end of the line. "I know I have it here somewhere . . ."

"I'll wait," Brighton said.

"Maybe it's in the other room. Anyway, can I send it to you? You always know just what to do with these things."

Brighton closed her eyes and pinched the bridge of her nose. "Scan it and e-mail it to me right now. I'll take care of it."

"You're such a good daughter. I never have to worry about you. Now, finish telling me about the article you were mentioned in. Did you get interviewed for one of those fancy business magazines?"

Brighton was still trying to recover from the mention of "IRS." "Guess again."

Her mother gasped. "The *Wall Street Journal*?"

"You're getting colder."

"*Forbes?* The *New York Times?*"

"Freezing. Ice-cold."

"Well, give a set designer a hint!"

"Stop at the grocery store, Mom. Pick up *People*, look at the ring on the cover, and prepare to be prouder of me than you've ever been."

"Why? What did you do?"

Brighton patted the magazine just to make sure all of this was really happening. "Something wildly impractical."

"Ooh, I *am* proud of you."

Brighton laughed. "You don't even know what it is."

"I trust you, honey. And it's time you learned to trust yourself. What's the point of being alive if you don't take a few risks now and then?"

chapter 37

$\mathcal{B}$righton was stuck in traffic on the New Jersey Turnpike, patiently waiting for her turn in a zipper merge, when her office mate Claudia called.

She pressed the button on the steering wheel to activate the car's hands-free phone system. "Hello?"

"Where are you?" Claudia sounded a bit frantic.

"Um . . ."

"Home, right? Francine said you had the flu."

Brighton knew that the sound of honking horns and construction vehicles must be audible on the other end of the connection. Not to mention Rory's heavy breathing from the backseat. "Why do you ask?"

"You picked the wrong day to call in sick, babe."

"Why? What's going on? Was the meeting—"

"Forget the meeting, Brighton." Claudia lowered her voice. "The best-looking man in the world is at the reception desk, asking for you."

Brighton inhaled sharply. "Did you happen to catch his name?"

"I believe it's Torrid McSwelterson."

Brighton reached back and rested her hand on Rory's giant head. The feel of his warm, coarse fur helped to calm her. "Would you please ask him what he wants?"

"No," Claudia whispered. "He's so attractive that I can't even talk to him. I have hottie-induced muteness."

"Fight through it," Brighton urged. "I need you to find out what he wants."

"Is that her?" She heard Jake's voice on the other end of the line. Rory must have recognized it, too, because he lifted his head and stopped panting.

Claudia didn't speak, but she must have nodded, because Jake said, "Find out where she is."

"I can hear him," Brighton told her friend. "And I'm stuck in a traffic jam on the turnpike. I'm on my way to Delaware. The jewelry store."

Claudia finally recovered her power of speech and relayed this information to Jake, who commanded, "Tell her I'll meet her there."

Moments later, Claudia snapped back to her usual confident self. "Brighton."

"I heard."

"You met that guy in *Delaware*?"

"Yes."

"Are they doing experiments with genetically engineered male models down there or what?"

"Stay with me, Claudia. What did he want? How did he seem?"

"He wants to talk to you. He seems very determined. And he had something in his hand."

"What was it?" *Did it look like divorce papers?*

"I don't know. I was too busy looking at his eyes and his mouth and his hair and his—"

Brighton gave up trying to get any answers out of her friend. She ended the call and surveyed the gridlock in front of her. The next exit was only a few yards ahead. She could get off the highway and turn back . . . or she could keep going and see Jake again.

Reaching for her turn signal, she felt the same rush of terror that she'd had when she'd heard his footsteps on the stairs that last night in his dark, empty mansion by the sea. But this time she refused to run away.

She put her left hand back on the steering wheel and made a decision to hope. To love without fear of getting hurt. To desire with her whole heart and believe that he could do the same.

The little red Prius next to her slowed to let her into the merging lane of cars. She turned the wheel and took her foot off the brake as the road ahead of her started to clear.

For better or worse, everything was about to change again.

Jake, leaning against the side of his gray pickup, was waiting for her when she arrived at the Naked Finger. He held an orange dog leash in one hand and a small black box in the other.

Brighton put the car in park and took a moment to collect herself before getting out. She wasn't ready for this, but she didn't need to be—it was already happening. Life and love were trickling in despite all her defenses.

She shielded her eyes from the midday sun with one hand as she opened the driver's-side door. "How did you get here before me?"

He straightened up and gave her that rakish smile. "I have my ways. You know this."

"And why do you have a leash? You don't have a dog."

"Yes, I do." He jerked his chin toward the Subaru's backseat, where Rory was writhing with glee.

Brighton opened the hatchback, and Rory leaped out and barreled directly into Jake's knees.

"He's my dog," she insisted, but her words lacked conviction.

"He's *my* dog." Jake leaned down to pat Rory's side.

"You can get another dog," Brighton tried. "You can buy any dog you want."

"I want *this* dog. We've had some great times together." Jake clipped the leash onto Rory's collar.

Brighton came closer to examine the orange nylon. "Is that a fancy handcrafted leash from Hermès?"

"Six bucks from Target." When he straightened up, she noticed the glint of stainless steel on his wrist.

"I see you got the watch."

"Yesterday." He unbuckled the brown strap, motioned her closer, and flipped the watch over to examine the smooth metal on the back of the case. "You didn't engrave it."

"Well," she said, inching closer, trying to breath in his clean, woodsy scent without being too obvious about it, "that's not really my place."

"I want you to engrave it." He pressed the watch into her palm. The metal was still warm from the heat of his body. "I want to start the heirloom thing with you."

She closed her fingers around the steel and leather and held on tightly.

He lowered his head and murmured into her hair. "It's going to be part of our history."

"Do you want me to cry?" She dabbed at her eyes.

"I don't want you to cry." He pulled her into his arms. "I want you to marry me." He opened her hand again and replaced the watch with the little black box. "Brighton Smith, will you do me the honor of not divorcing me?"

She opened the lid with trembling fingers to discover a small, round orange gemstone mounted on a dainty platinum band.

She glanced up at him. "Is that a Mexican fire opal?"

Jake nodded and slipped the ring onto her finger. It fit perfectly.

"I love it." She stretched out her arm, admiring the jewel. Then she looked back at his face. "What changed?"

"You left."

She ducked her head. "Yeah, about that—"

He slid his finger under her chin. "I didn't know what that meant. But then you sent the watch, and I had a realization: I love you. I need you. I can't live without you."

She gave up trying to hold back her tears.

"I've been trying to plan all these grand gestures that don't involve money. That's harder than you might think."

She looked at the six-dollar dog leash. "But you did it."

"Are you saying yes?" he demanded.

It wasn't the kind of ring she expected. It wasn't the kind of proposal she would have planned. But it was perfect. "Yes."

They kissed as passionately as they could, given that a pony-size dog was trying to worm his way in between them.

"But wait—there's more." Jake took her hand and turned it so she could see the side of the ring.

Brighton looked closer and saw that the ring, while deceptively simple and tasteful from the top view, had a little symbol on the side gallery. Instead of plain metal prongs, there was intricately detailed scrollwork.

She started to laugh as she examined the tiny silhouetted outlines in orange and green pavé sapphires. "It's a bottle of Gatorade." She stopped staring at her ring and went back to staring at him. "You put a ton of thought and effort into this."

He leaned down to scratch Rory's ears. "Without love, it's just rock and metal."

She couldn't stop admiring the ring. "I guess we should call the attorney and tell him we'll never be filing the separation papers." She lowered her hand and smiled mischievously. "Although . . ."

Jake quirked an eyebrow. "I'm listening."

"We could go back to Vegas."

"Vow renewal?"

"Exactly. But this time, do it right." She stood up, envisioning her ideal wedding. "No drunken shenanigans at the drive-through. We'll take our time and plan a real ceremony with a real dress and a real cake and a real commitment. Something *meaningful*."

He nodded, his expression serious. "So . . . Elvis?"

She pointed two fingers at her eyes, then his, to indicate their psychic link. "Soul mates."

Three months later

"*D*id I pack the blue suede shoes?" Brighton huddled into her soft cashmere turtleneck and surveyed the pile of luggage on the tarmac. Sunlight dappled the pavement as a patch of clouds drifted by overhead.

"Yes." Jake slid one arm around her waist and urged her up the steps and into the jet. "You packed the blue suede shoes. You packed everything."

Rory bounded up behind them, trotted over to his favorite leather seat, and curled up for a nap.

"I feel like I forgot something." Brighton pulled her packing list out of her pocket and scanned the text. "Let's see: I packed my gown, your suit, Rory's stuffed bunny . . ."

Jake took the list away. "If we forgot something, we'll buy it in Vegas, Type A."

She bit her bottom lip. "I'm going to Type A you later."

"I look forward to it."

She buckled into the same seat she'd sat in on their first flight to Vegas, but something was off. She couldn't quite get comfortable.

Jake picked up on her distress and went into problem-solving mode. "What?"

She furrowed her brow. "We're doing this all wrong."

He leaned forward. "Explain."

"Well, we're all packed, we've reserved a penthouse suite, we booked a chapel . . ."

"Yeah?"

"But it's broad daylight. And also, we're sober."

"Brighton. Do you really think I'd take you to Vegas with a case of champagne?" He looked wounded. "I came prepared, but it's a five-hour flight. Pace yourself."

"Oh." She sighed with relief. "That's better."

He went to talk to the pilot and when he returned, she handed him the large beribboned box she'd carried on board with her. "Here, I bought you a wedding present. I was going to give it to you after the ceremony, but I can't wait."

He accepted the box with a mix of gratitude and confusion. "You didn't have to get me anything."

"Yes, I did."

"I don't need anything."

"Yes, you do. Open it."

Jake untied the bow and peeled off the silver wrapping paper. He kept glancing up at her, searching for cues. Then he lifted the flaps of a brown cardboard carton to reveal . . . "It's a Windbreaker."

"Lined, insulated, waterproof, and virtually windproof." She pointed out the hidden zippers in the bright blue jacket's seams. "Look, you can put hand warmers in the pockets."

"Thanks?" He sounded so bewildered, she had to laugh.

"Keep going," she instructed.

He pulled out a pair of hiking boots, a heavy-duty flashlight, and a coffee table book on log cabin interiors.

"After Vegas, we're going to Montana," she announced. "You'll finally get to see all that acreage you own. Fresh air. Babbling brooks. Park ranger role-play. It'll be hot." She leafed through the pages of the log cabin book. "And you can start thinking about what kind of house you'd like to build. For *us*, not for resale value. I did a bit of research and found some names of architects who design lodges and cabins up there. We can meet with two or three of them while we're up there. Oh, and check this out." She found the little canister at the very bottom of the box.

He read the label and started to laugh. "Bear repellant?"

"You laugh now, but you'll thank me when you're staring into the glistening maw of a grizzly on some backwoods trail."

He turned the canister over to read the label. "They still have grizzlies in Montana?"

"Yep. According to my research, grizzlies are recolonizing some of the grassland up there. They also have black bears, mountain lions, bobcats, and lynx, although the thing you really have to watch out for is moose."

He put the book and the canister aside. "According to your research."

"You mock my research, but I'm going to build you your dream house and save you from a bloodthirsty moose."

"I would never mock your research."

"Then why are you looking at me that way?"

"I'm not looking at you. I'm kissing you." And then he was.

Across the cabin, Rory sat up and whined, pressing his nose against the little round window.

Brighton got up to see what he was looking at. When she put her head next to his and glanced out the window, she saw a huge shaggy black dog standing on the edge of the tarmac.

"Is that . . ." She reached for her handbag, digging for her phone so she could take a photo.

But when she looked back, the black dog was gone. Rory wagged his tail and gave her a conspiratorial canine smile.

She rejoined her husband, who was poring over pictures of log cabins. "It's official—*now* you have everything you need. Including bear repellant."

"Then, let's go. We'll beat the house at blackjack, honeymoon in Montana, and live happily ever after."

"Happily ever after," she agreed. "Against all odds."

"A statistical anomaly?"

"Also known as true love."

put a *ring* on it

BETH KENDRICK

QUESTIONS
FOR DISCUSSION

1. Brighton and Colin have a huge fight about a zipper merge that, you know, isn't really about a zipper merge. What small things do people do (or not do) that ultimately turn into deal breakers?

2. Does love at first sight exist? How long should people know each other before making a major commitment such as marriage?

3. Are there friendships in your life that you can pick up right where you left off after months or years apart? What makes those relationships so resilient?

4. It's karaoke night at the Whinery. What are you singing at the top of your lungs?

5. Brighton and Jake have very different perspectives on money, stability, and spending. Does the way we think about money say a lot about the way we view ourselves?

6. If you were Jake Sorensen–level rich, would you work? What would you do?

7. Do you have the equivalent of "twelve-dollar strawberries" in your own life? What items or events are worth splurging on?

8. Brighton tells Jake she loves him, then flees when she hears him coming back up the stairs. What do you think he would have said to her that night if she'd stayed?

9. Will Genevieve and Javier have a successful marriage? How would they define "successful"?

10. If you could design a piece of jewelry to mark a significant event in your life, what would it look like and what kinds of materials would you use?

11. If you were going to write a follow-up story about Kira, what would her story be?

brighton smith's official screw-up summer playlist

"Settlin'"—Sugarland

"Single Ladies (Put a Ring on It)"—Beyoncé

"Waking Up in Vegas"—Katy Perry

"Can't Stop"—MoZella

"A Sky Full of Stars"—Coldplay

"You Go to My Head"—Ella Fitzgerald

"Can't Buy Me Love"—The Beatles

"Keep It to Yourself"—Kacey Musgraves

"Fool's Gold"—Fitz and the Tantrums

"Gravity"—Sara Bareilles

"(Sittin' On) The Dock of the Bay"—Otis Redding

"Bright"—Echosmith

"Blue Suede Shoes"—Elvis Presley

Don't miss Beth Kendrick's charming novel

new uses
for *old* boyfriends

Available from New American Library

chapter 1

The last thing Lila did on her way out of town was sell her wedding rings.

When she arrived at the pawnshop, she looked flawless—she'd made sure of that before she left her custom-built brick house for the last time. Her honey blond hair was freshly straightened, her nails impeccably manicured, her blush and mascara tastefully applied. Her blouse matched her skirt, her shoes matched her handbag, and her bra matched her panties because, as her mother had always reminded her, if a terrible accident should ever befall her in a grocery store parking lot, she would be on display to a whole team of paramedics and hospital workers.

But as she pulled her diamond rings out of her purse, all Lila could think about were the things that didn't look right. The dark roots that were starting to show where her hair parted. The visible tension in her face from months of clenching her jaw at night. The pale stripe on her finger where her rings had been. And even worse than the flaws she couldn't hide were the ones she could. Out in the parking lot, her white luxury SUV awaited. Spotless and brand-new and jam-packed with the last remnants of her life she'd managed to salvage from the divorce.

For a solid two minutes, Lila kept her hands in the pockets of her stylish rose pink trench coat and listened to soft jazz on the sound system while the store employee scrutinized every facet of the diamonds. Beneath the glass display case, rows of rings sparkled in the light, each one representing a promise exchanged by two people coming together in trust and faith and hope. Lila tried to imagine the men who had proposed with these rings: rich and poor, old and young, each of them in love with a woman they believed to be as unique and dazzling as these jewels.

And they had all ended up here: the relationship boneyard. An "estate jewelry" storefront sandwiched between a dry cleaner and a pet groomer in a suburban strip mall.

The clerk finally looked up, clicking her tongue. "The setting's very dated, but the stone itself is decent."

Lila blinked. "Dated? Decent? That ring was on the back cover of *Elle* magazine the month I got engaged."

"And how long ago was that?"

"Well. Seven years." Lila squinted to read the employee's name tag and tried a different approach. "Norma. I appreciate that you have a business to run and a family to support, but look at the cut and color of this diamond! The stone was imported from Antwerp, the setting is really quite classic—"

"If I've learned one thing in this business, it's that everything goes out of style eventually." The saleswoman lowered her loupe and tilted her head, her gaze shrewd. "The whole 'timeless classic' line? It's a marketing myth."

"But the cut." Lila cleared her throat. "It's exquisite."

Norma lifted one corner of her mouth. "Do you happen to have the GIA certification papers?"

"Not anymore." Lila knew she was being assessed for weakness. How desperate was she for cash? How much did she value this touchstone of her past?

What was the bare minimum she would accept?

She should lift her chin and meet the other woman's gaze, but she couldn't. She'd been completely depleted—of confidence, of certainty, of the will to stand up for herself.

"We can sell the diamond, but the setting will have to be melted down and refashioned." Norma put on her glasses, picked up her pen, and wrote a few numbers down on the pad in front of her. "Here's what I can offer you."

Lila glanced down at the figure and swallowed back a sigh.

"I know it's probably not what you were hoping for, but the fact is, diamonds just don't hold their value." Norma's tone was both apologetic and insincere.

"But that's less than a third of what my husband paid for it." Lila hated how tentative and soft she sounded. Then she corrected herself. "My *ex*-husband, I mean." She flattened her palm on the cool glass case and tried to rally as she stared at the number written on the pad.

You can do this.

She knew better than to accept an opening offer. She needed to negotiate.

You have to do this.

But she glanced up at the jeweler through lowered eyelashes, her eyes watering and her lip trembling. All the fight had been drained out of her. The spark inside had flickered out.

"I . . ." Lila trailed off, cleared her throat, forced herself to start again. "I'll take it." The amount wasn't enough to save her, but she needed every bit of cash she could get right now. So she let go of all her old hopes and dreams and prepared to take the money.

Norma half smiled, half sneered. "Let me write you a check."

An electronic chime sounded as the shop's door opened; then a shrill feminine voice rang out. "Holy crap! You're Lila McCune. I love you! I'm your biggest fan. Marilyn Waters." A short, wind-blown woman in a green turtleneck shook Lila's hand, squeezing tightly. "I can't believe this! Do you live around here?"

"Until recently." *Like this morning.*

Marilyn turned to the jeweler and demanded, "Did you know she's a celebrity?"

Norma's sneer got a little sneerier. "No."

Lila bowed her head. "Oh, I'm not really—"

"She was the late-night host of my favorite shopping channel for three years." Marilyn turned back to Lila. "You probably don't recognize my voice, but we've spoken on the air. I called in a few times, and you were so nice. You made me feel good about myself when I was fat and hormonal and losing my damn mind."

Lila was beaming as she struggled to reclaim her hand. "It's a pleasure to meet you in person—I love connecting with callers. What were some of your favorite items?"

"Oh, Lord, I bought so many things. When I was up with my first baby, I watched you every single night. I was exhausted and healing from a third-degree tear, but your show was really soothing. This woman can sell anything to anyone," Marilyn informed the jeweler. "Crystal Christmas tree ornaments and fancy French sauté pans and this amazing cream that gets rid of the calluses on your heels. Works like magic. Would it be okay if I take a quick picture with you?"

"Of course." Lila summoned her cheeriest, camera-ready smile.

"One more, just in case." Marilyn clicked her camera phone three times in rapid succession. "I can't wait to put this up on Instagram! My sisters are going to be so jealous."

While Marilyn fiddled with her phone, Lila sidled over to Norma and murmured, "Make the check out to Lila Alders, please. A-L-D-E-R-S."

Norma raised one finely penciled brow. "I thought you were Lila McCune?"

"I was. Now I'm back to my maiden name."

Marilyn clicked off social media and rejoined the conversation. "So, what happened, Lila? You're not on the air anymore."

"My contract was up, and, um, my agent and I decided it was time to transition." Lila's jaw ached. "I'm exploring some new opportunities."

"Ooh! Like what?"

"Like . . ." Lila had never been so happy to hear her phone ring. "Would you please excuse me for a moment? I have to take this." She pressed the phone to her ear and walked toward the front window. "Hi, Mom."

"Where are you right now?" her mother demanded.

"I'm at the engagement ring boneyard."

"The where?"

"I'm selling my rings."

Her mother made a little sound of disappointment. "So you won't be here for dinner?"

"No. Sorry I'm running late; it took me forever to pack up the car and then I had to drop by my attorney's office to pay off my balance."

"Well, now you can put it all behind you." There was a pause on her mother's end of the line. "Did you get a good price for the rings, at least?"

"No." Lila forced herself to relax as her temple started throbbing.

"How much?" Her mother's voice stayed light and airy, but Lila detected an urgent undertone. "Approximately?"

"Why do you ask?"

"Oh, no reason." Another pause. "We'll talk about it when you get here."

"Talk about what?"

"Nothing. Drive safe, sweet pea. I can't wait to see you." Her mother hung up before Lila could say anything else.

When Lila returned to the glass counter, Marilyn was frowning and nibbling her lower lip while Norma examined a hair comb fashioned of tarnished metal.

Lila stepped closer to Marilyn and asked, "What's that?"

"It's a hair comb," Norma said flatly.

"It belonged to my great-aunt," Marilyn confided. "And her mother before her. It's not really my style, but I thought maybe we could find a buyer who would really appreciate it. Stuff like this should be worn, you know? Doesn't do me any good collecting dust in a drawer."

"It's beautiful." Lila peered over Norma's shoulder. The comb was shaped like a flower atop two thin prongs. "What's it made of?"

"Steel. Dates back to the early eighteen hundreds." Norma sounded disapproving. "Not interested."

Marilyn's whole body folded in a bit. "But it's vintage."

Norma remained impassive. "Worth a hundred bucks, max. Try listing it on eBay."

Marilyn took back her family heirloom with evident shame.

"Well, *I* love it." Lila straightened her shoulders. She ran her fingers along the faceted edges of the flower's petals. The steel had been cut like a gemstone, designed to look dainty despite its strength.

"You do?" Marilyn's voice was barely a whisper.

"Absolutely. Tell you what—I'll give you two hundred dollars for it." Lila opened her wallet, realized her current net worth stood at thirty-seven dollars and three maxed-out credit cards, and closed her wallet. "Let me go cash this check really quick."

The sparkle returned to Marilyn's eyes. "Keep your money. Just give me your autograph and we'll call it even. It will be such a thrill to know that somewhere out there, *Lila McCune* is walking around wearing my great-aunt's comb."

"Oh, I couldn't—"

"I insist." Marilyn gave a little hop of glee.

Lila accepted the metal comb and slid the prongs into her hair. "Thank you, Marilyn. I'll make sure it always has a good home."

"I want it to be with someone who loves it." Marilyn shot a hostile look at Norma. "Someone who understands that everything doesn't have to be made out of platinum to be worth anything."

For the second time in ten minutes, Lila's eyes welled with tears. She hugged Marilyn, said thank you a dozen more times, and hurried back out to the parking lot before she lost her composure.

The woman on TV who kept you sane in the middle of the night isn't supposed to have a nervous breakdown in the middle of the afternoon.

The prongs of the metal comb were biting into her scalp, and she reached up and pulled it out of her hair, then unlocked her car with a click of her key fob.

"Oh, Lila, wait!" Marilyn's voice called. "If I could just trouble you for one more thing before you go."

Lila startled. In her hasty attempt to shove the comb back into her hair, her thumb hit the button to open the SUV's back gate.

A jumble of linens, clothes, shoes, books, file boxes, and a lamp tumbled out onto the asphalt.

Marilyn stopped midstride and looked down at the mess, then back up at Lila with an expression that was equal parts shock and pity.

"I'm transitioning," Lila explained in her perky, late-night shopper voice as she picked up a fragment of the shattered stained-glass lampshade. "I'm considering my options."

chapter 2

*S*teady, pounding rain drenched the windshield of Lila's SUV as she made the drive to Black Dog Bay, Delaware. The night sky was starless, the roads were treacherous, and Lila stayed in the right-hand lane of the highway, praying that she wouldn't skid on an oil slick or scrape a guardrail or misjudge her braking speed.

She wanted to turn on the radio and take a sip of coffee from the travel mug resting on the console, but she was too afraid to release her death grip on the steering wheel.

Buying this car had been a mistake; she could admit that. A huge mistake. Almost as huge as the vehicle itself.

Once upon a time, in her heyday of hawking callus cream on late-night cable, she had driven a sporty little black coupe. She'd never given a second thought to issues like braking speed or turning radius.

And then, ten months ago, her father had died. And after the funeral, she'd come home to the news that her producers had opted not to renew her contract. Six weeks later, her husband had explained that, while he would always love her on some level, he was not actually *in* love with her. Because he was in love with someone else.

The morning after Carl broke the news that he was abandoning her for something new, Lila had decided she deserved something new, too. And Carl deserved to pay for it. She'd stalked out of the house, roiling with rage, and driven to the nearest auto dealership.

"I want the biggest car you have on the lot," she told the first salesman she saw. "Fully loaded: leather seats, sunroof, power everything."

The salesman didn't miss a beat. "Backseat DVD player?"

"Sure, why not?" she'd replied, though she had no children. She didn't even have a dog. There'd be nothing in her backseat but baggage after Carl sold the house she'd spent five years decorating with custom flooring and fabric and furniture.

"Do you have a color preference?" the salesman asked as he led her toward a line of shiny new vehicles.

"No." She pulled out her checkbook. "Let's just get this done before my husband closes the joint accounts."

And that was how she'd ended up with this all-wheel-drive behemoth with an interior large enough to set up a pair of sofas and a coffee table. This sumptuous, supersafe SUV—or, as she privately referred to it, the "FU"-V.

She'd driven back home in a spurt of renewed optimism, feeling invincible.

Then she'd turned into the circular driveway in front of their stately brick home and realized that she had blind spots the size of a small planet and insufficient clearance to maneuver the vehicle into the garage. She'd had to park outside and slink in to face the scorn of the man who'd vowed to love her in sickness and in health, for richer or for poorer.

Except that man hadn't been waiting for her in the house. He'd vanished, taking his laptop and golf clubs with him, leaving a certified letter from his accountant explaining that because his businesses had been "gifted" to him by his father, she wouldn't be entitled to any portion of his company's equity or revenue going forward.

All her outrage and optimism sputtered out after that, followed quickly by her savings, because Carl did indeed freeze the joint accounts.

But she still had this FUV, cocooning her within steel crossbars and countless air bags as she cruised down Coastal Highway 1. She had a world of comforts at her disposal—heated leather seats, climate control, enough cup holders to accommodate a case of cola, and, of course, the backseat DVD player. She'd signed the purchase agreement thinking that she was buying a guarantee of safety and protection.

Ding.

She instinctively tapped the brake as she glanced at the dashboard. An orange alert light in the shape of an exclamation point was blinking. She had no idea what that meant, but she knew it was bad.

Reminding herself to stay calm, she tried to watch the road ahead and maintain her speed.

One hazard light wasn't the end of the world. She could call Triple A. How did the Bluetooth system work, again?

Ding.

Another light illuminated—this time, the engine temperature alert.

Ding.

The oil level alert.

Ding.

The battery life alert.

BEEP BEEP BEEP.

The antitheft alert blared to life at eardrum-shattering decibels.

Lila didn't realize she was yelling until she heard the sound of her own voice in her ears in the split-second pauses between beeps and dings.

Her fingers gripped the steering wheel so tightly her wrists trembled. She tried to focus on the road, but all she could see in front of her was a cluster of red and orange lights, announcing crises she hadn't even imagined.

She glimpsed a gas station on her right and swerved into the parking lot, skidding on the wet pavement and jumping the curb in her haste. For a moment, she worried the enormous hulk of machinery would simply topple and roll over, but it righted itself with a shudder.

The cacophony of beeps and dings continued. She threw the transmission into park and started jabbing at buttons on the dashboard and key fob. Nothing changed—the lights kept blinking, the alarms kept blaring.

She heaved the door open and jumped out, stumbling on the retractable assist steps that automatically unfolded.

"Shit!" She fell into a gasoline-scented puddle. Though she managed to catch herself with her hands, the water splashed onto her cheeks and collar.

The car alarms kept sounding.

She grabbed the edge of the massive metal hood and pulled. Nothing budged. She could barely see at this point; her hair was plastered to her face in the icy downpour.

"Stop." A calm, authoritative male voice filtered through all the honking and dinging. A hand pressed down on her shoulder. "Give me your keys."

Shaking and breathless, she whirled around to face a man wearing a baseball cap and a dark wool jacket. He smiled at her and held out his palm.

Lila hesitated for a moment, worst-case scenarios flashing through her mind. If she handed over her keys, this guy could steal her car. She'd be stranded here, shivering and alone.

Without the three-ton vehicle that she could barely drive.

Good.

She pointed toward the driver's-side door. "They're in the ignition."

The man stepped onto the metal ledge, reached into the SUV's cabin, and cut the engine.

Everything stopped at once—the dinging, the honking, the panic and despair.

Lila listened to the raindrops spatter against the pavement during the long, lovely pause.

Then the engine rumbled to life again as the man turned the keys in the other direction.

She started to protest, but the words died on her lips when she realized that she could *hear* the engine now. She could also hear the steady squeak of the windshield wipers. All the alarms had been silenced.

And the guy that had done the silencing was now staring at her.

She took a faltering step back.

He kept right on staring. "Lila?"

She took another step back.

He took off his hat, and suddenly those features fell into place in her memory. The brown eyes and thick hair and the deep, teasing voice. "Lila?"

"Ben?" She clapped a hand to her mouth, suddenly aware of how bedraggled she must look. "Ben!"

Without another word, he opened his arms to her and she ran to him, closing her eyes as she pressed her cheek against his shoulder. It had been years since he had held her, but she suddenly felt sixteen again, hopeful and shy but safe.

"What are you doing here?" Something about the way he asked this made her wonder how much he'd glimpsed of the FUV's contents.

"I promised my mom I'd come stay with her through the summer," she mumbled into his jacket. "She's been having a hard time with everything."

His arms tightened around her. "I heard about your dad. I'm so sorry. He was a great guy."

"Yeah, it's been a tough year. But we're hanging in there." She looked up at him.

He cupped her chin in his hand. "It's so great to see you."

"What about you?" she asked. "I thought you were still in Boston."

"I moved back last month. I'm taking over my dad's company. We're starting some new projects down by Bethany Beach."

She was grinning now, not her camera smile but her real smile. She knew she looked toothy and ridiculous, but she couldn't stop.

Because the first boy she'd promised to love forever was smiling down at her with what could only be described as adoration. "You changed your hair."

She nodded. "I went blond a few years ago."

"It looks great. You always look great, Lila."

"Oh, please." She pulled away, trying to straighten her hair and her shirt and her earrings all at once. "I'm a drowned rat."

Ben shook his head. "You get prettier and prettier. Listen, here's my card. We should get together sometime and catch up."

She forced her lips into a more demure expression as her mother's voice resounded in her head: *Don't be too eager. There's nothing a man likes more than a woman who has other options.* "Thanks. I'd like that."

"You're staying with your mom?"

She nodded.

"Take it easy on the drive into town, and get your car checked out, okay?" He nodded at the SUV. "This model has a lot of electrical problems. Probably a short somewhere."

"How do you know?"

"My foreman used to have the same car. Emphasis on *used to.*"

Lila climbed back into the FUV, buckled her seat belt, and just sat for a few minutes. Relishing the heated seats and warm air gusting out of the vents. Watching the dashboard for any more emergency lights.

Reeling from the unexpected gift she'd just been given.

Finally, she put the FUV into gear and started back down the highway to her hometown. And five minutes later, when she passed the quaint clapboard sign adorned with the silhouette of a Labrador retriever—WELCOME TO BLACK DOG BAY—she removed one hand from the wheel, turned on the radio, and scanned through the static until she found a song she could hum along to.

Maybe coming home wouldn't be so bad, after all.

Photo by Anna Peña

Beth Kendrick is the author of twelve women's fiction novels, including *New Uses for Old Boyfriends*, *Cure for the Common Breakup*, *The Week Before the Wedding*, *The Lucky Dog Matchmaking Service*, and *Nearlyweds*, which was turned into a Hallmark Channel original movie. Although she lives in Arizona, she loves to vacation at the Delaware beaches, where she brakes for turtles, eats boardwalk fries, and wishes that the Whinery really existed.

CONNECT ONLINE

bethkendrick.com
facebook.com/bethkendrickbooks
twitter.com/bkendrickbooks